Berkley Prime Crime titles by Kylie Logan

Button Box Mysteries

BUTTON HOLED
HOT BUTTON
PANIC BUTTON
BUTTONED UP

League of Literary Ladies Mysteries

MAYHEM AT THE ORIENT EXPRESS

Chili Cook-off Mysteries

CHILI CON CARNAGE

Praise for the Button Box Mysteries

Panic Button

"I enjoy this series so much, and with each book, the stories get better. Character development is key in a mystery series, and it's nice to see that Josie remains both a strong woman and hones her sleuthing skills, showing that she is intelligent about much more than buttons. As I said in a review of the first book in the series, if this book had a 'Like' button, I'd click on it for sure."
                                            —MyShelf.com

Hot Button

"An unusual hobby provides the backdrop for this mystery that combines textile arts and history in a unique way . . . Eccentric characters at the convention add interest to the narrative as does the history surrounding the fabled Geronimo button."   —*The Mystery Reader*

"Who would ever have thought that buttons and murder would go together like peanut butter and jelly? . . . The second Button Box Mystery is a fascinating cozy starring an interesting cast."   —*Genre Go Round Reviews*

Button Holed

"Kylie Logan's *Button Holed* is absolutely terrific! I love it, and can't wait for the next installment in the series."
        —Diane Mott Davidson, *New York Times* bestselling author

"This is the opening act of an engaging amateur-sleuth mystery series, and if this book is any indication, readers have a special and original new series to enjoy. The protagonist is independent and resolute . . . a woman who refuses to be Button Holed."   —*The Mystery Gazette*

continued . . .

Buttoned Up

KYLIE LOGAN

BERKLEY PRIME CRIME, NEW YORK

THE BERKLEY PUBLISHING GROUP
Published by the Penguin Group
Penguin Group (USA) LLC
375 Hudson Street, New York, New York 10014

USA • Canada • UK • Ireland • Australia • New Zealand • India • South Africa • China

penguin.com

A Penguin Random House Company

BUTTONED UP

A Berkley Prime Crime Book / published by arrangement with the author

Berkley Prime Crime Books are published by The Berkley Publishing Group.
BERKLEY® PRIME CRIME and the PRIME CRIME logo
are trademarks of Penguin Group (USA) LLC.

For information, address: The Berkley Publishing Group,
a division of Penguin Group (USA) LLC,
375 Hudson Street, New York, New York 10014.

ISBN: 978-0-425-26594-9

PUBLISHING HISTORY
Berkley Prime Crime mass-market edition / December 2013

PRINTED IN THE UNITED STATES OF AMERICA

10 9 8 7 6 5 4 3 2 1

Cover illustration by Jennifer Taylor.
Cover design by Annette Fiore DeFex.
Interior text design by Kristin del Rosario.

For artists everywhere who believe even something as small as a button can be beautiful. And for those who are willing to suspend disbelief enough to consider the possibilities in the world we see—and the one we don't.

ACKNOWLEDGMENTS

Every book is an adventure, especially when the author decides to throw in the kinds of fanciful elements I've used in *Buttoned Up*. I had such fun with this book, and I thank my wonderful, talented, and generous brainstorming group—Shelley Costa, Serena Miller, and Emilie Richards—for helping to give it shape. I'm also grateful to Roger and Russell (hosts of the best Halloween party in Cleveland) for chatting about the book. Russell, you're going to recognize something familiar in these pages. Thanks for the idea!

As always, I'm also grateful to the wonderful button collectors I've met along the way. They are knowledgeable and interesting people, well-read and so informed on all things button-related, it takes my breath away!

Chapter One

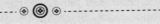

THERE'S A FINE LINE BETWEEN ARTIST AND CRACKPOT.

One quick look around the Celestial Spaces Gallery, and I knew Forbis Parmenter wasn't just walking that line, he was tippy-toeing over it ever so tentatively. Blindfolded. And probably with a glass of Jim Beam in one hand.

My words escaped on the end of a sigh of utter astonishment. "I've never seen so many—"

"Buttons. Yeah." At my side, Nevin Riley looked around, too, and truth be told, I'm pretty sure he was even more astonished than I was. His blue eyes were narrowed, and his usually ruddy complexion skirted green and headed toward ashen. "You sure this guy bills himself as an artist?" he asked. "Because I'm pretty sure I've arrested people like this. You know, screwballs."

It was so close to what I'd been thinking that had I been

with anyone else, I would have been surprised. With Nev, not so much. These days, Nev and I always seemed to be on the same wavelength. It was nice. Reassuring. And not the least little bit unnerving.

Not like the exhibit of Parmenter's works in front of us.

"Of course he's an artist," I reminded Nev, because, really, the process of gluing so many buttons on so many various and sundry objects must have been tedious, and the pictures (birds and fish and flowers) and geometric designs (zigzags and circles and squares) made out of those buttons were intricate, and the color combinations were astonishing. That qualifies as art, right? "Anyone who can take buttons—"

"Thousands and thousands of buttons." Nev glanced over the heads of the people gathered in front of the installation to our right, the first in the exhibit, billed in the brochure we'd been handed as we entered as *Vudon Me Wrong: The Daring, the Decorative, and the Devilish Art of Forbis Parmenter.* This particular piece was a bulky chest with thick, squat legs. The side panels were covered with brown and black buttons that twirled and swirled like a tornado on steroids. The drawers of the chest were decorated with stripes of buttons in shades of blue and red and surprising splashes of yellow. They were open, and each was mounded with buttons that spilled over the sides of the drawer and landed in little buttony puddles on the marble floor.

Plastic buttons.

Metal buttons.

Glass buttons.

Wood.

All shapes. All sizes. And in every color of the rainbow.

Even I—who love buttons and whose life's work is the

Button Box, a shop that specializes in antique and vintage buttons—felt as if I'd been dropped smack-dab in the center of a very weird dream.

"Josie?"

The sound of someone calling my name snapped me out of my button daze, and I turned to find a woman winding her way through the crowd and headed in our direction. I knew at once that she must be Laverne Seiffert, secretary here at the Chicago Community Church, and in charge of the gallery space that helped pay the church's bills.

"I'm so glad you made it!" Laverne grabbed my hand and pressed it. She was a middle-aged African American woman with a warm smile and eyes that danced in the reflected light of the spotlights that had been installed to throw halos of illumination around Forbis Parmenter's work. I'd never met Laverne in person but we'd talked on the phone plenty of times in preparation for tonight. I knew she was friendly and efficient. If her turquoise-colored suit and paprika and gold paisley silk scarf meant anything, she also had an eye for art as keen as Forbis Parmenter's.

With a little motion, she waved us to the far aisle, away from the art installation that took up a good portion of what used to be the main altar area of the old Roman Catholic church. These days, as in many cities, the historic churches of inner-city Chicago were empty of parishioners and the buildings were being sold off to smaller congregations. Except for the stained-glass windows, which must have been magnificent in daylight, the church had been stripped of its ornamentation; the old statues and side altars were gone. When the faithful of the Community Church weren't using the building for their services, it did double duty as a gallery.

"It helps keep the lights on," Laverne once told me. "And it doesn't hurt to get some new blood in here. Maybe our visitors will see all the wonderful things we're doing in the community and join in to help."

"You brought it, right?" The trill of excitement in Laverne's voice brought me out of the memory and I saw that she was so fidgety, she shifted from foot to foot on the gorgeous pumps that matched her Chanel-inspired suit. "You've got the button?"

"Right here." I patted my purse. "I'm as ready as I'll ever be. Only . . ." I glanced around. There were knots of people in front of the various artwork and a hum of anticipation that echoed around the church with its pointed Gothic arches and Romanesque columns. "I don't see Forbis. Where's the guest of honor?"

Laverne pressed her lips together. "Not here yet, and I've got to admit, the man's making me a little nervous. Then again, I'm not used to a show like this. We're new," she added, with a look at Nev because she'd told me all this when first we talked. "We only made the decision to use the church as a gallery space about six months ago, and we've had exactly two shows since then. One was from the local senior citizen center and the other featured artists from a nearby college. This is the first . . ." The breath Laverne pulled in trembled with anticipation. "This is the first time we're playing with the big boys on the real art scene." We heard one of the side doors of the church slap open, then shut, and automatically we all looked that way.

Along with Laverne and Nev, I studied the man who'd just strolled in. He was tall, with dark hair just graying at the temples. Wide shoulders. Narrow hips. A face that wasn't anywhere as near handsome as it was craggy, with a nose that was a little too big, and a chin that was a little too weak. He was wearing a tux that fit so well, it had obviously been made just for him. The overhead lights glinted off the studs on his shirt. Black onyx rimmed with silver. OK, so not technically buttons, but close enough for me to notice.

Laverne grabbed my arm with both hands. "Well, that pretty much proves what I was just saying. That's Victor Cherneko."

Even I knew the name. But then, when things were slow at the Button Box, I was known to skim the local news in the *Tribune*, and things like charity fund-raising galas always caught my eye. "He's the billionaire philanthropist, right?" I asked Laverne.

"And a big patron of the arts." She practically swooned. "I guess it's official. We're a real gallery, and now, I'm officially a nervous wreck!"

"You're doing fine," I told her, and then I said, "The church is beautiful," to help get her mind off her jitters.

I guess it worked, because Laverne beamed with pride. She looked away from Cherneko so she could look around the church. "It is, isn't it? We were lucky to get it for a song, that's for sure. And luckier still that we have an active and faithful congregation. Someday . . ." She sighed. "Someday I'd like to see this place filled to the rafters on Sunday mornings. Right now, we hold our services in the basement, which isn't all that shabby by any means, but it's not as magnificent as this space. Not as expensive to heat, either," she added with a wink that explained the real reason for the basement services. "Wouldn't it be something if someday we had standing room only and a choir so big, we had to use the loft up there to hold them all?"

I followed her gaze to the back of the church. The place was cavernous and because the exhibit was housed at the front, the back pews and the second-story choir loft were lost in shadow.

"That's all a someday dream, good Lord willing," Laverne added. "And we've got to start somewhere. Lucky for me, I've got a silver tongue and I was able to convince the church board of the benefits of holding art shows here. You should have seen Reverend Truman's face when this exhibit was set up earlier in the week!" When Laverne's throaty laugh came out louder than she intended and ricocheted back at her, she pressed one neatly manicured hand to her lips and glanced around, hoping no one had noticed. "When I arranged to have the exhibit here, I played it nice and cool, only told him it was artwork and talked up Forbis as the newest darling of the art world. Which is true, as you know. Man came out of nowhere and he's got the art world by the tail. The reverend, he never asked exactly what kind of artwork we'd be showing, and so I never told him. When he saw that the subject of this particular exhibit was voodoo . . ." A smile cracked her solemn expression. "I told him to pray—and get over it. Then I reminded him that the church is getting twenty percent of the price of any of the art that's sold. That changed his mind fast."

"Forbis's work is always . . ." I searched for the word and found my vocabulary sorely lacking.

"Bizarre?" Nev suggested at the same time he snagged a little sandwich from the tray of a passing waiter.

"We prefer provocative," Laverne said, but the way her eyes shimmered told me even she didn't take the word one hundred percent seriously. "At least that's what I told Reverend Truman. I pointed out that the work will help spark discussions about religion and about the enslaved people who practiced the various forms of voodoo like this vudon thing Forbis Parmenter has focused on. We're even going to invite some of our Haitian neighbors in for a discussion a week from Wednesday. Discussion is good, right?"

"Twenty percent of the profits is better." Because Laverne had been so forthcoming, I knew she'd get the joke, and she did. "From what I've read, Forbis's showings in other cities have been—"

"Dagnabbit! You can't talk to me like that!"

The voice that interrupted what I was going to say was distinct for a couple reasons. First of all, it was loud, and it bounced through the church like a flat stone skipping over water. Second—

"I ain't done with you so don't you dare turn your back on me. I've got a mind to walk outta here and tell the whole world what you done."

"That accent is unmistakable," I said, looking from Laverne to Nev. "I recognize it from talking to Forbis on the phone. That's him, and he sounds plenty mad."

Nev was already looking around but like I said, the building was enormous and like so many old churches, it had dozens of chambers and anterooms, one main aisle with a smaller aisle on either side of it, who-knew-how-many nooks and crannies, and a row of pillars marching down the main aisle that were plenty big enough for people to stand behind unseen.

Where Forbis's voice actually came from was anyone's guess.

The fact that he was spitting mad wasn't.

"This is the end!" That voice—the words rounded by Forbis's Southern roots—bounced around us like a handball striking a wall. "I ain't takin' this no more, and you ain't givin' it, that's for certain."

"Oh, dear." Laverne chewed her lower lip. "That doesn't sound good. I'd better . . ." And before she could say exactly what she'd better do, she scurried away.

"Sounds serious," I said to Nev, though since Laverne hurried away, we hadn't heard another word out of Forbis. "You don't suppose—"

"That there's something mysterious going on?" Nev brushed crumbs off his hands and, because I knew he wouldn't notice or if he did, he wouldn't care, I took care of the crumbs that had landed on the orange tie he'd worn with gray pants and a navy sport coat. "No mysteries! Whoever this Parmenter character was yelling at, the fight's over, right?" For a minute, we both stood in silence and strained to hear Forbis's voice again and when we didn't, Nev nodded. "So it's official. The fight's over, no harm done. We are having a night out. And I'm not letting you get entangled in any more murders."

"From your mouth to God's ear." Just to hedge my bets, I glanced up at the nearest stained-glass window when I said this. "No more murders." I repeated the words I'd been saying to Nev in the months since one of my customers was killed outside my shop and I helped find out whodunit. "But that doesn't mean we shouldn't find out what's going on and who Forbis is fighting with. It could be serious."

"There's a security guard here."

Wise words, but Nev knew he couldn't get away with them. Not when we'd both seen the security guard when we walked in, and we both knew that the man was eighty if he was a day, and so frail-looking, one good puff of wind off Lake Michigan would blow him clear to Iowa.

"I'm not saying we should stick our noses where they don't belong," I assured Nev.

He crossed his arms over his chest. "But . . ."

"But if something's wrong and you don't help–"

"If something's wrong and somebody needs my help, I'll be only too happy to oblige. I'll even take a quick walk around and make sure nobody's in trouble if that will make you happy. After that, all I want is a chance to enjoy an evening out with you without murder and mayhem getting in the way."

"And all I want . . ." I didn't need to think about it for more than two seconds, I knew it was true. I'd helped the cops with that customer's murder a few months earlier, and I'd assisted in a couple other investigations, too. That didn't change a thing. "All I want is to live the button life."

"And let's just add another one of those sandwiches! Ham salad. It was really good." Nev spotted a waiter over near the exhibit and grabbed my hand, and together we headed that way. While he took care of two of the little sandwiches, I checked out the nearest art piece. This was a set of tribal drums and like everything else, the hourglass-shaped drums were covered with buttons.

"You don't suppose he uses actual historic artifacts for his work, do you?" I asked Nev but true to his word, he'd walked away to do a quick turn around the church and I found that I was talking to myself. I flipped open the exhibit brochure to see if it answered my question, and mumbled, "These things are replicas, right? Forbis wouldn't use artifacts that are hundreds of years old."

"Absolutely. Yes, he absolutely does."

The answer came from a woman standing at my side and studying the drums like I was, and I turned that way. She was taller than me, which is no big accomplishment, and as willowy as a reed. When Forbis contacted me six weeks earlier and arranged to buy the button that was in my purse—the button that I would present to him when he arrived and he would use to complete one of the artworks in the show—I'd treated myself to a sleeveless black sheath dress and a black shrug. The outfit screamed *art gallery*, and apparently, I wasn't the only one who heard it. This woman, too, was all in black, though her dress was shorter than mine and cut low enough in front to accent the smooth swell of her breasts. Me, I'd decided to stand out in the crowd by adding Grandma Roba's string of pearls to my ensemble. This woman didn't need to accessorize. Her eyes were green and nearly almond-shaped, her hair was long, sleek, and dark, and scooped over one shoulder, and she was leggy enough to turn heads.

When Nev walked back up to join me, she turned his all right, and when she caught sight of him, her mouth fell open.

"Nev!"

"Evangeline!"

Their voices mingled and after one second of utter surprise, Nev and Evangeline fell into each other's arms. A quick hug, a quicker peck on the cheek, and they stepped back, beaming and still holding onto each other's hands.

"What a wonderful surprise," Evangeline crooned, and apparently it was, because Nev turned red all the way to the tips of his ears.

"Evangeline . . ." He untangled himself from her and put a hand on my shoulder. "This is Josie Giancola. Josie, this is Evangeline Simon, an old friend of mine."

Evangeline's laugh was as chipper as bird song. "Not so old," she protested, "though it has been too long since I've seen you, Nev. I know you're still on the job." She looked my way and lowered her voice as if Nev wasn't there and we were sharing a secret. "He's got cop in his blood, that's for sure. I can't imagine he'd ever do anything else."

I was about to mention that not only was Nev a cop, but the best one in Chicagoland, but Nev and Evangeline didn't give me a chance. Questions poured out of her, and Nev, usually as talkative as a stone statue, answered and threw in a couple dozen of his own.

When they both finally stopped to take a breath, I saw my chance and jumped at it. "You're an art fan?" I asked Evangeline.

Nev answered for her. "She's an expert," he said, and in response Evangeline blushed ever-so-prettily. "Not in art, though I bet she knows plenty about that, too. In this vudon thing." He smiled at her. "Right?"

Evangeline stepped closer to the drums we'd both been looking at before Nev walked up. "I'm an anthropologist," she explained. "My area of expertise is the cultures of the enslaved peoples of the Barrier Islands along the Atlantic coast."

"Where Forbis is from," I said.

Evangeline nodded. "When I heard about an art show

that included vudon, I had to come see what all the excitement is about."

"She's being modest." I hadn't even realized Nev had ducked away for a moment until he came back with two glasses of champagne. He handed one to me and the other to Evangeline. "When it comes to the Barrier Islands and the people who lived there, she's the world's leading expert," he said. "Like you are about buttons, Josie."

"You know buttons?" Evangeline's question was straightforward enough but I didn't fail to notice the way one corner of her perfectly bowed lips pulled to the side.

"I know antique buttons," I informed her. "In fact, I've got one button for the display with me."

"Josie's part of the opening ceremony," Nev told Evangeline.

It was my turn to be modest. "Just a small part. The way I understand it, Forbis is quite the showman. He needed one more button to complete one of these pieces . . ." I let my gaze rove over the drums and beyond them to what looked like some sort of altar. I hadn't been told which piece my button would be added to, and on first glance, it was impossible to see where there could possibly be a blank space. So many buttons, so many colors, I bet I could look around for hours and never find the place where this one last button belonged.

"Forbis wanted just the right button so he contacted me," I told Evangeline. "Once he shows up, I'll present him the button and he'll put it in place. Then, officially, the exhibit will be open."

"And this button . . ." Evangeline took a sip of champagne. "It has some connection with vudon?"

I laughed. "Nothing that mysterious! It's just a plastic button, manufactured some time in the last thirty years. It cost Forbis exactly one dollar and fifty cents."

Evangeline's eyes went wide. "Then why—"

"Who are we to question an artist?" I asked. "I e-mailed Forbis pictures. Literally, thousands of pictures. He was looking for a button of just the right size and just the right shade of red. Fortunately, I had it in my inventory."

"Josie's got lots of buttons in her inventory," Nev told her.

"Fascinating."

As far as I could tell Evangeline meant what she said, but I couldn't help but wonder if somewhere down the line, I'd be the subject of some academic study: The Effects of Button Accumulation on the Subnormal Acculturation of Gatherers.

"You can be a big help to me, Josie," Evangeline said. "As we walk around the exhibit, you can tell me about the buttons."

"Only if you explain vudon customs to me," I countered.

She laughed, and side by side, we began our tour of the installation.

"The religion is quite intriguing," Evangeline said as we stepped away from the drums and in front of a large box covered top to bottom with buttons. "There is an interrelation between vudon and the voodoo practiced in places like New Orleans and the vudou of Haiti. They share the same pantheon of gods and spirits, but vudon has idiosyncratic elements that set it apart. The enslaved people who were brought to the islands combined their ancestral African religious practices, tenets of Catholicism, and the spiritual beliefs of the Native Americans who were the first inhabitants of the Barrier Islands."

I love history. I guess that's no big surprise since I love old buttons so much. I'd always been curious about other cultures, too. This was really interesting stuff. But what I didn't get . . .

Another quick look around the gallery only heightened my confusion.

"I appreciate it all from a historical perspective," I told Evangeline. "And I get Forbis's thing with buttons. Well, sort of, anyway. He's an outsider artist, one of those dreamers whose work doesn't quite fit in the box of regular art. I've seen pictures of his work before and he usually covers stuff like cars and clothing and furniture with buttons. But this emphasis on vudon—"

"That's what I'm here to try and figure out, too," Evangeline said. "My original supposition was that he was offering a commentary on the paradox between cultural practices and man's push-pull relationship with history and modernity. We say we're all about technology, but there's something about the ancient religions that speak to us, something that speaks to us on a gut level, whether we want to acknowledge it or not."

"And here I thought the guy was just a nutcase!" Nev beamed a smile.

"What I was going to say," Evangeline said and her smile was as wide as Nev's—that is, until she looked around again and it wavered a little around the edges. "I was going to say that now that I've seen the exhibit, I'm not so sure of any of that. The whole thing makes me uneasy." A shiver skipped over her shoulders. I guess that's why she slipped her arm through Nev's. "I get the feeling the artist is not as concerned about tapping into the cultural and ethnic significance of vudon as he is simply poking fun at it. Although this big box here . . ." She studied the exhibit in front of us, a cube that stood about ten feet high. "I can't imagine what Parmenter is trying to convey with this piece. The colors are certainly significant." When she bent forward to point out a series of red and green stripes, she naturally took Nev with her. "In vudon, colors are allegorical. Green, of course, represents life. And red symbolizes death. But in my considerable experience, large cubes have no significance in the religion and big boxes played no role in religious ceremonies."

"Maybe this will help explain." I pointed to a sign (completely made out of buttons, of course) to the right of the exhibit.

"Press the Button," it said.

Which didn't help a lot considering how many buttons surrounded us.

Never one to be put off—especially when I had the chance to study buttons, buttons, and more buttons—I let my gaze roam over the sign, and it actually didn't take me very long to catch on to what I'd bet any money Forbis thought was one heck of a whopping joke. The sign, see, was made entirely out of glass buttons—almost. There was one shell button all by itself over to the side.

I pressed it.

A whirring noise from inside the big box startled not only me, Nev, and Evangeline, but the rest of the crowd as well. My gaze was fixed on the box, but I could feel the space behind me suddenly fill with people who, like us, were anxious to see what was going to happen. We held our collective breaths and when the top of the box popped open, we all flinched as if we'd choreographed the move.

The whirring continued and like a jack-in-the-box in slow motion, a figure rose into the spotlight.

Good thing Nev was standing between me and Evangeline; I grabbed onto his free arm. But then, I don't think anyone could blame me. The button-covered statue that ascended from the box was one of the most terrifying things I'd ever seen.

It was eight feet tall and its arms were out as if it was reaching for each person in the audience. It's eyes were black and sunken, its face was that of a skeleton and since it was covered with what I recognized as mother of pearl buttons, it glimmered in the overhead lights like bone. Its hair, row after row of black buttons strung onto wire, bobbed as the statue rose up. Like it was twitching. Like it was alive.

"It's Congo Savanne." On the other side of Nev, Evangeline's voice choked out of her, as unwavering as the look she gave the statue. "He's a powerful *petro loa*; that is, a fiery and aggressive spirit. He's fierce and strong and angry and he grinds people up with his teeth and eats them."

"Yeesh." I would have known this was a malevolent spirit even if Evangeline hadn't told me, and I backed up a step and would have kept on going if there wasn't a lady right behind me staring up into the terrifying, button-covered face of Congo Savanne. I glanced passed Nev toward Evangeline. "You still think Forbis is trying to be funny?"

"I think . . ." She finished off her champagne and when she was done, she was back to being her old self, straightforward and friendly. With a laugh, she handed her glass to

Nev. "I think I'll hit the ladies' room before the festivities get started. I'll be right back."

It wasn't until we heard another series of whirring gears and the statue of the loa sunk back inside the box that I felt as if I could shake off its fierce spell. "Creepy, huh?" I said to Nev.

Who, unfortunately, had picked that exact moment to glance toward where Evangeline had disappeared.

"I didn't mean her," I blurted out, embarrassed. "I meant the statue. Evangeline is nice." I gave him a playful poke. "You didn't tell me you hung out with anthropologists."

My glass was empty, too, and Nev took it out of my hand and deposited it on the tray of a passing waiter along with Evangeline's glass. "We don't exactly hang out," he said. "I haven't seen Evangeline in a couple of years."

"She's very smart," I said, because it was true and because I was dying of curiosity and knew the best way to find out what I wanted to know was to keep Nev talking. "And she's very pretty."

"She is."

"And you don't exactly strike me as the type who sits around talking about cultures and old religions." I knew this for a fact; Nev and I had been dating for just about a year and I knew he wasn't into brainiac stuff. Sometimes, even talk of button history and collecting made his eyes glaze over. "How do you two know each other?"

"Oh, just from around." Nev shrugged away the significance of the comment. "Evangeline is—"

"What?" She was back and with a fresh coat of lipstick accentuating her smile. As if she'd never left, she slipped her arm right where it had been, through Nev's. "What's he saying about me?" she asked, turning to me. "Because my guess is whatever it is, it's not true."

"Nev's nothing if not one hundred percent honest." It was one of the things I appreciated most about him. After all, I'd once been married to a guy who specialized in lies. Knowing Nev always had been and always would be aboveboard—about everything—was one of the reasons I liked him so much.

"And one hundred percent trustworthy." Evangeline added to my assessment of Nev's character at the same time she turned Nev around and piloted him over to the next item in the exhibit, an altar decorated with buttons. "That's why you didn't look surprised when he introduced us, right? Nev's already told you all about me."

When I didn't answer, she looked up at Nev. "I'm sorry," she said and I didn't doubt her for an instant. Evangeline's face was pale. "You and Josie look so comfortable together, I just assumed you'd been dating a long time. I figured she knew all about us."

"And I'm feeling a little like everybody knows where this is going except me." Three cheers for a bravado I suddenly wasn't feeling; I kept my voice light and airy even though my insides felt as if I'd guzzled a Slurpee in record time. "Somebody want to clue me in?"

Nev, apparently, didn't.

But that didn't stop Evangeline.

She adjusted her arm to hang onto Nev a little tighter. "I just assumed you knew," she said. "Nev and I, we used to be engaged."

Chapter Two

SLACK-JAWED IS NOT A GOOD LOOK FOR ME.

I froze—yes, slack-jawed—and stared at Evangeline just long enough to see those gorgeous green eyes of hers go wide with horror. I didn't know the secret, and she'd let it slip from her lips. The poor woman was mortified!

Not nearly as much as I was.

I couldn't have been paralyzed for more than a second or two, but it felt like a lifetime. Every muscle tensed except for my stomach, which was twitching like a son of a gun, I finally forced myself to pivot toward Nev, and in that one moment before the emotion took over and swamped me like a tsunami, I was more curious than anything else. What would I see registered in his blue eyes? Embarrassment? Anger? Indifference? What excuse would he offer for keeping this huge piece of his past from me all this time?

I never had a chance to find out.

Before either Nev or Evangeline could open their mouths again—and before I could close mine—a hand grasped my upper arm and a voice I recognized from phone calls (not to mention that argument that had echoed through the church just a little while earlier) drowned out the thrumming of my blood inside my head.

"There you are, sweetheart! Why, you are as cute as a spotted puppy under a red wagon, just like I knew you'd be. I been lookin' all over the place for you."

"Forbis." How I managed to say the name when my mouth was filled with sand, I don't know. I'm also not sure how I pulled off a smile. Apparently, it wasn't as anemic as I feared because Forbis beamed back like a lighthouse.

We stood eye to eye, me and Forbis, and he was stick-thin and seventy-five if he was a day. The publicity photo that appeared on his website and on the back of the exhibition brochure had been taken by a pro, that was for sure. It somehow managed to downplay his prominent nose, the large ears that didn't lay anywhere near flat against his head, and his flapping jowls.

"You got my button, don't you, darlin'?"

"Button?" Even to me, my voice sounded as if it came from the depths of some deep, dark cave. Not acceptable. Not in public. Not when the Button Box's reputation—and mine—were on the line. I shook myself out of my daze. "Of course I have the button," I told Forbis.

"Perfect red button," Forbis said, with a look toward Nev and Evangeline as well as the rest of the crowd that had gathered around now that the guest of honor had finally made his appearance. "This lady here . . ." He patted my shoulder. "If y'all ever need buttons, she's your go-to girl!"

I appreciated the publicity and smiled at the crowd. Notice I said *the crowd*. I wasn't sure what was going to happen when my eyes finally met Nev's so I made sure I didn't look his way.

"Root beer barrel?"

When Forbis stuck something in front of my nose, I flinched and hoped I didn't look as weird cross-eyed as I was sure I did with my mouth hanging open. When my eyes finally focused, I realized it was one of those old-fashioned hard candies that looks like a brown barrel and is flavored like root beer.

I declined. With the knot of emotion in my throat, I was pretty sure the combination of root beer flavoring and sugar would not yield pretty results.

Forbis unwrapped the candy and popped it in his mouth. "Can't get enough of these things," he told me. "Morning, noon, and night. I'm pretty sure it's what keeps me so sweet." He winked.

Corny, yes, but truth be told, I was glad. If I thought about corny, I didn't have to think about getting bushwhacked, and if I didn't have to think about getting bushwhacked, I could pretend—almost—that everything was fine and my world hadn't just turned upside down. Some of the tension melted from my shoulders. This time when I smiled at Forbis, it didn't feel as if my face would crack. "Would you like to see the button?" I asked him.

He nodded, and looked at the crowd. "Gonna have to ske-daddle!" he told them. "A surprise is a surprise, and I ain't

21

ruinin' this one. Go on. Shoo!" Coming from anyone else and aimed at a gallery crowd—which, let's face it, can sometimes live up to its snooty reputation—this might not have gone over well. But Forbis was so darned cute with that Southern drawl—I'd bet a dime to a donut it wasn't so much fake as it was exaggerated—and wearing a gray suit that was a little too baggy, he was the picture of the eccentric and lovable artist, and nobody had the heart to argue.

The crowd that surrounded us drifted away, including Evangeline and Nev. Last I saw of them, Nev took a second to glance over his shoulder at me. Was that regret I saw in his eyes? Or was I being as imaginative in my own pathetic way as Forbis was when it came to buttons?

"So . . ."

I snapped back to reality to find him tapping one foot against the stone floor. He was wearing sneakers. The big, ugly expensive kind. Royal blue high-tops with neon orange laces.

Forbis sucked on the root beer barrel in his mouth. "Let's see that there button!"

I reached into my purse and took out the box I'd brought along with me from the shop and he lifted the little red button from the bed of cotton where it had been swaddled and held it up to the light. "It's a beauty! Perfect for finishing my work."

I looked over his shoulder toward the exhibit. "And it's going . . . ?"

Forbis chuckled. "You'll see, sweetie. You'll see!"

"You ready, Forbis?"

A man joined us and Forbis handed the button back to

me. "Told you I'd take care of this myself," he grumbled without a glance at the man.

"You did, and I said that wasn't acceptable and promised I'd help, remember?" The man stuck out his hand for me to shake. He was middle-aged, with a round pleasant face, doughy features, and thinning hair. "Richard, Richard Norquist," he said by way of introduction. "I'm Forbis's agent. We . . ." He glanced toward Forbis who was looking down at his sneakers and grinding his root beer barrel between his teeth. "Forbis and I appreciate your help."

"That's what I'm here for," I told him, but when I glanced at Forbis to see if he appreciated the comment, he was still looking down at his shoes. No doubt, the atmosphere had changed since Richard joined us. I wondered why, and then I wondered about that argument we'd overheard earlier.

Right before I came to my senses and realized it was none of my business.

"Buttons are my business," I told them and reminded myself. "And Forbis, your use of buttons . . ." Once again, I allowed my gaze to drift over the exhibit. I didn't pause—well, at least not too long—when I saw Nev and Evangeline with their heads together near the vudon ceremonial drums. "It's all amazing," I said, and even I wasn't sure if I was talking about the news Evangeline had just dumped on me or Forbis's work.

"He's a genius." This cheery commentary was provided by Laverne who scampered over to join us. She put a hand on Richard's arm. "Need proof? Over there." She looked over her left shoulder toward a man who'd just walked in and was looking over the brochure.

He was tall and though I am not inclined to exaggeration,

I will admit that my first impression was this—gorgeous. I mean, really. Hair the color of the night sky. A face that was all planes and angles. A sense of style that told me that while he might attend art shows, he wasn't one to go along with the crowd; he was the only one who'd come to the black-tie-and-suit affair in faded jeans that hugged every muscle of his body and a black T-shirt with the name of a rock group called Silverlights emblazoned across the front.

"Gabriel Marsh." Laverne whispered the name. Or maybe it was a sigh because like me, she had an appreciation for true perfection when she saw it.

"The journalist?" Richard's shoulders shot back and he turned to look at the man. "We have attracted attention," he purred. "Marsh only writes about the crème de la crème, and he usually doesn't bother with regional shows." He tugged his suit jacket into place. "If you'll excuse me, I'll go introduce myself. That is, Forbis . . ." When he turned toward the artist, Richard's smile was tight. "If you don't mind."

"Knock yourself out," Forbis told him, and once Richard walked away, he added, "Please."

No doubt Laverne felt the tension, too. That would explain the smile that froze on her face in the moment before she shook away her bewilderment. "Are you ready to get started?"

Forbis looked at me.

"Say the word." I slung my purse over my shoulder, the better to hold on to the box with the button in it. "I'm ready whenever you are."

Forbis was ready, too. Or at least he was once he grabbed a glass of champagne from a passing server. He took a gulp and Laverne climbed the one step that separated the body of the church from the main altar area.

"Ladies and gentlemen," she made a graceful motion in our direction. Not at me, of course, but to focus attention on Forbis. "This is Forbis Parmenter." The crowd applauded and Forbis grinned like a schoolkid who'd been kissed for the first time. "And he's going to do something that I understand is a little unusual in the art world. You see, the exhibit in front of you . . ." Again she motioned, this time toward the strange collection of vudon artifacts. "You may not have realized it as you looked around, but the exhibit in front of you isn't quite finished. It's going to be in just a moment. And the artist himself is going to finish it while you watch."

I guess that was our signal because Forbis poked me and started toward the exhibit. I followed one step behind, not exactly sure where we were headed. When he finally stopped in front of the big box with Congo Savanne inside, I whispered a silent prayer. I hoped the one button he wanted to place wasn't on the statue. No way I wanted to get that close to the terrifying thing.

Lucky for me, the one blank spot in that whole sea of buttons was on the front of the box and now that I had an idea where to look, I found it pretty easily. A bit of bare wood showed through the sea of buttons, and it was exactly the right size and just the right shape to fit the button I carried. The red plastic button would be at the center of a flower, and the surrounding petals were shades of orange and gold. I couldn't help myself. From back behind the velvet rope that kept the gallery-goers from getting too up close and personal with the artwork, the buttons had been fascinating. But this close . . .

I pulled in a breath of pure wonderment.

This close, and surrounded by so many thousands of buttons, I will admit it, I was in button-lover's heaven!

Forbis took another sip of his champagne and said a few words to the crowd about what he called his "artistic process" and the lightning flashes of inspiration that led him down the button path to begin with. While he was at it, I took the opportunity to revel in the riot of buttons. There was a yellow glass button just below where my red one would be placed, and I recognized it as a moonglow, one of those charming buttons manufactured in Europe in the middle of the twentieth century that's made of light-gathering satin glass and topped with clear colorless glass. When moonglows are done right, the results are ethereal, and this one was no exception.

But it was the button just to the right of where my little red plastic gem would spend the rest of its life that really caught my attention. Was it ceramic? As casually as I could so as not to draw attention to myself, I leaned nearer. Certainly ceramic, and handmade, too, from the looks of it. This ochre-colored button was marked with what looked like shaky alphabet letters and I itched to get closer to see what they said. I promised myself when the ceremony was over, I would ask Forbis for permission to study the button more closely.

"Button?" Forbis held out one hand, and I had no choice but to pay attention. I removed the red button from the box and dropped it into his hand, and with another sip of champagne to mark the occasion, he held out the button, back side up.

And waited.

I wasn't sure for what until I saw Richard scramble away from Gabriel Marsh's side, a tube of contact cement in one hand. He dabbed cement on the underside of the button and backed away.

Then we were ready.

Forbis leaned closer to the box to put the button in place, and after that . . .

Well, I've thought about it a lot since that night, and I still can't say for certain what happened first. Maybe it doesn't matter. Not as much as the fact that all the color drained out of Forbis's face and he jerked back as if he'd been zapped by an electric line. That's when the champagne glass slipped out of his hand and shattered on the marble floor.

"Forbis?" Automatically, I stepped forward, my hand out to steady him, but by that time, it was already too late.

His hands shaking and a sheen of sweat on his brow, Forbis pointed at the box. "Le bouton, le bouton," he wailed. Then he turned and bolted off the altar.

"Well, I'll be darned. I thought that art show was going to be a real snorer. If I knew there was going to be that much excitement, I would have gone with you!"

It was the next morning and I was back in the Button Box, straightening the display case that was filled with horn and antler buttons. Not that the case needed straightening. But with all that had happened the night before, I'd decided early on that the best way to deal with the day was to keep busy.

I straightened a little more.

"So what did you do?" Stan showed up at the door of the shop even before I was officially open for business. He'd brought coffee and bagels, and he'd toasted the bagels in the mini-kitchen in my back workroom. Now, he brought one over to me—raisin, drizzled with butter and sprinkled with cinnamon. Just the way I like 'em! If I didn't know better, I'd think Stan had used his retired-cop powers of deduction and knew I was nursing a broken . . .

What was it, exactly?

Heart?

Ego?

Or was it just my trust radar that was out of whack?

Even I wasn't sure, I only knew that wherever I'd been struck by Evangeline's thunderbolt of an announcement, it still hurt like hell.

"So . . ." When I didn't take the paper plate with the bagel on it out of his hands, Stan poked it in my direction again. "After this Forbis character ran out, what did you do?"

I took the bagel and went over to sit at my desk. "I went after him," I explained, but not until I took a bite, chewed, and swallowed. It was the first thing I'd eaten since the art show and I was surprised how easily it went down. Whatever had been broken there in the Chicago Community Church, it apparently hadn't affected my appetite. "Or at least I tried."

I thought back to the night before. Once the crowd shook off the shock of seeing Forbis scream and run out, a hum of questions filled the air. I didn't wait to hear any of them. As quickly as I could, I headed down the main aisle and out the front doors of the church.

Gabriel Marsh was already out on the steps that overlooked the main drag and the convenience store across the street.

"Bloody hell! He's bolted."

A Brit. Didn't it figure? The hunk who was Gabriel Marsh would have made a perfect *Masterpiece* hero.

"Did you see which way he went?" I asked.

"Didn't see him at all." Just to be sure, Marsh glanced up and down the street, his fists on his hips. "By the time I got out here, he'd already vanished." Since I was looking up and down the street, too, I didn't exactly see Marsh look my way, but I knew exactly when he did. That would be when my temperature shot up a degree or two.

"Do you suppose Mr. Parmenter is simply a temperamental artist?" he asked.

"I barely know the man."

"But you do have an opinion."

I dared a look at him. Fortunately, the streetlight in front of the church was out, and Marsh's face was lost in shadow. I think if I reminded myself how completely delicious he was, I wouldn't have had the nerve to speak. "My opinion doesn't matter," I told him. "Because that's all it is, an opinion. I think it's pretty obvious that Forbis was upset."

"And you were standing right next to him. What happened?"

The scene in front of the Congo Savanne box had happened only a few minutes before and either I'd already gotten the facts jumbled, or I hadn't had a time to process them so that they made any sense.

I shrugged, and because I really didn't have any more to offer, I stepped toward the church doors.

Marsh sidestepped into my path. This close and with the

help of the light of the flashing neon sign from across the street that declared the convenience store a purveyor of "Drinks, ATM, and No-Contract Phone Service," I saw that his eyes were the same gray as the aged stone facade of the church.

"He's got a reputation. They say there's nothing he loves more than drama and publicity," he said, and I didn't have to ask who we were talking about. "Do you suppose what happened in there was a bit of performance art designed to make us all speculate and dither?"

"Like we're speculating and dithering right now?"

A smile tugged one corner of his mouth, but he hid it quickly enough beneath a cool so complete, I wished I had my winter coat in spite of the steamy summer temperatures. "I'm British. I never dither."

"And I never speculate."

"Because you're afraid I'll quote you."

"Because I don't have anything to say."

"Maybe when you've had some time to think about it—"

"Maybe." I dodged past him and went back inside the church.

When I finished telling the story of what happened the night before, Stan laughed. "Oo-wee! I can't imagine you being so hard on the poor guy, Josie. You're usually so polite."

"Marsh is a journalist." I finished up the first half of the bagel and took a sip of coffee. "I wasn't trying to be tough, I just remembered what happened when that actress was killed here at the shop." I made it a rule to try never to look at the spot where I'd found that body soon after I opened the Button Box, but this time, I couldn't help myself. My gaze slipped over the short expanse of hardwood floor in front of my desk and to the Oriental rug in muted shades of red, green, and blue that covered a good portion of the front of the shop. "The press caused plenty of problems then," I reminded Stan. "I don't need a repeat when it comes to Forbis's over-the-top behavior."

"Right you are." He drained the last of his coffee from his cup. "So where did this Parmenter character disappear to?" he asked.

My sour expression should have been all the answer he needed, but when that didn't seem to be enough, I explained. "Richard Norquist, Forbis's agent, said he was sure Forbis was just trying to squeeze all the fun he could out of the opening. He said Forbis loves to make people talk and he was sure that's what the whole thing was about. Richard insisted that we all stick around and enjoy the exhibit and, of course, he said all the works were for sale and he'd be happy to talk to anyone who was interested. But after what had happened with Forbis . . ."

Again, my mind drifted to the night before. Though Laverne had done her best to chat up the knots of people gathered around the exhibit, and Richard had gone around talking a little too loud and laughing a little too much, the mood had been ruined. Slowly, the crowd had broken up and drifted out the doors.

"And Nev, what did he say?"

Stan was bound to ask, and really, if I was on the ball, I would have been ready with an answer. The way it was, I tried to say enough to satisfy him without saying too much about everything that had gone on the night before.

What had Nev said?

He'd closed in on me just as the crowd was beginning to

break up. He was alone, and a quick look around told me Evangeline was already gone. "We have to talk."

"We do." It wasn't the clever comeback I'd hoped for, but then, I was worried about Forbis and about what had happened over at the exhibit. Besides, I wasn't sure there was a clever comeback in the *honey, I used to be engaged* category that would suit the purpose. "You didn't see where Forbis went?"

"That wasn't exactly what I was thinking we need to talk about," Nev said.

"I know." I tried for a smile. "We could stop for a cup of coffee on the way home and—"

His phone rang.

Evangeline was right when, earlier in the evening, she'd said Nev had cop in his blood. He lived and breathed his work and since it was important work, that was all right with me. I'd never seen him take a shortcut, never seen him shirk his duties. But I swear, right about then, the last thing he wanted to do was answer his phone.

With a pained expression on his face, he answered anyway, and apologized as soon as he ended the call. "There's been a shooting over near Humboldt Park. I'm sorry, Josie. I've got to go. I could take you home and—"

"Not to worry." I gave him a peck on the cheek. "I'll get a cab."

I crunched into the other half of my bagel. "Nev didn't see anything, either," I told Stan. "Nobody did. Forbis just vanished."

"And nobody's heard from him since?"

Something told me that Stan already knew the answer to this because while he was toasting our bagels, he must have heard me on the phone. I'd called the hotel where Forbis was staying and asked for his room. There was no answer.

"I e-mailed him last night when I got home, too," I told Stan. "And again this morning before I left my apartment. I haven't gotten a reply."

"So maybe this crazy Forbis guy . . ." Stan had eagle eyes and thinking, he narrowed them. "Maybe something really did happen to the guy."

"Maybe." I chomped down the last of my bagel, took my plate and Stan's into the back room, and came back brushing my hands together.

"So what are you going to do?" Stan asked.

Like I said, he might be retired, but never let it be said that Stan isn't as sharp as a tack. I know him well, and I knew he knew my answer even before I said it. "I was thinking of going back over to the church," I said. "If you're not busy this morning . . ."

It was raining when I left the apartment that morning, and I'd left my slicker on my desk chair when I walked in. He held it up so I could slip my arms into it.

Within half an hour, I was back at the church. I found Laverne behind her desk in the office next to Reverend Truman's and as best I could, I explained why I was there.

"If I could just look around a little," I suggested. "Maybe I could—"

"No worries!" She popped out of her chair and led the way down the corridor and to the side door that led into the church. She unlocked the door, opened it, and stepped back to let me walk in first. "I don't think you'll find anything," she said. "Richard and I, we looked around last night before we locked up, but I can see how you'd be worried, about the

33

buttons and about sweet little Forbis. That was mighty peculiar, wasn't it, the way he took off out of here like the devil himself was on his heels?"

"Exactly what I was thinking." Maybe it was some sort of subliminal suggestion, but the moment Laverne mentioned the devil, I found myself drifting toward the Congo Savanne exhibit. The red button I'd brought to finish the work, the one Forbis had dropped when he bolted, was on the floor. I bent to retrieve it, and groaned.

It had landed back side down, and the contact cement Richard had applied to it had stuck it to the floor.

I stood up. "No sign of the broken champagne glass."

Laverne nodded. "Had Bob, our maintenance guy, clean that up before we turned off the lights and locked up last night. Didn't want to worry about somebody forgetting the glass was here and maybe stepping on it this morning." She looked over the area and shook her head. "It was mighty odd what went on here last night. You think it has something to do with all these buttons?"

"I wish I knew." I looked over the exhibit. The sign that said "Press the Button" was a little crooked, and I reached to straighten it. When I did, I hit the shell button and the whirring started up from inside the box. "Dang," I mumbled.

Laverne and I were on the same wavelength. "Oh, we're going to have to look at that nasty statue again!" she moaned.

And though neither of us wanted to, we couldn't help ourselves. We stood side by side, listening to the whoosh of the hydraulic lift inside the box, waiting for Congo Savanne to make his appearance.

We saw the button hair first, dark and springy.

Then the opalescent sheen of the buttons that covered the statue's forehead.

Then . . .

Laverne grabbed my arm and held on so tight, I was pretty sure I was going to have a bruise. Her voice was high, and choked with panic. "Is that . . . ?"

It was.

As the statue rose, we saw that the *petro loa* was not alone. There was something tied to the statue.

Someone.

Gray suit. Blue high-top sneakers with neon orange laces.

Forbis's skin was pale and glazed, like the mother of pearl buttons on Congo Savanne's face. That is, except for his eyes and his mouth.

Those had been glued shut with buttons.

Chapter Three

"Sorry."

It was the first thing Nev said to me when he arrived at the church an hour after Laverne and I discovered Forbis's body. Call me shallow, but even though we stood ten feet from the art installation and watched a team of crime-scene techs swarm the area with their cameras and their evidence collection kits, I was grateful that he had his personal priorities in order. He needed to apologize, I mean what with the whole Evangeline situation. I was glad we could get that out of the way right up front so we could concentrate on the body propped in Congo Savanne's arms.

"You keep finding bodies. It's just not fair."

"That's what you're sorry about?" OK, when I spun from facing the altar to gaping at Nev with my fists propped on my hips, my words shouldn't have come out quite so crisply.

But hey, I'd just had something of a shock, what with finding Forbis dead and all. I had an excuse.

Nev was a professional, he didn't.

"You thought I was talking about Evangeline."

Like I said, he's a professional, and he's supposed to be good at reading people. He didn't need me to tell him he was right on the money.

Nev poked his hands into the pockets of his raincoat. The belt was untied, and it dragged on the floor. "I never told you about Evangeline because there's nothing to tell," he said. "I knew her way before I met you. We were engaged, but things didn't work out. It's over. It has been for a long time. End of story."

"Just like that."

"Just like that."

"But don't you see, Nev . . ." The last thing I needed to do was attract attention to what we were talking about when what we were talking about was supposed to be murder. I glanced around to make sure no one was looking our way, and even though nobody was, I made sure I kept my voice down. "If you keep big chunks of your past from me, I can't get to know the real you. It's important because everything that's ever happened to you makes you the person you are today and—"

And his phone rang.

This in and of itself was not all that unusual. After all, the poor guy's always on call, and this is a big city that can sometimes be violent. We'd had plenty of late-night movies and cups of coffee and dinner sandwiches interrupted by crime.

When he answered one of those calls, though, he never turned his back on me.

KYLIE LOGAN

Fortunately, churches have great acoustics and this one was no exception. "Just got called to a crime scene," I heard Nev say. "I can't really talk right now."

Once he ended the call, he turned back to me.

"I hope you told Evangeline hello from me," I said ever so sweetly.

"How did you—" He shoved his phone in his pocket. "It doesn't mean anything."

"It means she has your cell number."

"Just like a few hundred other people do."

"Were you engaged to all of them, too?"

Oh yes, this was a bitchy little comment on my behalf, but come on . . . no one could blame me! I was more than willing to be an adult and discuss this whole ex thing sensibly and calmly. Heck, I had an ex myself! Trick is, Nev knew all about Kaz. He had, right from the start.

Maybe Nev realized all that and, consequently, didn't want to talk about it. Maybe he was simply dodging. Whatever the case, when Laverne caught his eye from where she was standing with her arms wrapped around herself, next to one of the gigantic pillars that lined the main aisle of the church, he used the opportunity to head that way and, not so coincidentally, to effectively let me know that the subject was closed.

Since I hadn't been told to stand back and mind my own business, I went along, too. Not to worry; I wasn't looking to pick a fight with Nev because of Evangeline. I was curious. About Congo Savanne. And Forbis. And those buttons that held his eyes shut. I got over to where Laverne stood just as Nev asked her, "What time did you get to the church this morning?"

She wiped tears from her cheeks with the back of one trembling hand. "Got here early, about eight or so. But I was in the office the whole time. There's always so much to do first thing in the morning. I check phone messages from the night before, make sure there aren't any urgent e-mails, make coffee. There was no reason for me to come in here to the gallery. And even if I did . . ." Her gaze slid toward where the crime-scene techs were circling the Congo Savanne statue, snapping pictures and taking measurements.

Nev stepped to his right so that she couldn't see past him to the grisly scene.

Laverne sniffled. "I didn't come in here until Josie showed up."

Nev's steady gaze turned to me. "And Josie showed up because . . . ?"

I shrugged, and since I knew that wouldn't satisfy him, I said, "I was worried about what happened here last night." Then, just so he didn't get the wrong idea, I added, "I was worried about Forbis. He seemed so upset when he ran out of here. I wondered what was wrong. I e-mailed him last night when I got home and never heard back from him. And I called his hotel this morning and he didn't pick up." Though Laverne was standing at a spot where she could no longer see Forbis's body, I wasn't so lucky. I watched a tech take a close-up shot of those buttons glued to Forbis's eyes and mouth, and I shivered. "I guess I know now why he didn't answer his phone."

"If he's been dead that long." It was the sort of noncommittal comment Nev would have made to any witness, not to the woman who'd helped him solve three cases, and I bristled, then told myself to get a grip. This might be Nev's job, but I had no doubt that it was just as stressful for him as it was for the rest of us, especially since he'd seen Forbis alive and well less than twenty-four hours earlier, just like we had.

I thought back to the night before and to the scene in front of the box that held the terrifying statue, about how Forbis had taken a few sips of his champagne before he dropped his glass and ran. He was frightened, paranoid, but let's face it, he couldn't have been afraid of the buttons, right? That meant he saw something or someone else that sent him screaming into the night. But if he'd seen something odd, I would have, too. I was standing right next to Forbis.

Unless his mind was playing tricks on him.

"Do you think he could have been poisoned?" I asked Nev.

I should have known he wouldn't speculate, not at this stage of the game. "He had a couple of drinks, didn't he?" Nev looked toward the altar, then back at Laverne. "When Forbis dropped his glass, there was champagne everywhere. It's been cleaned up. Did you—"

Laverne nodded and told him what she'd told me earlier. "Had Bob, our maintenance man, mop up before we left last night. Couldn't leave champagne on the floor. Never thought somebody was going to die and that champagne . . ." She swallowed hard. "You think there really might have been poison in it?"

"Can't say. We won't know until the medical examiner does an autopsy." Nev softened the comment with a tiny smile designed to put Laverne at ease and get her mind off murder. "But I would like to talk to Bob if he's around."

"Doesn't come in this early," Laverne said, and just as she

did, one of the side doors that led into a hallway that ran the length of the church slapped open. It was relatively quiet in there, what with us talking in hushed whispers and the crime-scene techs working at their jobs, so the sound of the door was like rifle fire. Automatically, we all glanced that way. There was a window in the hallway directly beyond it, and the man who took a step into the church, then froze, was silhouetted against its light. Because of the wash of sunlight behind him, it was hard to tell for certain, but it looked like he was wearing dark gray pants and a matching shirt, like a maintenance man would.

"Oh, look. Perfect timing. It's Bob. You can talk to him right now, Detective!" Laverne raised a hand and waved. "Bob! Come on over here. Bob!"

Bob stood motionless. That is, right before he backed up a step into the hallway, and the door banged shut.

"Well, he probably was surprised to see so many people in here," Laverne said, staring at the closed door. "Bob's a quiet kind of guy and not very good with crowds. He's probably on his way to my office now to find out what's going on."

"You can be sure I'll catch up with him." Nev said, and just to be sure, he called to one of the uniformed cops standing nearby and told him to go after Bob. "For now, let me ask you, Ms. Seiffert, what do you suppose happened here last night?"

"Me?" Laverne's hand fluttered against the honey-colored top she wore with black pants. "I . . . I don't know. It's so very terrible, it's hard to even imagine. But you saw what went on here last night. Both of you." Her gaze darted from Nev to me. "You both saw exactly what I saw. Forbis was here, and he was so excited. And then his little ceremony

41

started and then . . ." She threw her hands in the air and let them drop back down. "Then he ran out. And Josie, you went after him."

"Did you?" This was news to Nev, but then, he'd been talking to Evangeline at the time I raced down the aisle to try and catch up with Forbis, so I guess he never noticed.

"I looked out front," I told him and remembered what Gabriel Marsh had told me. He hadn't seen Forbis outside, either, and he'd gotten out there first. "There was no sign of Forbis." I looked around at the vast interior of the church. "Maybe he never left."

"It's possible," Nev conceded, and then asked Laverne, "If he stayed here in the church, was there anywhere for Forbis to hide?"

"Just about a thousand places." She looked around, too, as if that should have been enough to remind both Nev and me of just how big the old church was. "He could have been anywhere. Or he could have ducked out one of the side doors and not the front door," she added for my benefit. Her dark eyes filled with tears. "All that matters is that the poor man is dead. I'm sorry. I really am. But I can't explain any of it. I don't know anything."

"You know Richard." At this point, I wasn't sure how Nev might take a little bit of my amateur interference, but I was willing to take a chance. When it came to asking questions, Laverne needed a little tender loving care, and she deserved it, too. Unlike a certain button purveyor, she hadn't been entangled in murder before. "What can you tell us about him, Laverne?"

"Richard . . . I . . ." Laverne chewed her lower lip. "How do you—"

"Last night when Richard introduced himself," I reminded her. "When he walked over to where you and Forbis and I were talking, the first thing you did was put a hand on his arm. It was a friendly gesture and not something you'd do to a stranger. You obviously know the man."

"Yes, of course. I didn't mean it to be a secret or anything, I just didn't understand how you knew." She looked at Nev, then looked away again quickly. "A few months ago I was paging through a magazine and ran across an article about Forbis. Well, you can imagine that it caught my attention." For a moment, a smile relieved her somber expression. "He was certainly a character! The article mentioned that he was going to have a show in Chicago. It also mentioned Richard's name and said he was Forbis's agent. Richard and I, we're old friends."

"But if you never found out about Forbis until the show here was already scheduled, how—"

Laverne knew where I was going with the question and answered even before I had a chance to finish it. "The show was originally scheduled for a place called the Mango Tango Gallery in Wicker Park. I was so excited that Richard was going to be a part of something so fascinating, I called him and suggested maybe we could do something here at the church in conjunction with the show. I was thinking maybe he could pull a few strings and convince Forbis to stop by and talk about his art. I thought we'd do coffee and cookies and have a meet-the-artist night, you know, that sort of thing. And I thought that one night of the show, we might even rent a bus and take folks over there. After they met Forbis and heard about his work, I knew they'd be interested."

"But you ended up hosting the show here." Yes, it was

obvious, but sometimes it doesn't hurt to point out the facts. If I didn't, I knew Nev would. "That's a long way from coffee and cookies."

Laverne nodded. "It all happened so suddenly. When I first mentioned the meet-the-artist idea to Richard, he said he'd think about it but . . . well, you know how it is when you expect a person to be as enthusiastic about one of your ideas as you are. He was being polite and I thought it was just for old time's sake. But then Richard called back and I thought, hallelujah, he changed his mind. He wants to do the evening of coffee and cookies. But he didn't."

It must have happened weeks before, but it was obvious this still baffled Laverne. She screwed up her face and shook her head. "Richard told me that the show at Mango Tango had been cancelled. Just like that, out of the blue. He said he was looking for another gallery to host the show and he had plenty of places that were jumping at the chance to do it, but the first person he thought of was me." She held out her hands, palms up. "So here we are. I was thrilled to show off Celestial Spaces and so grateful when Richard said the church could share in the profits from any sales. Then this . . ." Again, her gaze traveled in the direction of the altar. "It was supposed to be so wonderful, and a springboard for discussion and a way to bring the neighborhood and the community to our church. And now this horrible thing has happened."

"So why was the show cancelled at Mango Tango?" Nev's turn to ask, maybe because he knew I would if he didn't.

Laverne shrugged. "All Richard ever said was that the owner there . . . some man named Burt or Bart, some name like that . . . all Richard ever said was that he was unreasonable. Some sort of art world prima donna. Richard was thrilled that we could accommodate the show. And we were thrilled to host it! Anyway, that's how Richard explained why he wanted to move the show here."

"You don't actually believe him, not completely." No, I'm not psychic, but one woman can read another woman's emotions as sure as shootin'.

Laverne proved I was right on the money when she grinned. "I thought maybe . . . Like I said, Richard and I were old friends. I thought maybe once he knew I lived here and that I was involved with Celestial Spaces . . . Well, I think he might have moved the show here on purpose. You know, so we could rekindle our friendship. And to help out the church, of course."

Nev had been scribbling in a little notepad, and he stuck it back in his pocket and looked around. "There was a security guard here last night during the show."

"Yes, but he didn't stay. Not all night," Laverne told us. "The church was locked up nice and tight. We didn't think we needed more security than that and, frankly, we can't afford it."

"Which makes me wonder how if Forbis did leave, he got back in here," I said and looked Nev's way. "Unless there was some sign of a break-in?"

Apparently not. "Who has keys?" he asked Laverne.

She laughed. "Keys? I can see you've never been involved in your church, Detective. In any church, everybody has keys, and this place is no exception. Reverend Truman, our minister, he certainly has keys. So does Bob, the maintenance man you saw a minute ago. The grounds staff does because they're always coming and going, and me, of course.

As church secretary, I have a set. So does our choir director, the president of our board, and anyone who's ever served on a committee. Then there are the workers we hire for the jobs Bob can't handle. A lot of times, there can't be someone here to meet them, you know, if someone comes in to fix something electric or to mess with the plumbing or whatever. When that happens, we just leave a key outside for them and they use it and put it back where they found it when they're done."

"So anybody could have a key," I said.

"Pretty much," Laverne said.

Nev and I exchanged looks. For this, I was grateful. It meant that, at least for now, we had put aside the Evangeline question and were back in investigating mode. Investigating was good. Investigating was all about logic, and with any luck, I could keep my emotions in the background where they belonged. At least until Nev and I had a chance to sit down and have a real heart-to-heart.

Even before Nev said, "I think we need to talk to Reverend Truman," I was already headed for the door. Yep, we were back to being a team and thinking alike. I didn't even realize that it felt as if a hand was squeezing my heart. Not until the pressure let up.

We found the minister in an oak-paneled office with bookcases on two walls and a window that looked out over the parking lot. He was an African American man in his sixties with gray hair, and he looked decidedly unclerical in khaki pants and a green golf shirt. When we walked in, he had a dust rag in his hands, and he was rubbing away at the side of his desk.

"Be with you in a minute." He tossed the comment over his shoulder at us. "Just can't stand the thought of a mess in here. Whatever this is, it wasn't here when I left yesterday evening, that's for sure. And now there's this white greasy stuff all over the side of my desk."

Nev stepped forward and whisked the dust rag out of the minister's hand before he could take another swipe. "It might be evidence," he said.

"Oh." Reverend Truman had a round, pleasant face and bulging eyes. "Oh," he said again after he'd had a moment to think about it. "I'm sorry. I never thought it might be important. After what happened here last night . . ." His gaze drifted to the hallway and the gallery beyond. "I prayed, of course. I prayed for the poor man's soul and the soul of whatever monster did this to him. And then I couldn't keep still. I had to do something and cleaning up seemed like the right thing to do. I never thought—"

"It's OK." Nev had plastic evidence bags in his pocket and he took one out and dropped the rag into it, then took a look at the smudge on the desk. "You're sure this wasn't here yesterday?" he asked.

"I would have noticed." The reverend nodded. "Yesterday was Thursday and Thursday is cleaning day. We can't afford to have a crew come in and do the work. We each clean our own offices." He looked toward Laverne for confirmation. "I cleaned this place top to bottom yesterday. Dusted, vacuumed. I would have noticed something smudged on my desk, that's for sure."

"We'll get the techs in here," Nev told him. "And they can take samples."

"You think . . ." The reverend's gaze slid toward the smudge. "You think the murderer might have—"

"We don't know, Reverend. Not yet. For now . . ." Nev put the evidence bag with the dust rag in it into his pocket. "We're wondering about keys to the church. Who has them?"

"Everybody!" Reverend Truman confirmed what Laverne had told us a little while before. "We're a small congregation and running a church and a food pantry and the little thrift store we maintain to bring in a few extra dollars and the gallery, of course . . . well, it's a lot of work. Pretty much anyone who's ever helped has a key."

"I'll need a list of those people," Nev said and the reverend looked to Laverne, who nodded. "And I'll need to know if there are extras."

"Extra keys?" For a moment, Reverend Truman seemed confused by the question. "Well, there are . . ." He walked around to the back of his desk and opened the top drawer. "There are these." He took out a key ring with three keys on it. "And these," he said, taking out a second key ring. "These are the ones we leave when the utility companies need to come in, you know to check the water meter and such. And, Laverne, didn't we give that other extra set to somebody? Was it Miss Maud from the choir? I think it was. And then of course there are the keys over there . . ." He dropped the key rings back in his desk at the same time he made a vague gesture toward the door. "We always keep those on the nail right inside the door. Just in case anybody needs them for anything."

Both Nev and I looked that way, and we both saw the nail the reverend was talking about.

Just like we both saw that it was empty.

Reverend Truman realized it just as we did, and his mouth dropped open. "They were there last night," he said. "I'm sure of it. Before I went in to the gallery to take a look at the show, those keys were hanging right there inside the door." He hurried around to the front of the desk and headed over to the door, but before he could get too close, Nev stopped him.

"There could be fingerprints," Nev said.

The reverend froze. "Then you think the murderer was in here."

"It would have been easy to slip in here during the show," I pointed out. "There were lots of people in the gallery and no one would have noticed if someone slipped out and came in here. It would be pretty easy to pocket the keys and use them to get back into the church after we were all gone."

Reverend Truman dropped his chin onto his chest and squeezed his eyes shut. "And kill that poor artist. God forgive him."

"Except he would have had to get Forbis back here to the church to begin with." I wasn't sure anyone wanted to hear this bit of theorizing on my part, but I felt it was only fair to bring it up. "Forbis left. So how did the killer get him to come back to kill him?"

"Unless he wasn't killed here. He could have been killed somewhere else," Nev suggested and I knew he was right.

"But if he was, it would have been a heck of a lot easier to leave the body wherever that somewhere was." Nev didn't argue so I went right on. "Which means there was a very particular reason the killer wanted Forbis found where he was, and the way he was. I mean, with those buttons on his eyes and mouth. It's like he was sending a message."

One corner of Nev's mouth twitched. "Maybe he was an art critic."

Chapter Four

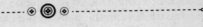

ONE OF THE CRIME-SCENE TECHS CAME IN AND ASKED NEV to come into the gallery, and this time I knew better than to poke my nose where it clearly didn't belong. It was one thing working alongside Nev to think our way through an investigation. It would be another altogether if the techs, uniformed cops, and other detectives there to do their jobs thought I was an interfering buttinski.

Rather than stand there with nothing to do, calling attention to the fact that I was hanging around where I didn't belong, I stepped back into the church. Nev was taking a look at the body. Me, I went in the other direction.

Just like I had the night before, I walked down the main aisle of the church, stopping now and again to imagine all that had happened after Forbis dropped his champagne glass and ran. As long as I was at it, I looked around and wondered what Forbis had seen when he raced by.

Pews.

Nothing but row after row of pews.

Though if someone had decided to duck into one . . .

The thought struck, and I stopped and thought back to the scene. Though the art installation was brightly lit, it was pitch dark here in the body of the church, and even if I'd bothered to look around as I raced outside, I doubt I would have seen Forbis if he'd sidestepped into one of the pews and scrunched up to hide.

But why?

I took another look around the church. From here, about halfway down the aisle, there was a clear shot to the old altar area and the box where Congo Savanne lurked. If Forbis really had run away from the exhibit just as a stunt designed to attract attention to himself and his artwork, this would have been an ideal place to watch the show. From here, he could see the stunned expressions on peoples' faces when they realized the star of the show had just taken off like a bat out of hell. He might not have been able to hear exactly what they said, but he would have been able to catch the excited hum of their conversation, just like I could hear the overlapping voices of the crime-scene techs at work around the exhibit.

This was a possibility Nev and I hadn't considered and, wondering if it was actually feasible, I sat down in the nearest pew to think.

I stood up again just as quickly when I realized how slick the wooden pew was.

Of course! It made perfect sense. Laverne said that church

services were conducted in the basement. Which meant that except for the art shows up front, most of the old church went largely unused and wasn't cleaned often. This pew was coated with dust and that meant the others were, too.

Quickly, I headed to the front of the church, then back down the aisle, glancing left and right as I did. If Forbis crouched down in any of the pews, he would have left a smudge in the dust, just like I had when I sat down.

Only he hadn't.

He didn't.

Except for the spot where I'd just sat down, the light that flowed in through the stained-glass windows showed that the dust was undisturbed, a slick, smooth coating on each and every wooden pew.

Sure I was disappointed that my hunch hadn't worked out, but I am nothing if not determined. Ask all the friends and family members who'd given me weird looks when I told them I'd decided to quit my admin job at an insurance company and open up my own button shop. Ever practical, I knew it was time to move on to Plan B.

This would actually have been a really good idea if I had a Plan B.

Grumbling, thinking, and grumbling some more, I wandered out the door at the back of the church and into the vestibule. There was no use going outside. I'd been out there the night before—me and hotness personified, Gabriel Marsh—and I knew there wasn't anything to see. Not anything that would help me figure out what happened to Forbis, anyway.

I was just about to throw in the towel and go back into the church when I realized all wasn't lost. There were other possibilities. Two of them, in fact. To the left of the main doors was an alcove that contained a baptismal font, and to the right, the stairs that led to the choir loft.

Like so much of the church, the baptistery was dusty and obviously unused. That left the choir. I took the steps two at a time, and by the time I got up to the loft that spanned the width of the church, my heart pounded and I was breathing hard.

I didn't turn on the lights. That would only have attracted the attention of the cops swarming the art exhibit and, for now, I wanted to keep this little piece of the investigation to myself. If it panned out, I would certainly mention it to Nev. And if it didn't, well, there was no use in him knowing that I'd tried and gotten nowhere.

Then he'd only have another reason to compare me to beautiful and brilliant Evangeline.

I slapped the thought out of my head. It was unworthy of me. Not to mention small-minded. Besides—a slow smile spread across my face—Evangeline might be an expert when it came to vudon and Barrier Islands culture, but I had it all over her when it came to buttons, not to mention murder.

The thought firmly in mind, I took a look around.

There was a rose window to my left, a long way off and directly opposite from where the old altar used to stand. With the morning light streaming through, it was breathtaking, but I tried not to get distracted by the pools of blue and purple and red that stained the old wooden floor. The night before, the choir loft would have been completely dark and not as easy to negotiate.

There were five rows of pews up here, each a little higher than the one in the row in front of it. That made sense, of course, both from the perspective of the congregation, who could look back and see the singers, and for the singers themselves, who would have a bird's-eye view of the services. There was an aisle between the two sets of pews and directly at the end of it, a big old organ, its pipes arrayed on either side of the rose window.

I checked the pews, just as I'd done downstairs. It wasn't hard to find the smudge in the pew on the left, three rows back from the railing that looked out over the church. It was at least three feet long and it rippled from the front of the pew to the back, like someone hadn't just sat down there, but more like that someone had shifted back and forth. Or maybe tried to scrunch down to hide.

Oh yes, someone had been in the choir loft, and recently.

Another glance around and I knew exactly who that someone was.

There it was on the floor just next to the pew, its plastic wrapping caught in a particularly vivid ray of golden light so that it winked and flashed at me.

A root beer barrel.

I HURRIED BACK downstairs, and this time I didn't worry about looking bad; I found Nev and told him what I'd seen up in the choir loft, and he sent a few of the techs up there.

"Good work." When he smiled at me, I smiled back. It felt good, comfortable, and I was just about to tell him so when Richard Norquist walked into the church.

Talk about bad timing!

A team from the medical examiner's office was just

lowering Forbis's body down from the statue, and Richard took one look at what was going on and turned as white as those buttons on Congo Savanne's skull.

Nev and I exchanged glances and we knew we were on the same page: if Richard fainted and cracked his head on the stone floor, we'd have another problem that we didn't need on our hands.

"Mr. Norquist, you really shouldn't have come here." Nev got to Richard before me and put a hand under Forbis's agent's elbow to pilot him to the nearest pew. Richard sat down so hard, the thump reverberated up to the painted angels who looked down at us from the high ceiling. "What are you doing here?"

"I'm . . . I'm . . ." Like Laverne had earlier, Richard stared at the body, and Nev, just like he had before, moved to block the view. I was struck by his thoughtfulness. That, and his desire to keep the conversation on track and to keep Richard Norquist from falling completely to pieces.

Richard passed a hand over his forehead. "I'm . . . I'm . . ." He swallowed so hard, I saw his Adam's apple jump. He looked up at Nev, his eyes wide. "I'm sorry. What did you ask me?"

"I asked what you're doing here. How did you know about Forbis?"

"I . . . I didn't." Richard pressed a hand against the front of his navy blue windbreaker. "Laverne called. She didn't say what was wrong, she just said I should get down here. She sounded so upset . . ." He pulled in a breath, and like he'd just woken from a very sound sleep and a very bad dream, he shook his head. "I thought maybe the church had been broken into and some of the artwork was gone. Or that a pipe had burst and there was water damage. I never imagined . . ."

Richard leaned to his right so he could see around Nev. "Do you think Forbis was murdered?"

"Somebody glued buttons to his eyes and mouth and put him in with that statue." I did my best to keep from sounding cynical, but it wasn't easy. "Do you really think—"

"Where were you last night, Mr. Norquist?" Nev interrupted me, and maybe that was a good thing. No doubt the irony of my words was lost on Richard Norquist. "After Forbis Parmenter left the show?"

"I . . . I . . ." Richard thought back. "I stayed around for a while. You know that." He looked at me, then Nev. "And you do, too, Detective. You were both here. Forbis ran off—"

"And where do you suppose he ran to?" Nev asked.

Richard's doughy features accordioned in on themselves. "I figured it was a stunt. I thought Forbis was looking for attention. I just thought he ran out of the nearest door and hit the closest bar. You don't think—"

"You haven't told us where you were," Nev reminded him.

Richard took a moment to collect his thoughts. "Like I said, I stayed around. I did a little networking. You saw me, certainly. Detective, I talked to you and that very pretty woman you were with."

Since I was outside looking for Forbis, the very pretty woman was obviously not me. I gritted my teeth.

"I reminded folks that even though Forbis wasn't around, they were still welcome to look at his work," Richard continued. "I told them they could certainly still make purchases. That woman you were with, Detective, you remember, she asked for prices on a couple of the pieces."

Investigation, I reminded myself, and repeated the word like a mantra.

The investigation was what was important.

"Did anyone buy anything?" I asked him in the name of the investigation.

Richard shook his head. "It really fried me, I'll tell you that. Forbis pulls these crazy publicity stunts, and he doesn't even stop to consider that they don't build interest in his work, they just turn people off. Like that time in Asheville when he had those models dressed as old-fashioned housewives—you know, wearing aprons and housedresses and high heels—show up at the exhibit that featured buttons on household goods. Everyone was so taken with these five gorgeous models, much more than they were with blenders and mixers and vacuum cleaners covered with buttons. Forbis just doesn't get it. If he's going to get anywhere in the art world—" He thought better of the comment.

"If Forbis *was* . . . If he ever was going to get anywhere in the art world, he knew the drill. The way to become popular is to get some of the movers and shakers to buy your pieces. That's how this business works. People with big bucks. You know, investment bankers. Actors. Actors are great for business. Once a movie star buys a piece, everybody else thinks it must be real art. If we could get that to happen, I knew the world would beat a path to our door."

"And last night . . ." Nev gently nudged him back on the path where we'd been headed before Richard took a major detour.

"Well, after all that drama from Forbis, no one made an offer on any of the pieces. I could have wrung his neck!"

Richard realized the error of his word choice just a second after both Nev and I had. His already pale face went a little paler.

"I didn't mean that," he said. "I mean, I did, but only as a figure of speech. You understand?" He didn't care if I did; he looked at Nev, his eyes pleading.

"So you were angry." It went without saying, but Nev, was a good interrogator. He knew it was important to let Richard know that he understand how Richard felt. "But not angry enough to try and find Forbis and figure out what he was up to. Unless you did find him."

It took a moment for what Nev wasn't saying to sink in. "Me?" Richard squeaked out the word. "I didn't. I swear, I didn't."

"But you didn't go after him," I said. "And that seems odd since you're his agent. I barely knew the man, and even I tried to find Forbis."

Was that a roll of the eyes from Richard?

I pretended not to notice.

"You tried to find Forbis because you'd just met the man and you were taken in by that good ol' country boy act of his." Richard shook his head, but whether he was disgusted with me for admitting what I'd done or with himself because he'd once been taken in, too, I didn't know. "Believe me, if you'd known him as long as I have, you would have been glad to see him disappear for a while. Only . . ." Richard's wide-eyed gaze traveled back to Nev. "Not like this."

"And how long have you known Mr. Parmenter?" Nev asked.

Richard thought about it. "We met years ago. Ten. Twelve maybe. I was representing another artist down in Georgia and her work was being presented at one of the local galleries. Forbis had a couple pieces there, too, and he tried to interest me in representing him."

"You weren't impressed with buttons?" I tried to keep the acid from my voice, but let's face it, when people start dissing buttons, it's bound to get me riled up.

"Oh, he wasn't doing the button thing then," Richard said. "Back then, Forbis was what I like to call a serious artist. He worked in oils."

"Painting?" It didn't exactly fit with the notion of the weird outsider artist I knew.

"Oh yes, landscapes mostly," Richard said. "He did beach scenes, ocean scenes, scenes around that old plantation home of his back on the island. You both met Forbis. You won't be surprised to hear that he thought he was brilliant. The Barrier Islands' answer to Michelangelo."

We were talking art, and art is a little outside Nev's area of expertise. I felt perfectly comfortable taking over, at least for a bit. That's why I prodded Richard, just a little. "And you thought . . . ?"

Richard shrugged. "His work was OK. Just OK. It wasn't especially inspired, and it certainly wasn't brilliant. He had average technique. A so-so understanding of color. None of it was very exciting."

"And so you weren't interested in representing him."

"I didn't see there would be any money in it," Richard said matter-of-factly. "So why would I waste my time? About five years later . . . well, I guess that was about when Forbis realized he was wasting his time, too. He tossed his easel and his oil paints and started in on this whole crazy button thing. When he contacted me again and I saw what he was up to—"

"So you do think it's art?" Nev asked.

"And you did finally realize Forbis was brilliant?" I said.

Richard apparently wasn't sure which question to answer. That would explain why he sidestepped both of them. "Hey, I've got bills to pay and a credit card balance just like everyone else," he said. "It doesn't matter if I thought what Forbis was producing was art. Or if he was brilliant. Truth be told, I thought the guy was a certified nutcase. But that didn't mean people wouldn't buy his stuff. It's different. It's weird. And a lot of collectors, they like weird."

"Are any of them weird?" Nev asked. Then because it looked as if Richard wasn't sure what he meant, he added, "Was Forbis having trouble with anyone? Did anyone have a beef with what he was doing?"

"With the buttons?" Richard barked out a laugh, then looked at me to see if I was offended. I was, but I didn't let on. "I can't see anybody getting worked up about buttons."

"How about someone getting worked up about vudon?" I asked.

Richard shook his head. "This was a brand new show. No one had ever seen it before. Forbis's last show was classic cars covered with buttons. The one before that, that was the one with the household items. Who would care so much about a couch covered with buttons that they'd want to kill someone over it?"

"Just so I have this straight . . ." Nev pulled a small, spiral-bound notebook out of his pocket and flipped it open. "What exactly did you do for Mr. Parmenter?"

"What an agent does." Richard nodded. "I handled sales. I arranged shipment when a piece was sold. I put out feelers to the art community so that I could book shows for him."

61

"Speaking of shows . . ." I sat down next to Richard. "Laverne told us that this show was originally scheduled at another gallery. What happened?"

Richard pulled at his left earlobe. "The guy was a real flake," he said. "That Bart McCromb over at Mango Tango. Promised us the moon for the show and backed out of every one of those promises. And the gallery?" He clicked his tongue. "In the famous words of Bette Davis, what a dump! When I got to Chicago and went over there, I just about had a cow. I was so excited. Finally, a big show in a big city. We were bound to attract plenty of attention. Then when I realized Mango Tango was just a hole in the wall, well, I'll admit it, I didn't know what to do."

Richard shifted uncomfortably in his seat and I pictured the dust in the pew getting smudged. "I like to come across as a mover and a shaker," he said. "I mean, that's part of my job, right? Art critics and buyers, they want to think they're dealing with the cream of the crop, so I've got to put on a show, just like Forbis does. Did." He cleared his throat. "Truth is, I've always worked with small, regional galleries. Never with a show on this scale and never in an art mecca like Chicago. When I realized what I'd gotten us into with crazy Bart and that refuse heap of a gallery, I was sick to my stomach. I didn't know what to do. Then I remembered Laverne."

"She'd talked to you about having Forbis here as a guest," I said.

Richard nodded. "And I realized I'd just had my salvation dropped in my lap." He cringed and looked around. "Pardon the pun. So I saved my bacon and at the same time, I realized I could do a little good. The church is definitely a worthy cause and with Forbis's star rising, it wouldn't hurt us to donate a portion of the profits to this place and get a tax write-off in return. Besides . . ." He glanced away. "Laverne is an old friend, an old girlfriend. We dated back in college and I thought, well, I thought it wouldn't hurt to get together with her again. You know, just to see if any of the old spark was still there."

"Was it?" I knew Nev wasn't going to get too personal, or show off his soft, romantic side, so I did him the favor of asking. "What did you do after the show was over last night, Mr. Norquist?"

Richard's smile was fleeting. "We went for coffee, me and Laverne."

"And you didn't come back here to the church?"

He shook his head. "Laverne locked up before we left. We got in a cab, had coffee over near my hotel, then I put her in another cab and sent her home. I didn't hear from her again until this morning. You know, when she called about . . ." Again, he peeked around Nev. "About this."

"When Mr. Parmenter ran out of here last night . . ." Nev was holding a pen in one hand, and he used it to point down the aisle in the direction Forbis ran. "What did you think?"

"That he was crazy. That he was ruining a good thing. That he should have known better."

"And before that, what did you see?"

Richard looked across the church. "I was standing over there. You remember. You both saw me. Ms. Giancola, you walked up to the front with Forbis—"

"And you came over and dabbed some cement on the back of the button I brought with me," I added.

"That's right. Then I stepped back over to where I was

to begin with. The next thing I knew . . ." Richard made a face. "I'll admit it, when I saw Forbis wince, I didn't think a thing of it. He was a twitchy old guy, or at least he liked to pretend he was. I think he thought he was being cute and folksy. But then he dropped his glass and yelled, 'The button, the button' and ran out of here, and I admit it, I was as stunned as everyone else."

"Until you decided it was all for show and you got angry," Nev said.

"Not angry, more like disgusted," Richard said. "But not disgusted enough to kill Forbis."

We were right back where we started from. Nev told Richard that he was free to go, but that he shouldn't leave town any time soon, just in case he could help with the inquiry.

"What do you think?" he asked me once Richard was out of earshot.

"I think we've got it all wrong," I said, considering what Richard had just said. "Forbis jerked back. Just like Richard said. And we all know he dropped his champagne glass. But you know, Nev, Forbis didn't say, 'the button, the button' like Richard said he did. I was standing right next to him so I know. What Forbis said was 'le bouton, le bouton.' It's French and yeah, it means, 'the button, the button,' but you know what? To me, Forbis didn't seem like the kind of guy who'd just naturally start suddenly speaking French."

Chapter Five

I ACTUALLY DO HAVE A REAL JOB. AND A REAL BUTTON SHOP to keep open, running—and in the black. As intriguing as Forbis's murder was, I knew it was best to leave solving the crime to the professionals so I could concentrate on what I knew and loved best, buttons.

Besides, I'd learned that murder takes its toll on me. Like I mentioned earlier, I'd been involved in three cases previously, and with each, I found it nearly impossible to shake the pall of tragedy that followed in the wake of death.

So much potential lost. Not just when an artist like Forbis is killed, but with every life lost. So much sadness.

That next day at the Button Box, I knew I could kill two proverbial birds with one stone. Which, now that I think about it, probably wasn't the best metaphor to use in regards to the situation. It was, however, true. I could concentrate on the shop and on the customers who came and went that Saturday and at the same time, I would use the opportunity to calm my mind and find familiarity and comfort, as always, in the sanctuary of the restored brownstone with its soothing sage green walls, tin ceiling, hardwood floors, and old library card catalogue file cabinets along every wall, each drawer filled with buttons.

Ah, buttons!

There is nothing like buttons to soothe this collector's soul.

By the time I helped a woman who was looking for just the right button to use as a closure for a purse she'd knit and felted, rearranged a couple shelves that didn't need it, and re-catalogued all the buttons in the drawers where I stored my Wemyss (that's pronounced *weemz*) Ware—those delightful earthenware buttons produced in Scotland at the end of the nineteenth century and distinctively decorated with wonderful things like cabbage roses and dogs—I was breathing easier.

That is, until Nev showed up just as I was about to close and ruined everything.

Oh my, that came out sounding all wrong!

I didn't mean Nev ruined everything because he came into the Button Box.

I mean he ruined everything because as soon as he walked in, I saw that he had papers in his hand and that look in his eyes that said he was thinking about his case and needed to bounce ideas around.

My vacation to tranquility came to an abrupt halt and my heart began a cha-cha in my chest.

"The list of people invited to the opening Thursday night." He held up the papers briefly before he tossed them down on the antique rosewood desk where my computer sat. "I thought you could look through it and tell me if there are names of any button collectors you recognize."

"Hello, Nev."

It took him a moment, but when he caught on, his shoulders drooped and he made a face. "Sorry. Hello." Nev hurried over and gave me a quick kiss. "My lieutenant's riding me about this case and you've seen the newspapers, right? Between the vudon connection and those buttons glued to Forbis's eyes and mouth . . . well, the media is making a circus out of this. The brass isn't happy about it."

"That means you've been working like mad and you didn't even take the time for lunch today. Or breakfast, I bet." It's not like I was guessing. One quick look and I knew Nev hadn't even changed his clothes since I saw him at the church the day before. That meant he hadn't been home, that he'd been running since he'd first responded to the call at the Chicago Community Church. He was even more rumpled than usual, and the belt of his raincoat was still dragging. When he slipped off the coat, I tugged the belt through the loops to even it up all the way around, thus restoring order, at least in this little corner of the world.

Before I said another word, I went into the back workroom and pulled out a jar of corn and black bean salsa, a bag of corn chips, and a couple of paper plates. I'd run out earlier in the day for the express purpose of buying comfort food so I could eat it in front of the TV once I got home, but hey, keeping Nev going was more important and I'd still get my comfort-food fix. I filled our plates and because I didn't like the thought of salsa mingling with my buttons, I called Nev into the back room.

He brought the guest list along with him and while he polished off his plate of chips and salsa in record time, I looked it over.

"There are a few collectors from the area," I told him, and pointed out the names. "I spoke to all of them briefly when we first got to the art show. Remember? In fact, they'd heard about Forbis's exhibit from me and I'm the one who called Laverne and had them added to the list. They're all nice people. As far as I know, there isn't one who would have a gripe against Forbis. In fact, none of them had ever even met Forbis."

"Except he got his buttons from somewhere, right?" Nev talked with his mouth full, swallowed, and took a glug from the can of ginger ale I'd put out for him. "If some of those buttons belonged to one of them and—"

"I did some research last night," I told Nev, and pointed to my own pile of papers that I'd left on the counter near the mini-fridge. "According to what I found online, Forbis got his buttons from garage sales and estate sales near where he lived in Georgia. And when he couldn't find enough—because let's face it, there couldn't possibly have been enough, what with all the buttons he used in his work—he ordered them directly from button manufacturers, most of them in China. He bought so many, they were more than happy to give him wholesale prices."

"Which means none of the buttons at the exhibit were very valuable."

"I can't say." It was true, and thinking it over, I crunched into my own chips while Nev refilled his plate. "I'd have to take a closer look," I said before I realized I was insinuating myself back into the case. What about maintaining distance?

Not to mention tranquility? As tempting as it was, I knew it was more important to find justice for Forbis. Even so, I gave Nev an out. "That is, I'll take a closer look at the buttons at the exhibit if you'd like me to."

"Are you kidding?" The snack brightened Nev's spirits. He grinned. There was a blob of salsa on his green plaid tie and I dabbed it up with a paper towel, then wet another one and got rid of the tomatoey residue. Well, most of it, anyway. "If you could go back to the church one of these days and do that for me, that would be fabulous."

"So you think there's a button connection? That someone wanted one of the buttons in the exhibit?"

Nev wrinkled his nose. "Not really. I mean, if that was the case, why not just grab the button? Why kill the crazy artist? But I would like to cover all the bases."

"You think it's far more likely that someone had it in for Forbis?" He crunched into a chip. I chewed thoughtfully. "Why do people kill other people?" I asked Nev. Then, just so he didn't think I was being too philosophical, I added, "I don't mean because the killer hates the person, or the killer's evil or anything. I'm talking more about motive."

"That's easy enough." Nev settled on one of the high stools at the table. "Revenge, jealousy, greed, lust, hate. Motives are living proof that the deadly sins really exist."

"So we should ask ourselves who wanted revenge against Forbis."

Nev shrugged. But then, his mouth was full so there wasn't much he could say.

"Or who was jealous." To me, this sounded like a better motive, what with the fact that we were dealing with the art community. As a collector, I was on the very fringes. I sometimes sold my buttons to artists and discerning crafters and I'd seen how their vision of their art—not to mention some of their delusions of fame and fortune—could make their egos inflate to the size of hot-air balloons. "If there was another artist who's ideas Forbis was stealing, or who thought Forbis was getting all the attention he should have been getting—"

"Another artist who glues billions of buttons onto stuff like couches and drums?" Nev's pointed question gave me all the answer I needed.

"Greed, then. Richard said that since he started in on button art, Forbis was making money. Someone could have wanted it."

"Absolutely." I was so grateful to have finally hit on something Nev considered feasible, I smiled. "We're looking into Forbis's bank accounts, his expenses. All that stuff."

"What about lust?" Honestly, I had no intention of bringing up Evangeline so Nev shouldn't have looked so uncomfortable. Just in case I imagined it, I ignored it completely and answered my own question. "Forbis was a little old for a jealous lover."

"But we'll check that out, too," he assured me.

"Speaking of which . . ."

"Josie!" Nev groaned. "I told you there's nothing to talk about, not when it comes to Evangeline."

Since Evangeline wasn't what I was going to talk about, I froze. But then, I guess that could easily have been because there was suddenly a block of ice in my stomach. My words felt wooden. My legs suddenly wouldn't hold me, and I took a seat, too. "I wasn't talking about Evangeline." A little niggle of worry ate away at my composure. Maybe Evangeline was what we should have been talking about. "I was talking about Laverne and Richard. He said that back in college, they were a couple."

"Oh." Nev took another drink of ginger ale.

Sometimes, silence can be just as loud as any noise. And far more uncomfortable.

I got up and refilled our plates with chips.

"Maybe there's some symbolism for Forbis's body being found where it was," I said, desperate to say something, anything, that would relieve the thundering silence and get our conversation back on track. "You know, in the arms of that spirit who grinds up people and eats them. And with those buttons on his eyes and mouth."

"Well, I'm no profiler . . ." No, he wasn't and I wasn't either, but there was no doubt Nev was as grateful for the change of subject as I was. Some of the stiffness went out of his shoulders. "My guess is the buttons on his eyes and mouth pretty much are a giveaway. You don't just do that to someone, even someone you dislike enough to murder. Not unless you're trying to send a message."

"Forbis wasn't looking. He wasn't seeing. He refused to open his eyes." Theorizing, I dragged a chip through the salsa even though I knew I wasn't going to eat it. After Nev's comment about Evangeline, I wasn't so hungry anymore. "He said too much. He didn't say enough. Button your lip!" I brightened. "That's about as literal as you can get."

Nev finished off a chip. "But what was he supposed to button his lip about? It sure wasn't buttons because, I swear, nothing could make Forbis stop talking about or working with buttons. I did some online research, too, and it's pretty clear, the guy was a publicity machine. Any time he got the chance, he showed up at regional button shows and county fairs. He loved being the center of attention, and according to his agent, he just got another huge shipment of buttons in so it sounds like he had another crazy notion for more crazy artwork. Not that buttons are crazy," he added a little too quickly.

"I know what you mean," I assured him and I did, honest, even though I had to ungrit my teeth before I said, "You don't need to apologize. What we need to figure out . . ." I drummed my fingers against the table. "One of the things we need to do is figure out who Forbis was arguing with when he first showed up at the art show."

Nev had a full mouth so he nodded and held up one finger as a way of telling me to hold the thought. While I did, he took his notebook out of his pocket and scanned through the pages. "We know it wasn't Laverne," he said, "because she was with us when we heard the fight break out."

"And Richard?"

Nev looked through a few more of the pages. "After you left the church yesterday, I asked him. He said he'd heard the argument, too, and went to try and run interference, but he never did find Forbis or see who he was fighting with."

"Which leaves . . ." I picked up the guest list Nev had brought along and let the four single-spaced pages drift back onto the table. "A hundred or so other people."

"And the church staff," he reminded me. "Because Reverend Truman and Bob the maintenance guy and anyone else who was connected with the church isn't on the guest list and they were all in the building, too. And what about that journalist guy . . ." He skimmed through his notes and when he found what he was looking for, he stabbed the page with one finger. "What about this Gabriel Marsh? Journalists can be annoying. I mean, if he was asking Forbis questions that were too personal, that could explain a fight."

"Except . . ." I thought back to my own encounter with Gabriel on the front steps of the church. Though we hadn't been able to clearly hear the person Forbis was fighting with, I couldn't help but think we might have picked up on the accent. "He's English," I told Nev.

"And English people are too well-behaved to get into arguments?"

It was Nev's idea of a joke and, actually, it wasn't a bad one. As I'd quickly learned once I started dating Nev, cops are a literal bunch. Just the fact that he was able to joke around after working more than twenty-four hours straight said something about a sense of humor I wasn't always sure he had.

"I was thinking more like if it was Marsh, we might have heard his accent, but I guess not." I dismissed the possibility with a sigh. "We heard Forbis, but not the person he was fighting with. Too bad. Then we'd know if it was a man or a woman."

"And how do you know this Marsh guy is English?" Nev asked.

"When I ran after Forbis . . ." I popped open the top on my can of diet soda. "I found Marsh already outside looking for him. But of course, if Forbis was up in the choir loft the whole time, that explains why we never saw him. Unless . . ." This was something I hadn't thought about earlier. "Maybe Forbis didn't go upstairs when he ran off. Maybe he was up there way earlier. You know, like before any of us even got there for the show. Or maybe that's where he was when he was arguing with . . . with whoever."

Nev shook his head. He was a couple weeks past needing a haircut and a thick strand of his sandy-colored hair flopped over his forehead. "If Forbis was having that fight up in the choir loft, I'm pretty sure we would have known it. The acoustics in that church are really good. As for him being up there before anyone arrived at the show, after what you found up there, I did check that out. According to Richard, he and Forbis came over from the hotel together in a cab. They arrived at the church just as the doors opened for show attendees. Forbis waited in Laverne's office so he could make his grand entrance. If he'd gone up into the loft, we would have seen him cut through the church."

"So that is where he went when he raced off the altar. But why? Unless there was someone waiting up there for him?"

One corner of Nev's mouth pulled tighter. "There were signs of other footprints in the dust. Unfortunately, some of them were yours."

I hadn't thought of this, and my stomach soured. "Sorry," I said.

Nev finished his ginger ale and took the can over to my recycling container. "You couldn't have known, and besides, it doesn't really matter. We were able to eliminate yours because you were wearing heels. Obviously, Forbis wasn't, and neither was the other person who was up there. The prints look like they were made by men's dress shoes."

"So someone *was* up there with him."

"And maybe it wasn't an accidental encounter. Maybe Forbis had arranged to meet that someone there."

"Could that someone be the killer?"

I knew Nev hated not to have answers, so I could just about feel his pain when he had to admit that he had no idea.

"If Forbis's champagne was poisoned . . ." I said, but Nev stopped me.

"We don't know that yet. And I'm not going down that road until we do. We won't know the cause of death until the medical examiner completes his autopsy. When I sent that officer out after Bob yesterday, he couldn't find hide nor hair of the guy, but I finally tracked him down later in the afternoon. He confirms what Laverne told us. He not only mopped up the champagne, he used bleach to do it. If there was any evidence on the floor, that was sure to eliminate it."

Nev took his empty plate and tossed it in the trash. "Thanks for dinner," he said.

My plate wasn't empty, but I threw it away, too. "That's dinner? You need more than that if you're going to keep going."

"There's a vending machine back at the station." Nev made it sound like this was no big deal and that whatever he got there was an actual substitute for real food. Knowing his schedule, I was afraid that many times, it actually was. "But tomorrow night . . ." When I walked past, he stopped me and pulled me into his arms. "If I've made any progress on the case, maybe I can take some time and we can do dinner tomorrow night? Nothing fancy. Just someplace quiet where we can talk."

75

I felt a smile relieve some of the tension that had been building in me ever since Nev dropped the *E* word. "I could be talked into making marinara."

Nev loves my marinara. He grinned and kissed me quick. "I'll bring the garlic bread."

"And I've got the fixings for salad."

"This does sound like a real meal. And that calls for a bottle of wine. I'll take care of that, too."

Our conversation sounded just like all our talks did in the old days (that is B.E. . . . Before Evangeline) and smiling, I leaned my head against Nev's chest.

And nearly jumped out of my skin when his phone rang close to my ear.

"Sorry." He stepped back and took the phone out of his shirt pocket. "I've got the ringer set loud so I make sure I hear it."

He answered and this time, he didn't turn his back on me, and while he talked, I cleaned up the chips and the salsa.

"Really?" Nev asked the person on the phone. "You're sure about that?"

Of course I was curious about who he was talking to and why there was suddenly a vee of worry between Nev's eyes, but I didn't want to look too nosy. Or too much like I was worried it might be Evangeline. I grabbed my purse, and since Nev was wandering as he talked, I followed him out to the front of the shop, turning off lights and my computer as I went.

By the time he hung up, we were at the front door and I flipped the sign in the window that said the Button Box was now officially closed.

76

Even then, Nev didn't budge. His head cocked to the side, he stood at the door, and didn't say a word.

"Bad news?" I asked.

Nev shook himself back to reality. "Weird news." He tucked away his phone. "That was Manny from the medical examiner's office. They finished their autopsy on Forbis."

"It was poison, wasn't it?" I was so sure of it, I would have bet a boatload of buttons. "And dang, too bad Bob cleaned up that spilled champagne so well or you'd have even more evidence."

"No, it wasn't poison." Nev put a hand on the door. "Manny said there was no sign of poison or drugs or even alcohol in Parmenter's system except for that little bit from the champagne. He also said from what they could tell, Forbis never had previous heart trouble."

Like I said, I was curious. I leaned forward, urging him to spill the beans. "And heart trouble is important because . . . ?"

"Because if Forbis did have heart trouble, they would have seen old damage. At least that's what Manny said. He also said something about . . ." Nev paused to think and I knew he wanted to get the information right. He's nothing if not a ducks-in-a-row kind of guy.

"Manny said something about ventricular fibrillation and I don't understand it completely so don't ask me to explain until I find out more. But he said that's what killed Forbis. Ventricular fibrillation."

"He had a heart attack?" I suppose this should have made me feel better; we weren't dealing with murder. But there was still the matter of Congo Savanne and those buttons on

Forbis's eyes and mouth. If he'd died of natural causes and someone came along and did that to the body . . .

I shivered and wrapped my arms around myself. "We're not talking murder?"

Nev pressed his lips together. "I wish I knew," he said. "Because Manny said . . . well, what Manny said is that if he had to make an educated guess, he'd say that Forbis Parmenter was scared to death."

Chapter Six

DRUMS POUNDED IN THE DISTANCE.

They echoed all around me, and I wasn't sure if I was running toward the sound or away from it. I only knew that each beat reverberated in my body. My heart thumped. My blood throbbed. I couldn't catch my breath.

The drums kept up the incessant beat.

And I kept running.

It was dark and wherever I was, it wasn't any place I was familiar with. There were plenty of trees, and a path so thick with leaves, my footsteps were muffled. But this wasn't Lincoln Park over near the lake or Seward Park in the Old Town neighborhood where the Button Box is located. Somehow, I knew that instinctively. This was strange territory. Foreign and forbidding. I was lost, and scared out of my wits.

When I raced down the path, cold wisps of fog swirled

around me, ghosts in the darkness. They closed behind me, brushing over me with their skeleton fingers.

Behind me, somewhere back in the darkness, something thudded on the path. Or maybe it was just the sound of my stomach hitting bottom and bouncing back up again when I realized there was someone just a dozen paces in back of me. Someone following me. Someone closing in.

I picked up the pace. Or at least I tried to. My legs were leaden and each time I lifted a foot and plunked it down again, it felt as if I'd never have the energy for another step.

The drums, though . . . the drums never stopped.

They hammered in my ears and shivered in my breast-bone. They drowned out the noises behind me and I cursed each and every beat. The drums were so loud, I couldn't tell if I was still being followed.

I could stop. I could look. I would know for sure then.

My logical self knew this was the best plan. But I couldn't take the chance. This was no time for reasoning. This was all about animal instinct, and mine told me that if my pursuer was still back there, I couldn't waste a step.

One foot in front of the other. One breath, then a second, and my lungs were on fire.

Behind me, the air stirred, and the chill turned molten against the back of my neck.

The drumbeats deafened me.

Rap, rap, rap.

The sound penetrated my subconscious, mingling at first with those drums in the distance, then gaining strength and volume.

Rap, rap, rap.

My eyes were weighted down with bricks, and I had to fight to open them.

Rap, rap, rap.

It took me a minute to realize I was sitting in the plump and comfy armchair in my living room, right where I'd drifted off. The reading lamp on the table next to me was still on, and the art magazine I was scanning for any news about Forbis was still open on my lap.

I was home, and safe.

Like a swimmer coming up for air after being underwater too long, I gulped in a breath and let it out in a whoosh, then pulled in another and another.

It was a dream. All a dream. No one was chasing me, and there were no drums.

Rap, rap, rap.

But there was someone at my door.

Even though it felt like I was moving through quicksand, I managed to scoop the magazine off my lap and stand, and when the room did a one-eighty and my knees buckled, I grabbed the chair to steady myself. A few more quick, steadying breaths and I started toward the door, massaging my throbbing temples with my index fingers.

Eleven fifteen.

I checked the clock on the cherry sideboard that had once belonged to my grandmother. I couldn't have been asleep more than twenty minutes, yet it felt like I'd been out of it for days.

"Eleven fifteen." I checked the clock again, just to be sure and mumbled to myself, "Who in the world comes calling at eleven fifteen on a Saturday night?"

Stan.

The idea hit like a wave of ice water, and worried that something had happened to my neighbor, I made for the door as quickly as I could.

Rap, rap, rap.

"I'm coming!" I called, my voice dull and muffled. I shook my head to clear it and when that didn't work, I stumbled to the door and yanked it open.

"Stan? Is it Stan? Is something—?"

The words froze on my lips.

But then, finding gorgeous Gabriel Marsh standing in the hallway was something of a surprise.

"You were in bed." He looked me up and down, not as penitent as he was simply curious. Since I was dressed in capris and a T-shirt the exact color of his inky hair, I guess he thought better of his initial assessment. "Or not. Have I interrupted something?"

"Would you care?"

He grinned and looked past me and into the apartment. From where he stood, I knew he couldn't see much. When it comes to living space, I'm a pretty basic person, but then, this is Chicago, and even with the royalty check I get every month from the crazy movie I once did costumes for that has since become a cult hit, fancy is a out of my price range. "Vintage charm." I guess that's what my apartment could be said to have, what with the oak crown molding, the fireplace, and the leaded windows. But in reality, the place is not that different from the thousands of other apartments in the area: living room, dining room, two bedrooms, one bath. Thanks to a recent renovation, the kitchen is no longer Eisenhower-era, but no way Gabriel could see the granite countertops or new appliances.

And why would I want him to, anyway?

I ran a hand through my hair and forced myself to focus. "What are you doing here?"

"Bothering you, apparently." This may have been true, but it didn't stop him from stepping into the entryway before I could even think about closing the door in his face. "I need to talk to you."

"You could have stopped by the shop."

"At this time of the night? My dear lady, I hear you love your buttons, but no one's that dedicated."

"Of course I wouldn't be at the Button Box." I was still swimming to the surface to escape the remnants of the disturbing dream. Otherwise, I was sure I would sound more coherent. Or at least a little more intelligent. "The shop is closed tomorrow. You could come on Monday."

His smile was brighter than anyone's had the right to be at that time of the night. "That's the thing, isn't it? I'm afraid I'm not very good at waiting. For anything."

It was my turn to eye him. Like he had been at the art show opening, Gabriel was wearing jeans and a black T-shirt. His denim jacket had seen better days, but his sneakers were new. I remembered what Nev had said about the footprints up in the choir loft. Mine, Forbis's, and one more set that looked to have been made by a man's business shoes.

"How did you know where I lived?" I asked Gabriel.

Honestly, I thought he was going to say, "pish-tosh," and when he didn't—when he just gave me a sort of lopsided smile—I wasn't sure if it made me feel better, or worse. "I'm a reporter. It's my job to know things."

"You write for some snooty art magazine. It's your job to know the difference between ultramarine and cobalt."

The heat radiating off his smile reminded me of the fire I felt against my neck in the dream. I shivered. The way his smile inched up a notch, I think it was safe to assume it was a reaction he often got from women. "You certainly know your shades of blue."

"And you know . . ." I paused long enough for him to fill in the blank and when he didn't, I threw my hands in the air. "You're looking for information. About Forbis."

He held up his left hand and the bag he was carrying in it. "I brought Chinese. Shrimp lo mein, fried rice, spring rolls."

Shrimp lo mein is my favorite.

But don't think I'm so easily distracted. Just because a gorgeous hunk comes knocking on my door late at night bearing the gift of Chinese food does not mean I completely lose my senses.

Since my front door was still open, it was easy enough to waltz across the hallway to Stan's. He had a couple of TV shows he liked to watch on Saturday nights so I knew I wouldn't be disturbing him. When he answered the door, I didn't even bother to say hello, I just took his arm, walked him across the hall to my apartment, and waved a hand in Gabriel's direction.

"This guy stopped in to see me," I told Stan. "You getting a good look at him?"

Stan nodded. "Six one, one seventy-five. Mid-thirties. Scar above his left eyebrow." I hadn't noticed the scar. "What's he doing here?"

"He says he wants to talk."

Stan folded his arms over his chest. "Do you want to listen?"

"I'm not sure," I admitted. "But he's got lo mein."

"Lo mein, huh?" Stan pulled in a breath. By now, the air in the apartment was fragranced with the aromas of the food inside the bag. "You want me to sit in the living room until you polish off dinner?"

"That's probably not necessary. Give us forty minutes." Both Stan and I checked the clock. "Then come back."

"And if anything's wrong . . ." Stan's gaze moved over Gabriel with laser precision. "I never forget a face. Just so you know. I could find you in a heartbeat, fella."

With that, he turned around and walked out of the apartment. He didn't close the door behind him. In fact, he went into his apartment, brought a chair and a book out into the hallway, and sat facing my door.

Gabriel let go of a shaky breath. "I didn't expect reinforcements."

It was my turn to cross my arms over my chest, the better to step back and give him another thorough once-over. "I hope you didn't expect me to be stupid, either. And just so you know, Stan's an ex-cop. See that blanket he brought to cover up his knees while he sits out there?"

Gabriel looked over his shoulder at Stan who simply stared back.

"I don't have one doubt that he's got his service weapon with him," I told Gabriel. "After all, there's a murderer on the loose."

"You can't possibly think it's me." Like he had every right to be there, he strolled into the dining room and plunked the bag of food on the table that matched Grandma's sideboard. "Dishes?"

It was on the tip of my tongue to tell him that if he expected that kind of service, he'd come to the wrong place, but the food smelled divine and I hadn't had a bite to eat since I shared the chips and salsa with Nev. I went into the kitchen.

"I wasn't sure you'd be home. I thought maybe you'd be out with that cop boyfriend of yours."

I was just reaching into the cupboard for plates when I realized Gabriel had followed me, and I froze. But only for a second. I wasn't sure what kind of game we were playing, but I did know I didn't want to lose. I got down plates and took linen napkins out of a drawer. "You seem to know an awful lot about me."

"You've got a reputation." Another smile. "In the button community, that is. I will admit, when I heard you owned a button shop—"

My chin came up and I clutched plates and silverware to my chest. "What?"

"Well, it is a tad out of the ordinary."

"Which doesn't mean it's weird."

"No one said it was."

"And they better not ever."

I pushed past him and into the dining room, and set out the plates while he pulled white cartons of food out of the bag. He'd also brought along a bottle of wine. Before I could offer an opener, he pulled a Swiss Army knife out of his pocket and did the honors. There were wineglasses on the sideboard and I reached for three, and once he'd poured, I took one of the glasses to Stan.

Gabriel staked out the chair at the head of the table and I chose the one to his left. "You must have been pretty sure I'd be willing to talk," I said, looking over the feast. "Or is the lo mein supposed to take care of that?"

"When it is appropriate, I'm not above offering a bribe." He sipped his wine. My head was still pounding and I thought better of joining him, but one taste and I changed my mind. It was a pinot noir and pricey, if I knew my labels. A couple more sips helped clear my head. "As for the lo mein, it was a lucky guess. You look like a lo mein sort of girl."

"I'll take that as a compliment."

"It was meant as one." He heaped his plate with fried rice and chomped into a spring roll. "So . . ." He chewed. "That bit with Forbis at the art show, the dramatic dropping of the champagne glass and the race from the church, was it staged?"

"If it was, nobody told me."

"Then what did they tell you?"

I had an excuse for not answering—I had a mouthful of lo mein. I chewed, swallowed, and washed it all down with another sip of wine. "If you're looking for answers, you came to the wrong place. You should talk to the police."

"You found the body."

There was no use denying it so I didn't even try.

There were two sets of chopsticks in the bag and Gabriel scooped up fried rice with his as if he'd been born using them. I am not so adventurous or willing to make a mess; I played it safe and used a fork.

"Is it true?" he asked. "About the buttons glued to Parmenter's eyes and mouth?"

"Is that what the news reports said?"

"You know they did, or I wouldn't have the information. I've called your boyfriend any number of times to try and get a few quotes and a whole lot of information. He's either busy, or he doesn't want to talk to me."

"And you think I can put in a good word for you."

"I think you look like a woman who could use some fried rice on her plate." He did the honors and for a couple minutes we sat in silence, eating. When I was feeling more generous and less like I'd been ambushed, I'd have to ask Gabriel where he got the food. It was too delicious to be from one of the carry-out places in the neighborhood.

He finished off his fried rice and attacked a portion of lo mein. "You know buttons," was all he said.

"If you're talking about the buttons on Forbis's eyes and mouth . . ." Sitting in my dining room eating lo mein did not seem like the appropriate time to think of what I'd seen at the church. I tried to stay as objective as I could, as objective as I'd seen Nev at the scene of a crime. Turns out, I wasn't very good at it, but it did give me a better appreciation of what it must cost him to retain his professionalism in the face of human tragedy.

"What about the buttons?" I asked Gabriel.

His right eyebrow lifted just enough to let me know he hadn't expected me to be even this cooperative. But then, he didn't know how firmly I believed that two could play the same game. He wanted information from me? Well, I wanted the same from him. Namely, why. Why was an arts writer so interested in murder? And why was he so convinced that buttons were involved that he thought a payoff in the form of lo mein to a button dealer was going to get him somewhere? If he knew something I didn't know then I owed it to my investigation, not to mention to Forbis, to find out what Gabriel had up his sleeve.

"The buttons the murderer glued onto Forbis, were they valuable?" Gabriel asked. "Unusual? Striking? Was there anything extraordinary about any of them?"

I'd gotten a close-up look at the body once the techs took Forbis down from Congo Savanne's arms, and I closed my eyes, pictured the scene, and gulped.

"Sorry."

When he spoke, and I opened my eyes again, Gabriel was refilling my wineglass. "It's not easy, is it, staring death in the face?"

"You didn't ask about death, you asked about buttons. One button on each eye," I said, and this was not some deep, dark secret because I knew the media had already reported it. "One button on his mouth. They were generic. Generic plastic buttons. My guess is that they were cut off shirts and probably manufactured in the mid nineties."

"My guess is that isn't a guess at all." Gabriel acknowledged my expertise with a lift of his wineglass.

I took the compliment in stride. Just as I'd told Nev when he asked for my opinion at the church, if I couldn't say that much about the buttons the murderer had glued to Forbis's body, I'd be a poor expert, indeed. Rather than risk getting caught in the snare of Gabriel's admiring look, I stuck to the facts. "One of the buttons was red, one was yellow, and one was green. Vudon colors."

"And the other buttons?" he asked.

I nibbled my spring roll. "You saw the exhibit. There were thousands of them. They were . . . buttons."

"None more valuable than the others?"

"Oh, I'm sure some were." I thought back to what Nev had mentioned about the buttons earlier in the evening. He wanted me to go back to the church and check them out. This was not exactly information I was willing to share. Not until I knew what Gabriel Marsh was up to. Lo mein can only get a guy so far. Even a guy like Gabriel, who was as delicious as the dinner he'd brought with him.

I told myself to get a grip. I hadn't spoken more than a couple dozen sentences to the man and I already knew one thing about him—he was a lot like Kaz, my ex. In fact, he was way too much like Kaz. Handsome and snake-oil-salesman charming. I knew better than to get fooled. I'd been fooled once and once was enough for a lifetime.

"When you found the body . . ." Gabriel pushed his chopsticks through the fried rice on his plate. "You didn't happen to notice if any of those buttons were missing?"

"Any of the thousands and thousands of buttons on Forbis's artwork?" It should have been enough of an answer, but when all he did was sit there as if he was waiting for more, I sat back. "You're serious. You think Forbis's murder has something to do with buttons he used in his artwork."

"I didn't say that."

"You didn't have to."

"You're used to being the one who asks the questions."

"And I've got plenty." I took another sip of wine and realized my headache was still pounding, but not quite as much. For this, I was grateful. "Why do you care so much?"

He considered the question while he dished up more lo mein. His perfect body (there I was getting off track again!)

didn't seem to go along with his super-sized appetite. "It would make a hell of a story, don't you think?" .

"And you're that hard up for something to write about in an arts magazine?"

"Unless I'm not thinking of writing this particular story for an arts magazine."

Some of the fog cleared, and I would have slapped my forehead if I wasn't afraid that would make my head start pounding all over again. I should have seen it sooner. I would have if I was thinking more clearly. "You have delusions of grandeur! Is it a book or a movie deal you're hoping for?"

"With any luck, both. You can't deny it, a story like this has bestseller list written all over it. The eccentric artist, the mysterious death. Voodoo."

"Vudon," I corrected him. "And something tells me that's nothing more than a coincidence. Forbis's death can't possibly be connected to some long-dead religion."

"You mean you think Parmenter might just as well have been killed at any of his other showings. The one that featured home appliances, for instance." Gabriel's eyes gleamed. "It would have been bloody brilliant if the killer could have left him in a button-covered cooler."

It took me a second to realize he was referring to the fridge. I wondered if that scenario would have been any less disturbing than finding Forbis in the arms of the people-eating loa and decided it wouldn't have made any difference.

"I don't know what to think," I said, and I wasn't just talking about the case. It applied to Gabriel, too. "I only know that the poor man is dead and the cops are working as hard as they can to figure out what happened to him. I'm sure they'll be interviewing everyone who was at the opening. They'll want to know where you were after Forbis ran out."

He finished the last of the food on his plate and pushed it away. "With you on the steps of the church. Don't tell me you've already forgotten. I like to think I make a little better impression than that."

Yeah, like I was going to admit that! "What about after?" I asked him instead.

"After . . ." Gabriel finished the wine in his glass and didn't pour another. He reached back in the takeout bag, pulled out two fortune cookies, and tossed one to me.

He broke his cookie in half and ate it without bothering to look at the fortune. "After that, I was . . . occupied," he admitted, and I wondered if I was about to hear something I'd rather not and then realized what I was comfortable hearing didn't matter. Wine, women, and song? Whatever Gabriel had been up to, it wasn't as important as the truth.

"So you do have an alibi for the time of the murder."

He laughed. It was a deep, throaty sound and it shivered along my skin like those wisps of fog in my dream. Only hotter. "Even if I didn't, you know I'd say I did. As it happens, mine is legitimate, but impossible to substantiate. Not unless the person I was following knew I was following him. And really, I highly doubt that. I may be . . ." He searched for the right word. "I may be conspicuous at times, but I wouldn't be very good at my job if I couldn't follow people without being noticed."

"Your job as a writer for an arts magazine."

Smiling, he ate the other half of his cookie, then pushed

back from the table and stood. "You're smart. No doubt that's why the police have let you consult on other cases. You know people."

"I know buttons."

"Buttons . . . yes." He ambled to the door and when he saw Stan was still sitting where we'd left him, Gabriel pointed back to the dining room. "There's plenty left," he said. "Enjoy."

He was about to step into the hall when I stopped him. "You still haven't told me where you were, who you were following the night of the murder."

"Why, Richard Norquist, of course."

I remembered what Richard had told us back at the church. "Richard and Laverne. They went for coffee near his hotel."

"Is that what he told you?" Gabriel's gray eyes glinted in the hallway light. "You might consider asking him again. You see, he wasn't with the lovely Laverne. He was with Victor Cherneko."

I suppose I shouldn't have been stunned. People had lied to me before, especially in connection with murder. Still, the thought that Richard could have told such a story, both to me and to Nev, left me at a loss for words.

Unless Gabriel was the one with the penchant for story-telling.

Before I could ask, he was down the stairs and gone, and honestly, I just wasn't in the mood to chase after him. For one thing, it would have looked pathetic and for another . . . I pressed my hands to my head. The rumba was starting up inside my brain again, and all I wanted to do was put on my jammies and crawl into bed.

First, I helped Stan get his chair back inside his apartment, thanked him, and wished him good night. Then I realized I had a mess to clean up in my dining room.

I tucked away the leftovers, filled the dishwasher, and grabbed the bag and cartons to throw everything away.

It was the first I saw that Gabriel had left the fortune from his cookie still lying on the table.

I picked it up and read it.

"A clear conscience," it told him, "is the sign of a bad memory."

Mine?

I cracked open my cookie and popped half of it in my mouth, then was sorry I did. I needed a gulp of wine to force the cookie past the sudden lump that blocked my throat when I read my fortune. Too bad the wine did nothing to erase the memory of that dream that had knocked me so off-kilter, or the thought of Forbis propped in the arms of the vicious Congo Savanne.

"You will be forced to face fear, but if you do not run, fear will be afraid of you."

Chapter Seven

WHEN NEV IS KNEE-DEEP IN A CASE, IT'S NOT UNUSUAL for him not to call. After all, as so many TV shows say so many times, the first forty-eight hours of a murder investigation are the most important.

According to the medical examiner, Forbis had been killed in the wee hours of Friday morning. Which meant by Sunday, forty-eight hours had come and gone. I knew this. Just like I knew that because there had been no break in the case, Nev was harried, busy, and being pressured by his superiors, not to mention the media.

He didn't call.

And this shouldn't have bothered me.

But it did.

I spent Sunday doing laundry, cleaning the apartment, and trying not to think about it. As a thank you for his above-and-beyond-the-call-of-duty good deed the night before, I made dinner for Stan—pot roast, his favorite—and he declared my roasted parsnips the best he'd ever eaten. Coming from Stan, that is high praise, indeed.

After I cleaned up, I did some reading and since the remnants of that pounding headache still lurked in my brain and threatened to erupt at any moment, I made a cup of herbal tea with honey and went to bed early.

And still, Nev didn't call.

And I was worried.

Oh, it's not like I was concerned that he was in some kind of danger. Though he keeps it hidden beneath the rumpled clothes and the little boy smile, Nev is as tough as nails. He can take care of himself.

And it's not like I'm some kind of crazy, jealous girl-friend, either. At least I never had been. I knew Nev cared about me, just like I did about him. We had a special relationship and thanks to him, the places in my heart that had been left cold and empty by Kaz's lying ways had been filled with warmth.

But as much as I tried (and honest, I tried!), I couldn't stop thinking about Nev. Nev and Evangeline.

Believe me when I say I knew this was disturbed. Not to mention disturbing. It was so not like me that I knew I had to do something to shake loose from the thoughts.

By Monday morning, I'd had enough, and I vowed to keep myself busy in spite of the fact that the headache was back full force and no amount of pain relievers would touch it. I put a message on the Button Box website and another one on the shop voice mail that said I'd be opening a little later that day and with that taken care of, I headed on over to the Mango Tango Gallery.

As soon as I stepped off the Blue Line El, I remembered how much I love the Wicker Park neighborhood and wondered why I didn't make it a point to visit there more often. Then it hit me: Wicker Park is adjacent to Bucktown where Kaz lives. And adjacent is too close for comfort.

Still, I will admit that in spite of its proximity to my ex, Wicker Park is funky and fun. It's got about a million little independent shops and, of course, that's the kind of thing that gives this small business owner hope for the future. It's also home to a ton of gorgeous old churches and more—many more—neighborhood dive bars. I must have passed at least a dozen on my way over to the gallery.

Mango Tango was located upstairs from a tapas restaurant that, this early in the morning, wasn't open for business. Too bad. I looked over the menu posted in the window and promised myself a return visit. Goat cheese with honey and sweet onion? Be still, my heart! Oh yeah, I'd be back.

Unfortunately, it looked like I'd have to come back to talk to Bart McCromb at Mango Tango, too.

My hand was already on the door that led up to the second-floor gallery, when I caught sight of the note stuck on the window nearby:

Off to sunny St. Croix. See you next week.

It was signed simply, *Bart.*

So much for that line of investigation. I checked the open and close times on the tapas restaurant so I could hit both the gallery and goat cheese/honey heaven the next week, and headed over to the Button Box.

The first thing I saw as I approached the brownstone was Nev standing outside.

OK, I'll admit it, I'm not sappy and I'm nobody's definition (I hope) of a woman whose ego depends on the man in her life.

That didn't mean I didn't give Nev a mile-wide smile.

"You're late today." After a quick peck on the cheek, he stepped back so I could unlock the robin's egg blue front door. "I wondered what was going on."

I told him about Mango Tango. "Weird to think the owner went to St. Croix when he was supposed to be hosting Forbis's exhibit."

While I turned on lights and put out the sign that said the Button Box was officially open for business, Nev went into the back room and made a pot of coffee. "Maybe not," he said when he came back with a mug in each hand and we slipped right back into the conversation with all the comfort of a couple who knows each other's minds. "If Richard and Forbis moved the exhibit to the church, maybe this McCromb guy was left high and dry."

"You think McCromb might have been angry enough about it to kill Forbis?"

"I think . . ." Nev took a drink from his mug. He can drink coffee hotter and faster than anyone I know. I think it has something to do with cops and how they're always so busy and always on their way somewhere. He was halfway done with his coffee and I was still blowing on mine and taking tiny sips to test the temperature. "If McCromb was left high and dry without the exhibit he was planning, I think the guy was pretty smart to head on down to St. Croix for a week."

He was right, and I was seeing motives and menace where it probably didn't exist.

I told myself not to forget it.

"So, what have you been up to?" I asked the question because I honestly cared. I wasn't fishing, and I sure wasn't prying.

That didn't keep an image of Evangeline and Nev from flashing through my head.

I pushed it aside. "I mean about the case, of course. Is there anything you can tell me?"

"No progress." He drained the last of his coffee. "I wish I could say there was. The crime-scene techs tell me they haven't found anything very useful at the church. Have you had a chance to get back there and check out the buttons?"

I told him I hadn't, but promised I would, and soon.

Then I remembered what Gabriel Marsh had told me. "You might want to talk to Richard again," I suggested. "He told us he was out with Laverne after the show on Thursday."

Nev raised his eyebrows just a tad. In Nev's world, this is the equivalent of unbridled surprise. "And you know that's not true?"

"I know there's another version of the story. Richard might have been with Victor Cherneko. You remember him, the guy who was wearing a tux at the show. Laverne pointed him out, said he was some hotsy-totsy patron of the arts."

"And a prominent businessman." Nev nodded. "I was just reading something about him in the newspaper. His company built some new building downtown and there's been a dispute with the general contractor or the architect or someone. He's a mover and a shaker, all right. And you say Richard was with him after the show and not Laverne? How do you know?"

"Gabriel Marsh." It was all the explanation I had a chance to give before a customer came through the front door. She was particular and, honestly, I didn't hold that against her. When it comes to buttons, I am particular, too. Still, I didn't anticipate spending nearly an hour with the woman and dragging out every Czech hand-pressed glass button in my inventory.

While I took care of my business, Nev handled his own. He went into the back room and I heard him on the phone, no doubt going over the details of Forbis's death and following any lead that came his way.

No sooner had I bagged the woman's button purchases than Nev came back out to the front of the shop.

"What about Gabriel Marsh?" he asked.

It took me a moment to figure out what he was talking about and pick up the threads of the conversation. I did that, and put away the hand-pressed glass buttons while I talked. "He stopped over Saturday night," I said.

"The shop isn't open on Saturday night."

My hands stilled over the buttons. "Not here. He came to my apartment."

Nev crossed his arms over his chest. I pretended not to notice because, let's face it, the gesture was entirely too confrontational and, therefore, uncalled for. Then again, so was the slightly accusatory tone of Nev's voice. "Gabriel

Marsh was at your apartment. How did he know where you live?"

I shrugged. That pretty much said all I could say about Marsh finding me. While I was at it, I answered what I knew would be Nev's next question even before he asked it. "He was looking for information. Seems he wants to write a book about Forbis's murder."

"And you told him . . . ?"

"That I didn't know anything." I replaced the first batch of buttons in the old library card catalogue file cabinet where they belonged and got to work on the rest of them, sorting first by manufacturer, then by when they were made, then by color. "I wouldn't have even bothered telling him that much, but he brought lo mein and—"

"This Marsh character showed up at your apartment with dinner?"

It was a logical question, but blame it on my headache, I didn't like Nev's tone of voice when he asked it. I slammed the card catalogue drawer shut and spun around. "He was looking to butter me up. That's what the lo mein was all about. But like I said, it didn't work. He asked what I knew and I told him nothing."

"But you ate dinner with him. Jo . . ." Nev's exasperated sigh echoed through the Button Box. "There's a murderer on the loose, you know."

When I gritted my teeth, my head pounded just a little harder. "I'm well aware of that."

"But you let the guy into your apartment, anyway?" Nev ran a hand through his hair. "I can't believe you'd be so stupid."

I already had another handful of buttons and, truth be

told, had they been anything else—jewelry, coins, bits and pieces of ancient Egyptian artifacts—I would have flung them across the shop at Nev. But they were buttons, after all, and I treasure my buttons. My fingers closed tight around them. "What did you say?" I asked. Oh yes, it was a rhetorical question, so technically I shouldn't have needed an answer. But I wanted one. Along with an explanation of what on earth had possessed Nev to talk to me that way.

He rubbed his hands over his eyes. "I'm sorry. I didn't mean you were stupid. I just meant—"

"That what I did was stupid." I deposited the buttons in the proper drawer and slid it shut with a little more of a bang than I intended. It was my turn to cross my arms over my chest. "I know what I'm doing," I reminded Nev. I shouldn't have had to. "I've investigated murders before. And successfully, too. I'm not some dumb kid who—"

"I know, I know." He hurried over and looped his arms around my waist. "I'm sorry. Really." I guess the quick kiss he gave me was supposed to prove it. "I'm tired and I haven't had breakfast and you know how crabby I get when I haven't had my Cheerios. Besides, I'm worried about you, Jo. I know you want to help, but we don't know who this Marsh guy is."

When I was looking for information about Forbis in art magazines, I'd read a few articles by Gabriel so that wasn't exactly accurate. "He's a journalist," I told Nev. "That means he's naturally nosy. He was fishing for information. He didn't get any. But I got some from him." Usually, I like nothing better than standing in the circle of Nev's arms and resting my head on his chest. This time when I tried, my headache only beat harder, and I pushed away.

"Richard told us he went out for coffee with Laverne after

the show," I reminded Nev. "But Gabriel says that's not true. He says he followed Richard, and Richard was with Victor Cherneko."

Nev considered this. "Did he say why?"

I would have shaken my head but when I tried, it hurt too much and I guess that's why my questions came out filled with just a little too much sarcasm. "Why Richard lied to us? Or why Gabriel was following Richard? Or why Richard was with Victor?"

Nev winced. Then again, my words were as sharp as stones.

I pressed my fingers to my temples and tried to make up for it by saying, "It's looking like Richard's alibi might be a little shaky."

"Unless Marsh is lying."

So much for being conciliatory.

"Why would he?" I asked. "What could he possibly gain from lying to us about Richard and Victor?"

"You mean what could he possibly gain from lying to *you* about Richard and Victor," Nev jabbed back. The next second, like me, he realized he'd come across as too harsh. "That's what we don't know," he said, his voice a little softer, his words less stinging. "Don't you see? That's why I'm suspicious. OK, so we know Marsh is a journalist. That's all well and good. But other than that, we don't know anything about him. Who knows what his motive might be! It's not like we can suddenly trust him just because he shows up at your door with lo mein. It's not like he's some old friend or anything."

I don't think I was imagining it. Nev recognized his slip of the tongue at the exact moment I did. That would explain why we both got quiet.

When the phone rang, I nearly jumped out of my skin.

"Button Box." My voice was too breathy when I answered and took care of the customer on the other end who had a question about old military buttons. By the time I was done, I realized my knees were shaking. I plunked down at my desk, firmly refusing to look at Nev who stood over near the display case where my wooden buttons were kept, drumming his fingers against the glass.

Even then, we couldn't think of anything to say to each other.

One minute of silence stretched into two, and two dragged out to three. I hadn't had a chance to turn on my computer for the day so I did that and pretended that it took longer than it really did so that I didn't have to think of anything to say. That taken care of, I straightened a small (and very neat to begin with) pile of papers on my desk, deleted the message I'd put on my website earlier about how I'd open a little later that day, and checked my e-mails to see if there were any customer orders or inquiries waiting. There weren't.

And I still didn't know what to say to Nev.

I grumbled my frustration and blurted out, "This is ridiculous," at the same moment he said, "Josie, we really need to talk."

And once again, we found ourselves at an impasse.

I restraightened those papers near my computer.

Nev stalked over and dropped into the guest chair across from my desk.

"You're wrong about Evangeline," he said.

"Wrong about her being an old friend?"

"No, you're right about that. I told you that from the beginning. She is an old friend."

"She was more than that."

"Yes."

"And you never bothered to tell me about her."

For the record, Nev is not a sigher. He sighed. "I told you, there's nothing to tell."

"Except that you were going to marry her."

"I was."

"It's not like I'm upset or anything. Believe me, Nev, I understand. Neither one of us is a kid, and we didn't just fall off the turnip truck. We both have pasts."

"You have Kaz."

"Yes." Was it the mention of my ex that started the headache pounding with renewed energy? I squeezed my eyes closed. It didn't help. "Like I said, I understand that part. Honest, I do."

Nev pushed out of the chair and paced the width of the shop. The place is only twelve hundred square feet, all told, so there really wasn't a lot of room for him to walk between the library catalogue files to my left and the glass display cases on my right. "Then what are you so steamed about?"

How could I explain that I wasn't? My words bumped along to the rhythm of the pounding inside my brain. "All I'm trying to do is understand. To put your relationship with her in some kind of context. Right now that's hard because I don't know anything. For instance, how long have you known Evangeline?"

He didn't need to stop and think about it. "Eight years. We met when she was in grad school and I just got on the force."

"And how long has it been since you broke up?"

"Three years."

"And how long were you engaged?"

"Six months."

"And why . . ." It wasn't my imagination, the thumping in my skull intensified and I caught my breath. "Why did you break up?"

This, Nev had to think about, and he did it for so long I wondered if he was trying to find the words to explain, or if even he wasn't sure of the reasons. "We just sort of drifted apart, you know?" Obviously my stony expression told him I didn't. Nev made a face. "She was working hard to get her degree. She was traveling to do research. So right away, there was that strain on our relationship. I guess I tried to compensate by putting in as many hours as I could on the job, then taking extra details to put aside money for the wedding and the honeymoon. I thought I was doing it all for her, for us. Turns out all I was doing was making things worse."

"Sounds to me like she was just as guilty."

"Maybe." Not the definitive answer I would have liked. Nev's smile was bittersweet. "It's hard to explain a woman like Evangeline. She's really driven. Her career means a lot to her, and you know how it is with academics. They've got a lot of pressure to do research and to publish their findings. That's all fine, I understood that going in. I guess what I didn't expect was just how difficult it could be to deal with someone like her. I'm just a regular guy, just a cop. She's an amazing woman with this really, really big brain."

"Oh."

That single syllable should have warned him to stop right then and there, but Nev was on a roll and he wasn't paying any attention.

"She's the most intelligent person I've ever met," he went on. "She can make these lightning-quick correlations and her observations are brilliant. I guess . . . well, in the end, I guess I just didn't know how to deal with a woman who was so smart."

"Oh." I wasn't taking the chance that he was going to miss my point a second time. I rose from my chair, my palms flat against the desk. "So what you're telling me is that you're a lot more comfortable dating a dumb woman."

Nev, always a bit pale, went positively chalky. "I didn't say that."

"You didn't have to."

"I shouldn't need to."

"Or maybe you do need to. Did you ever think of that?"

He ran a hand through his hair and a curl stuck up at the top of his head. Another one flopped over his forehead. "I never said you were dumb."

"You said I wasn't as smart as Evangeline."

"What I said . . ." He hauled in a breath. "I said Evangeline was smart. It's true. But that doesn't mean you're not smart."

"You said you don't know how to deal with smart women."

Nev threw his hands in the air. "I don't. I mean, I do. I do when it's you."

The disclaimer came a heartbeat too late to make a difference and he knew it.

"Fine." Nev got up and whirled toward the door. "We're obviously not going to see eye to eye about this. How about we just talk another time?"

"How about it," I shot back and, funny, when the door slammed closed behind Nev, my headache disappeared.

Chapter Eight

It was Monday, and just for the record, Monday traditionally isn't the busiest day at the Button Box. That gave me the perfect excuse to close early. No, it had nothing to do with the knock-down, drag-out I had with Nev that morning. Honest! In fact, once he was out of the shop door, my mood actually brightened. I wasn't sure why, and I wasn't sure I wanted to know why. I only know that I spent the rest of the day in relative calm and blissfully headache-free. By four o'clock, I figured it was time to reward myself.

And these days, I could think of no better reward than a little investigating.

I headed over to the Chicago Community Church, and I was just in time to catch Laverne before she left for the day. Laverne and Richard.

"Hey." They were standing together looking at Forbis's

exhibit and I stepped inside the church and waved. "I didn't think I'd find you both here."

Richard gestured toward the huge box with Congo Savanne still standing tall (and ugly!) above it. "I've got to get all this stuff packed up and shipped out of here. Laverne and I were just trying to figure out the logistics." His shoulders sagged. "I'd hoped we'd sell more and have less to ship back. But hey, I suppose I should look on the bright side. There's still a chance for sales, especially now that the media is all over the story of Forbis's murder. There's nothing like a little sensationalism to drive up interest in an artist's work."

Laverne had the good sense to look embarrassed by the comment. Richard, not so much. In fact, he mumbled something about jacking up the prices and, rubbing his hands together, went and collected a clipboard piled with papers so he could take notes about his idea.

"So . . ." I knew I had to ask Laverne about what I'd heard from Gabriel Marsh, about how he'd seen Richard after the show and not with her. I just figured I should edge into things slowly. It was obvious she and Richard had history and just as obvious that reminding a person about the history they had with another person can sometimes ruffle feathers.

Not that I was thinking about Nev and Evangeline or anything.

"Do you have another exhibit coming in?" I asked Laverne.

"Not for another month. But then, we thought this one would be here longer. Our next gallery showing is artwork from the day-care center across the street." She grinned. "You know, I'm actually looking forward to it. These days, little kids' pictures of flowers and smiling suns sound a lot more appealing than vudon and buttons."

To me, nothing could ever sound more appealing than buttons, but I knew where she was coming from.

"You don't mind if I poke around, do you?" I asked. "I was hoping to take a close look at the buttons, and now that I know everything's going back to Georgia . . . well, it might be my only chance."

Laverne's smile said it all. "You know I don't mind. The way I see it, we owe you. You're the one who kept me from completely going to pieces when we found the body." A shiver snaked over her shoulders and jiggled the colorful beads she was wearing with a black suit and a teal shirt. "I suppose there's no way I can ever make that up to you."

"Occupational hazard," I said before I realized that made absolutely no sense to anyone who thought my only occupation was selling buttons. Rather than explain, I stepped up the single stair that separated the exhibit from the main floor of the church. "I'll stay out of the way," I promised. "I'm just going to take a few photos." I pulled my camera out of my pocket. "And a few notes about the buttons and how Forbis used them."

"Have a blast!" Laverne left me to it and walked over to where Richard was mumbling to himself about markups and profits. I took a deep breath and glanced around.

So many buttons, so little time!

I should have come hours earlier, that was clear right from the start. Forbis used thousands of buttons in his work, and each was more interesting than the last, at least to this button nerd. I started with a careful survey of the buttons on the ceremonial drums, taking photos, jotting down my impressions, and wondering if Forbis ever kept notes about where he bought the older buttons, and if Richard might be cajoled into looking through Forbis's files and sharing the information.

If this sounds more like busywork than investigating, it's no wonder. Aside from satisfying my button itch, my survey of the drums and the thousands of buttons on them was a stall tactic and I knew it.

If I was really going to investigate . . .

If I was really going to discover anything that could explain what had happened there in the Chicago Community Church a few days earlier . . .

If I was ever going to prove that I wasn't a wimp who was afraid of inanimate objects . . .

I pulled in a breath for courage, gulped down my uneasiness, and made the move. When I stationed myself in front of the Congo Savanne statue, my knees were a little rubbery and my breaths came a tad too fast. Too bad, so sad. If I was going to find answers, this was where I had to start. After all, this is where the mystery began and ended.

Keeping the thought in mind, I stepped back, then moved forward again, following the same path I'd walked side by side with Forbis that fateful Thursday night. We'd gotten about this far . . .

I stopped to check my position and looked to my right, to where Forbis had stood as we approached the statue to place that last button. "Right here," I mumbled to myself. "It was about right here that he dropped his champagne glass."

Yes, dropped his champagne glass, I reminded myself, and said those cryptic words, "Le bouton, le bouton."

"Le bouton." I spoke the words out loud, but since Richard and Laverne had moved to the far side of the exhibit, deep in a conversation about packing and loading semis, I figured nobody would care. "Le bouton?" Before I even realized what I was up to, I asked the question of the fierce loa who loomed over this particular part of the exhibit. The mother of pearl buttons on Congo Savanne's skull glistened and winked down at me. The black buttons Forbis had used to accentuate his sunken eyes were bottomless pits, and instinctively, I knew that anyone careless or foolish enough to get too close would be dragged down and never see the light again.

Still, it was impossible to look away. Just like it was impossible not to take another step closer to the people-eater.

It must have been the way my neck was kinked when I looked up at the statue; the blood whooshed in my ears and Laverne's and Richard's voices, hushed but distinct only a short time earlier, were suddenly as muffled as if they were lost in a fog.

This close, a spotlight caught the fearsome skull face directly from my right and the milky buttons on it gleamed as if the statue was sweating. A chill breeze out of nowhere ruffled the back of my neck and though the breeze couldn't have been strong enough to make it happen, I swore I saw the statue sway.

"Scared to death."

The words echoed through my head to the rhythm of those same drumbeats that had haunted my sleep on Saturday night. Nev had told me that the medical examiner said it looked as if Forbis had been scared to death, and staring into the face of Congo Savanne, I could see how it was possible.

My blood beat in my veins and my heart pounded so hard, I could practically feel the buildup of adrenaline that signaled fight or flight.

Only I couldn't have moved if I wanted to.

I was frozen to the spot. Paralyzed. All I could feel was the cold that settled in my stomach and sent out icy tentacles that infiltrated every cell of my body, then slowly but surely immobilized each and every one of them. I wondered if Forbis felt exactly this before his heart gave out. In those last moments, did he realize that once the ice penetrated every inch of him, it would be too late?

It wasn't until I felt myself pitch forward that I snapped out of the daydream and back to reality. I took a sharp breath, further grounding myself at the same time I distanced myself from the weird feelings that had engulfed me out of nowhere. I was never going to get anywhere in terms of my investigation if I let my imagination run away with me, and determined (even if I wasn't completely convinced), I looked up at the statue and growled, "Take that." Yeah, it was false bravado, but it worked. This time, I didn't feel any bizarre sensations, no crazy, out-of-nowhere chills. The message was clear: Congo Savanne or no Congo Savanne, it was time to get down to business.

The thought firmly in mind, I backed up, the better to get an overall look at what Forbis must have seen right before he ran up to the choir loft. At the same time, I took a careful look at the spot where the red button was supposed to have been mounted.

Just like last time I'd seen it, the place on the front of the box where that last button was destined to go was blank, and a bare bit of wood showed through the buttons that surrounded it. The red plastic button would have been at the center of a flower, and again, I studied the buttons that made up its petals. Every button was exactly as I remembered it. There was the yellow glass moonglow button just below where the red one should have been, the same brass button with a beautiful little butterfly on it above. To the right of center . . .

My breath caught, and I leaned closer. On Thursday night, the button to the right of the flower's center was ochre-colored ceramic, incised with curving lettering. It was odd, it was distinctive, and of course I noticed it the night of the murder because buttons are my life and one that unusual was impossible to forget. I'd told myself I was going to ask Forbis about it after our little button-installation ceremony was over, but, of course, I never had the chance. That was because on Thursday night, Forbis looked where I was looking right now, and he screamed, "Le bouton, le bouton" and ran.

"Except le bouton . . ." I inched nearer, my gaze trained on the spot. "If le bouton is the button I'm thinking it is, le bouton isn't here anymore."

In fact, what was there was a pretty but perfectly ordinary orange glass button, one I knew I hadn't seen the other night.

By this time, I was kneeling in front of the exhibit, the better to get a really good up close and personal look at what was—and wasn't—there. I snapped a few pictures before I touched a hand to the orange button.

"Tacky." As a test, I touched my fingers together. They were slightly sticky. "Like something was glued over this button," I told myself. "Yeah, something, all right. Like that ceramic button with the writing on it." Thinking this over,

I sat back on my heels, and it was a good thing I did. Otherwise, I never would have noticed something flashing at me from the base of one of the ceremonial drums on my left. Still on my knees, I scooted that way, bent nearer, and reached a hand around the nearest drum so I could close my fingers over the object. When I unfolded my fingers, I found myself looking down at a silver and onyx tuxedo stud.

"Just like the ones Vincent Cherneko was wearing the night of the exhibit," I told myself.

And added (like I needed to), "The night of the murder."

Curiouser and curiouser. Until I had a chance to mull it all over, I tucked the stud in my pocket and pulled myself to my feet. Laverne and Richard were nowhere to be seen, and like I said, I needed to talk to them about their alibi. Until I could, I needed time to think about the missing ceramic button and the shirt stud.

I looked around the church and realized that my timing was perfect. Standing on the old altar and facing where the congregation would have been, I saw that the afternoon light shone from behind that rose window up in the choir loft. A riot of glorious colors floated in the air above the pews. Gold, orange, red, green. Tiny dots of dust danced in the rainbow and, thanks to the sunlight, sparkled like fairy dust.

I am not a big believer in signs and coincidences, but I'm not a complete moron, either. And besides, I didn't have a better idea. I headed up to the choir loft to sit and think about all I'd discovered.

There, the soft colors flowing from the rose window washed over the organ and the risers where singers once belted out their sacred tunes.

"Forbis, Forbis, Forbis." It's not like I expected, or wanted, an answer from the Great Beyond, but heck, as I'd learned over the course of my other investigations, it never hurts to bounce ideas off another person. And when another person isn't around? Well, it doesn't hurt to do a little thinking out loud, either.

"What were you doing up here?" I asked. "Who were you hiding from? And did it have anything to do with . . ." I made my way to the front of the loft and looked over the railing and across the expanse of the church. The lights of the exhibit made those thousands and thousand of buttons glow like jewels. Of course, it wasn't the buttons that were there that I was thinking about. It was the one that was missing. And the one that didn't belong. "Does your murder have anything to do with that funny, ceramic button? Is that what you were referring to when you said 'le bouton'? And how did Victor Cherneko's shirt stud end up in the midst of all those buttons?" I listened to the nothing but silence that greeted my questions, sighed, and leaned against the railing.

Well, at least I tried.

The moment I put a hand on the railing, it slipped and I slid.

"What the—?" My feet tangled, and I would have gone down like a rock if I didn't throw out one arm and grab onto the organ to steady myself. I was grateful now that I was alone, and no one had seen the not-so-graceful pirouette. I was also curious about why I'd slipped in the first place.

I looked at my hand, then back at the railing. Both had the slightest traces of a slippery substance on them. White. Like the greasy smear we'd seen in Reverend Truman's office the day I found Forbis's body.

My initial reaction was twofold. I mean, after I stood

there for a couple minutes wondering what the heck was going on.

1. I fished a tissue out of my pocket and wiped my hand, then carefully folded the tissue so I could turn it over to the cops and tell them what happened and where I found the smudge.
2. I reached for my phone to call Nev.

Instinct is a funny thing. It was instinct that made me think of Nev first, that warm, comfortable feeling that fit me like a second skin and let me know that if I was confused, or in trouble, and especially if I found evidence in a murder, Nev was my go-to man.

But it was instinct, too, that made me stare at the phone for a moment, then tuck it back in my pocket.

Oh, I'd tell Nev what I'd discovered, all right. After all, when it came to murder investigations, I was as professional as I was when the subject was buttons. But I wasn't in the mood to talk to Nev. Not yet. Not until the sting of our morning argument wasn't quite so sharp.

"Josie! Is that you up there?"

My thoughts were interrupted by a shout from down in the church, and I turned to find Laverne on the altar, waving to catch my attention. "We're locking up," she called out, and just as I expected, the church had great acoustics. I didn't have to strain to hear even one word. "I'd hate to see you stuck inside for the night."

She wasn't the only one.

I scrambled downstairs and found Laverne alone. No Richard. Which now that I thought about it, was probably a good thing. I'd already asked him the question I was about to ask her. Before I did, I thanked her for the opportunity to check out the buttons.

"No problem." Laverne patted my hand. "The way it looks, Richard's not going to be able to get this stuff out of here for at least a few more days. Some to-do with the shipping company and how they already had dates set and how changing them is going to cost more." She fanned a hand in front of her face. "You'd think they were planning D-Day! The good news is that means you're welcome to come back anytime between now and when the stuff gets moved out of here. In fact, you could stay a little longer this evening, but I have a social justice committee meeting over at the food bank and—"

It was my turn to tell her it was not a problem at all. "I might be back," I told her, thinking of the tissue that was in my pocket along with Victor Cherneko's onyx stud. And wondering about that missing button. "But until then . . ." I paused, pretending like this was something that had just occurred to me. "I've been thinking about the night of the murder. You know, the way you see detectives on TV think over their cases."

Laverne barked out a laugh. "Then you're way smarter than me," she said. "I will admit, I tried. That first day it happened. I had this sort of Jessica Fletcher thing come over me, and I tried to look at what we know about Forbis and the murder and piece things together. It got me absolutely nowhere!"

"Well, I might be getting nowhere, too," I said, and cringed when I realized it actually might be true. "But I figured I should give it a try. I feel responsible, you know what I mean?

Just being here with Forbis that night, and being part of the ceremony and then finding his body the next day . . ." I didn't have to fake the shudder that trembled over my shoulders when I pictured Forbis with those buttons on his eyes and mouth. "I guess I've just been trying to keep myself busy, to make a sort of puzzle out of it so I don't think about how horrible it all was."

Laverne bent her head. "Amen."

"So I've been wondering . . ." Did I sound like a woman intent on solving a puzzle? Or like a busybody who had no business poking her nose where it didn't belong? "I've been asking people who were here that night, you know, about their alibis for after the show."

It wasn't my imagination. Laverne's eyebrows really did shoot up a bit. Maybe it was because she hadn't expected me to be quite so much of a busybody. Or maybe there was another reason. I made sure I smiled when I said, "I talked to Richard, so I know what he said. You know, about his alibi."

Laverne's smile froze around the edges. "Richard told you I was with him, didn't he?" She pulled in a long breath and let it out slowly. "Of course he did. Because that's exactly what happened. Why on earth would he tell you anything else?"

"That's exactly what he told me." It was true, so it's not like I had to feel the least bit guilty saying it. Which was only fair, since Laverne didn't look the least bit guilty, either. Was it because Richard had told her what to say in case anybody asked? Or because Gabriel Marsh, he of the hot-as-sin smile and tempting . . . er . . . lo mein, wanted me to think Richard was with Victor when he really wasn't?

I didn't know. And I wasn't going to find out standing

there with a vacant smile. Instead, I told Laverne I hope she had a good meeting at the food bank, said I might be back soon one of these days to look at the buttons some more, and headed out the nearest door. I was in the hallway that led to Reverend Truman's office when a man came around the corner and nearly slammed right into me.

"Oh!" The syllable of surprise escaped my lips just as I pulled myself to a stop so I didn't crash into the man and the industrial-sized bucket on wheels he was dragging along with the help of the mop in it. He was tall and stocky, and wearing dark gray pants and a shirt with an oval on it and a name embroidered on it in red: "Bob."

"Excellent." I don't think he was used to being greeted with that much enthusiasm by strangers. Bob's eyes went wide and he took a step back and away from me. "I'm Josie," I told him without bothering to explain who, exactly, Josie was or why it mattered. I poked a thumb over my shoulder. "I was just talking to Laverne. You know, about the murder. I was hoping I'd run into you, because I think maybe you can help me out."

He shook his head. "Don't know nothing. I already told the police that. I only work here. Didn't have nothing to do with that weird art exhibit. Just watched them set it up, and made sure the floors were washed and swept and the bathrooms were all in good shape for everyone who was coming to the show. After that . . ." Another shake of his head that made his beefy jowls swing. "I don't know nothing."

"I believe you." I offered him a warm smile, and even though it was designed to melt his wariness, his shoulders got rigid. "I was just wondering about the night you cleaned up the champagne and glass. You know, from when Forbis dropped his glass."

"Did my job, and did it right." His fingers closed over the mop handle in a proprietary gesture. "I told the cops that."

"And the next morning?"

He wasn't sure what I was getting at and, truth be told, I guess I wasn't, either. I only know that what happened the next morning was a little odd, and odd always struck me as something I needed to get to the bottom of. "The next morning when we were all here. You know, the morning they found that poor man's body." The *they* was no mistake, believe me. I sensed that with a man like Bob, it was best to keep things as impersonal as possible. I feared if he knew I was so intimately involved in the finding of Forbis's body, he'd tuck tail and run. "You stepped into the church, and Laverne and I, we were hoping to talk to you but when she called out to you, you walked away. Then the police looked for you and couldn't find you anywhere in the building."

"Talked to Ms. Laverne that afternoon." Now he was nodding, again and again, like a bobblehead doll on a dashboard. "Talked to the police, too and told them just what I told her."

"That's terrific." Remember what I said about instincts? Mine told me there wasn't anything else I was likely to get from Bob. I stepped back and turned away.

"Only you're wrong about that morning."

His comment brought me up short, and just as quickly as I'd turned away, I whirled back to face him. "The morning the body was found? What am I wrong about?"

"You said I was here." Now he shook his head again. I had to focus my gaze directly on the wall behind Bob's left shoulder or I was going to get dizzy. "Didn't come in that day until noon. Just like I was scheduled to."

I looked down the hallway, back toward the door that led

into the church. Clearly, I remembered Bob opening that door as Laverne and I stood talking in the church. Just like I told him, she'd called out to him and waved him over. And all he'd done is turn and walk away. "You walked in," I said. "And then you walked out again."

"Wasn't me." Bob's hands closed around the mop handle. "I swear, it wasn't." His gaze darted to the door that led into the church and his eyes went wide, his pupils huge. "You seen that crazy stuff in there, that stuff they're calling art. Maybe that's what this is all about. You know, the murder and all. Maybe what you saw was one of them things. What do they call them?" He ran his tongue over his lips. "Maybe that's what it was. Maybe it was a zombie."

Chapter Nine

I WAS A THEATER MAJOR IN COLLEGE, AND MY SPECIALTY was costume design. My all-encompassing passion, of course, was the buttons on those costumes, and ultimately, that's what doomed my theater career. I was too focused on detail, producers and directors told me. I was too worried about authenticity. I was too careful and too compulsive. At least when it came to the buttons the audience would see only from their seats.

At the time, this broke my heart, but I am nothing if not an optimist and fate proved me right. I worked on costumes for exactly one low-budget, silly movie, and *For Whom The Trolls Troll* became a cult hit that guaranteed me a big, fat royalty check every month. It was that check that made it possible for me to quit my nine-to-five and open the Button Box.

The other plus of my schooling was that all those years of costume design taught me a thing or two about drawing. I am no Michelangelo, but my work is better than passable. At the same time I hit the speed dial on my phone, I looked at my kitchen table and the better-than-passable drawing of the button I'd sat down and sketched the moment I got home from the Chicago Community Church.

"Nev." I usually didn't sound so jumpy when my main squeeze answered his phone. I told myself to get a grip and put the memory of our argument out of my head. It was a stupid fight, anyway, and what I had to tell him was more important than either of our bruised egos.

"I hope I'm not interrupting anything," I said, then added so he didn't think *interrupting* meant what it could have meant only it wasn't what I meant to begin with, "Are you still at the station?"

"Just got home." He sounded tired "What's up?"

I told him. About the missing button on the Congo Savanne art piece. About Victor Cherneko's onyx and silver stud and how I found it under the ceremonial drums. About the smudge of white, greasy stuff up in the choir loft.

"And there's Richard's alibi, too," I added even though I knew it was likely that bringing up that particular subject would also bring up the subject of Gabriel Marsh and that bringing up Gabriel might put us in the same loop of unspoken, unreasonable, and uncomfortable accusations we'd danced around earlier in the day. "I asked Laverne where she was after the show—"

"And she confirmed Richard Norquist's alibi, right?"

Nev didn't have to sound so pleased with himself. And he sure didn't have to explain why. If Laverne and Richard were telling the truth, it meant Gabriel was lying. Which meant Nev was right about not trusting him. Which meant I was wrong about everything, including eating lo mein with the man.

"Just because she said she was with Richard doesn't mean Laverne is on the up-and-up," I reminded Nev. I shouldn't have had to. Cops are notoriously skeptical. About everything. "In fact, I'm pretty sure she was lying."

"Because . . ."

"Because she looked uncomfortable when she told me how she went out for coffee after the show with Richard," I explained. "You know, like she didn't really want to say it, and maybe he'd asked her to corroborate his story. Of course she was uncomfortable! Laverne is clearly not the kind of woman who likes to lie."

"Impressions aren't evidence," he reminded me.

"But gut instinct has to play some role in investigating." I could have pointed out that he obviously believed this or he wouldn't have written off Gabriel as a no-good lowlife as quickly as he had.

"Anyway, I thought it was important for you to know all that," I said, because clearly, going around and around about Laverne wasn't going to get us anywhere. "It's important stuff, don't you think?"

"The missing button and the onyx stud and the smudge of greasy stuff? You bet it is. Thank you for thinking of calling to tell me about it."

Don't think I missed the fact that he left Laverne's and Richard's alibis off of the list. Or that the way he thanked me bordered on a little too professional. It was the kind of throwaway line that begged to be answered with a, "That's OK. Glad to help. Good-bye."

The thought twisted my insides and rather than give in to the pain, I blurted out, "I haven't eaten yet. I was thinking maybe you could come over and we'd pick up something. I drew a picture of that missing button and we could go through some of my references books and—"

"Wish I could." It would have sounded more like Nev meant it if right after he said it, he didn't hold the phone to his chest for a moment to say something to somebody. His voice was muffled, but I thought I heard the word *dinner*. "LaSalle's been kind of punky," he said, his voice—and his message—loud and clear now that he was talking into the phone again. "The vet's got late clinic hours tonight and she said if I stopped in, she could check him out."

I knew how devoted he was to the mixed breed dog that used to be a stray in the Button Box neighborhood until he and Nev found each other. I understood.

Of course I understood.

I only wished I could believe him.

I didn't bite my tongue quickly enough to prevent myself from saying, "Is that why you were just talking about going to dinner with someone?"

"Huh?" He was quiet for as long as it took him to figure out what I was talking about. Which wasn't long. I heard a rattle that sounded like small rocks against a hard surface. "LaSalle's dinner," he said, shaking the dog's metal food bowl again. "I told him to come get dinner before we leave to go see Dr. Sylvia."

"I figured."

I didn't.

"I know."

He didn't.

Another shake of the dog's bowl and Nev sighed. "He doesn't even want to eat," he said, "so you know something's wrong." I heard a muffled *clunk* as he set down the bowl. "I'll give you a call at the shop tomorrow, and we can talk about that button. You think the fact that it wasn't on that box with the creepy statue in it means anything?"

"I think . . ." I had my fingers pressed to my temples even before I realized my headache was back. "I think I'll talk to you tomorrow," I said, and ended the call.

Truth be told, Laverne and Richard weren't the only ones fudging the truth (if, indeed, they were fudging the truth at all). On my way home, I'd grabbed a small pizza from the Italian place on the corner, so my dinner invitation to Nev wasn't as much an act of hungry desperation as it was a stab at compromise. So much for trying to be an adult. I dragged the pizza box closer and looked over my drawing of the mysterious button while I finished off a couple slices of pepperoni, mushroom, and banana pepper.

My memory, it should be noted, is pretty darned good, especially when it comes to buttons, so there was no question, at least in my mind, that I got the details right. Though I'd drawn it much larger, the real ceramic button was about three-quarters of an inch across. That is, what we in the button biz consider a medium-sized button. The button was the off-yellow of a #2 pencil and to help bring it to life, I headed into my bedroom and dug under my bed for the set of colored pencils that I hadn't used in years. I found one just about the right ochre color and pushing the pizza box aside, colored in my drawing, then used my regular lead pencil to again go over the squiggly lines I'd used to represent the wonky letters that I'd seen incised on the button. Did they actually spell out a word? And was it in English? Or was what I remembered as letters actually some kind of primitive picture of some sort?

If only I'd had a chance to check out the button more closely before Forbis was killed and the button went missing!

If only I knew if the two incidents were related, and if the medium-sized ochre-colored button was what he referred to when he screamed, "Le bouton."

If only.

I'd already grabbed another piece of pizza before I came to my senses and realized I was full. Before I could give in to the temptation, I wrapped the leftover slices and put them in the fridge. My drawing of the button in hand, I headed into the living room, but not until I stopped and grabbed every button reference book I had in the apartment.

A few hours later, my eyes ached and my neck muscles screamed in pain from being bent over so many pages of so many books.

"And without luck, too." I grumbled and closed the last of the books. But remember what I said about me being an optimist. I had many more reference books at the Button Box, and a network of button expert friends around the world. Believe me, I intended to use them all.

That is, once this darned headache went away.

More grumbling, and a quick trip to wash up, get ready for bed, and pop a couple of aspirin. But even once I was tucked in under the blankets, sleep refused to come. Tired as I was, the day's events whirled through my head. I must

have been thinking about that crazy thing Bob the maintenance man said to me. How he wasn't at the church until
late on the day I found Forbis's body, so I must have seen
his zombie double.

That would explain why when I finally drifted off to
sleep, I swore I heard drumbeats in the distance.

SINCE NEV DIDN'T take the Laverne/Richard alibi-that-
maybe-wasn't-an-alibi thing seriously, I knew it was up to
me to check it out. This may sound easy, but let's face it, I
have a shop to run and customers who depend on me to be
there when they arrive at the Button Box.

I worked diligently at the shop all Tuesday morning,
checking in and cataloguing the buttons that were delivered
from a collector's estate in Cleveland, helping ladies from
a church group who were looking for inexpensive buttons
for craft projects they could sell as fund-raisers, and looking
over the photographs I'd taken the day before of Forbis's
artwork. By lunchtime, I was ready to roll.

"I close at six on Tuesdays," I told Stan.

Just as he promised when I talked to him early that morning, he'd shown up to babysit the shop for me, and now he
sipped a cup of coffee and checked out the front page of the
day's paper. "I know that, Josie."

"But I'll be back before then," I assured him. "Except if
I'm not, you can put the 'Closed' sign in the window and—"

"I know that, too." He was seated behind my desk, and
he looked up from his newspaper to me. "I've watched the
shop for you plenty of times."

"You have. I'm grateful."

"And I'm wondering why you're as jumpy as a june bug. You're usually cool, calm, and collected, Josie. Even when you're investigating. What's up, kiddo?"

I was about to head to the door and I forced myself to take a deep breath and slow down. "I guess I'm just trying to prove something," I admitted to Stan.

"To Nev." I hadn't mentioned the recent tensions between me and Nev to Stan, but I wasn't surprised that he'd picked up on what was going on. Stan is a retired cop, after all. He's great at reading people, especially when that *people* is me. "It's the way you're acting," he said, in response to a question I didn't have a chance to ask. "I know something's wrong. You want to talk about it?"

"No," I said, then dropped into the guest chair in front of my desk. "He's being unreasonable," I said.

"About the investigation?"

"About everything." My shoulders rose and fell along with the sigh that shuddered through me. "He's not listening to me about this alibi for one thing."

"Because of that good-looking British guy who showed up at your door the other night."

"I hardly know the man. Nev knows there's nothing between me and Gabriel Marsh. Not like there is between Nev and Evangeline."

I hadn't meant that last bit to slip past my lips, but once it did, I had no choice but to fill Stan in on the details.

He listened—Stan always listens—and when I was done, he scratched a finger along the side of his nose. "Your suspicions about Nev and this Evangeline sound about as flimsy as Nev's when it comes to you and Marsh."

I dropped my head into my hands. "I know. I just can't

help myself. It's like . . ." I looked up at Stan. "You don't believe in voodoo and zombies and things, do you, Stan? When you were a cop, did you ever see anything that made you think any of it might be true?"

He waved a hand and just in case I didn't get the message, he made it clear when he said, "Hogwash! Why would you think—"

"I don't. It's just that I know I'm not acting like myself, and I know zombies and all that stuff aren't possible, but it's sort of what it feels like. Like somebody else is in control of me. I don't like it."

"Then don't let it get to you. Remember what you told me, Josie, the day you and Kaz split? You told me that from that day on, no one else was in charge of you. That still holds true, you know. Maybe now more than ever. You proved you could get along without Kaz. You proved that you could open your own business and make it a success. You even proved you can conduct a murder investigation, and you've done it a whole lot better than some of the cops I worked with over the years. What you've got to prove now is that you can set aside these crazy ideas you're having about Nev and get down to business."

"You're right." I pulled in a long breath. "As of here and now . . ." I slapped the arms of the chair and stood. "I'm back to being the old Josie. Practical, dependable, and without all sorts of weird ideas flying through her head."

"That's my girl!" Stan stood, too, and walked me to the door. "Only remember, you're allowed some flights of fancy now and again when it comes to your investigation. Clues and facts, witness statements and evidence, that's all important. But sometimes, a detective's got to listen to what's in here." He pressed a hand to his heart. "And what's in here." He moved his hand down to his stomach. "Don't let anybody tell you it's not valuable."

I kept the thought in mind and within an hour, I was acting on the advice.

Gut instinct, along with that onyx and silver shirt stud in my purse, led me to Victor Cherneko.

THE OUTSIDE OF the new headquarters building for Cherneko Industries was jaw-droppingly gorgeous. Sleek lines, plenty of glass, steel beams that gleamed in the afternoon sun, just like the waters of Lake Michigan that I could see on the other side of the wide swath of perfectly manicured green space that surrounded the building.

The inside . . .

When I stepped out of the revolving door that led into the lobby, I looked in wonder at the huge blank wall straight ahead of me. I mean, really blank. While all around me, every other surface gleamed with steel and granite beauty, this wall with its plain white plaster stuck out like a sore and very homely thumb.

A problem for the architects, I told myself, and strode over to the reception desk where I told the young woman that I had an appointment and was escorted to the elevator that led up to Cherneko's offices.

More granite, more steel, and here on the forty-eighth floor, vistas that took my breath away. If it was a really clear day, I bet I could see across the blindingly blue waters of the lake all the way to Michigan.

I had an appointment.

I waited for thirty minutes before a woman with an unreadable expression escorted me to an office as big as my apartment.

"Ms. Giancola." Behind his sleek desk, Victor Cherneko rose and cocked his head, like he was trying to place my face. "You left a cryptic message with my secretary. Something about buttons?"

As I recall, my message wasn't as cryptic as it was purposely vague. Which made me all the more curious about why Cherneko had agreed to this meeting so easily. Curious, and a little suspicious. "I was at the Chicago Community Church the other night. At Forbis Parmenter's—"

"The exhibit. Of course." He came around the desk to shake my hand. "You're the young lady who brought the button that Parmenter was going to place on the exhibit. That is, before that whole ugly incident happened. And then the murder." He pressed his lips together and shook his head. His salt-and-pepper hair matched the charcoal, pinstripe suit he wore with a killer Italian silk tie in shades of moss and gold. "Such a terrible thing," he mumbled before he put a hand on my elbow and escorted me over to a sitting area complete with buttery leather couches and chairs and a wet bar. He did not offer me a drink.

"I have to confess to being a little confused," he said. "You said you had something that belonged to me. But we never met at the show, did we? I saw you, of course, during that little ceremony. But if we never spoke, how could you possibly have something of mine?"

The shirt stud was in my purse. I took it out and handed it to Cherneko.

"But where . . ." He turned the little stud over in his

fingers. "I knew it was missing, of course. I realized it as soon as I got home that night. But how—"

"That's what I'm trying to figure out. The police have asked for my help, you see, because of the buttons. I was at the church surveying the exhibit and that's when I found the stud."

His look was as level as his voice. He didn't even blink. "Surely not near any of those other buttons. I never left the floor of the church, never got close to the artwork."

The look I returned was just as even.

"Actually it was right under one of the pieces."

He pursed his lips. "Really. Well . . ." He didn't so much smile as he bared his teeth. "I suppose shirt studs can roll."

We both knew they could, just like we both knew they couldn't roll up a step to the area where the artwork was on display.

So I wouldn't be tempted to point it out, I looked at the photos displayed on the mahogany coffee table in front of the couch. One showed Cherneko reeling in a marlin as big as a Fiat. In another, he was standing in front of the Kremlin. A third . . .

I took the framed photograph off the table, the better to take a careful look at it. In this particular picture, Cherneko was dressed in shorts and a golf shirt. He was kneeling in the dirt, surrounded by children with big eyes and ragged clothes.

"I have a factory in Haiti." Cherneko plucked the photo from my hand and set it back where it came from. "There are a couple orphanages nearby that are close to my heart. I like to visit."

"That's really nice."

"So . . ." He stood, and the message was clear: I'd done what I'd come to do, it was time for me to hit the road. "Thank you for returning the stud. I appreciate your kindness. Perhaps our paths will cross again at another art show. Until then, if there's anything I can do to repay your kindness . . ."

I followed him to the door. "You could answer a question for me," I said. "That wall down in the lobby. Everything else is finished but that one wall—"

"Oh, that." He acted like it was no big deal, but I couldn't help but remember what Stan told me about gut instinct. Cherneko's cheeks got dusky, and my gut told me there was more to the story than he let on. "A dispute with the artist who was supposed to be completing the mural, nothing more," he said. "We're in the process of getting things sorted out now. Thank you again, Ms. Giancola. I'll have my secretary show you out."

"There is one more thing." To prove it, I stopped and refused to budge an inch, even when he backed up to give me clearer access to the door. "It's just a little thing, of course, but a man like you, I'm sure you understand. Little things are often important. I've been asking everyone who was at the show about their alibis for after."

A muscle jumped at the base of his jaw. "The police have already done that."

"Of course they have. That's their job. And it's not like I have any official standing in the case. I mean, I'm just the button expert. That's all they've called me in to consult on. Buttons. But it does kind of help me get a sense of things, you know?" He didn't and frankly, I didn't, either, so before he could point out that getting a sense of things had nothing to do with buttons and was, therefore, none of my business, I hurried right on. "And I did bring that stud back to you. You know, rather than turn it over to the police."

"You did. And I appreciate it." Cherneko put a hand gently to the small of my back, the better to escort me all the way to the door. "One of these days, I'll thank you with a drink. How does that sound? We'll go to Remondo's. That's where I was after the show. I stopped for a drink at Remondo's."

Remondo's.

It was on my way home so don't think I didn't take the opportunity to stop in. It wasn't hard for the bartender to remember Cherneko. He was a regular, and a big tipper.

"Sure he was here Thursday night," the man told me. "Late, and all dressed up in a tux. But then, Mr. C., he's usually coming or going to some fancy affair or another."

"Was he alone?"

The way the bartender's eyebrows elevated, I knew he was about to tell me it was none of my business.

I slid a twenty across the bar. "I'm just trying to get some facts straight," I said.

He palmed the money. "They sat over there," he said, pointing to a table in a corner. "Mr. C. and another guy. Maybe in his forties. With kind of soft features, you know. And thinning hair."

"Richard Norquist," I mumbled to myself.

"Richard. Yeah, that's it." The bartender nodded. "That's what I heard Mr. C. call the other guy."

"They stayed long?"

"Mr. C. did. Had a couple Drambuies before he called it a night. The other guy . . ." Thinking, he narrowed his eyes. "He walked in here carrying a package. About yea by yea."

He held out his hands to indicate something the size of a shoe box. "It was all wrapped up in brown paper. He sat down for a while, didn't order anything."

"And when he left?"

Three cheers for the bartender. He knew exactly what I was getting at. "The package stayed with Mr. C," he said.

I left Remondo's convinced that my twenty was well spent. After all, I knew a little more than I'd known when I started out that day.

For one thing, I knew Gabriel Marsh was telling the truth. He had followed Cherneko and Richard and they were definitely together.

For another, I knew that Richard and Laverne were lying, and that told me that whatever Richard was up to with Victor Cherneko, it was something he didn't want anyone else to know about. It also told me that Laverne was head over heels about the man. Go figure. She wouldn't have been willing to lie for him otherwise. I reminded myself not to forget it, and outside Remondo's I headed for the nearest El stop. It was only a little after four and as promised, I'd be back at the Button Box in time to relieve Stan and close the shop.

I knew one more thing about what happened on Thursday night, I told myself when I got on the train. I knew that shirt stud I found belonged to Victor Cherneko, and I knew Victor Cherneko hadn't been near the artwork during the show, no one had.

That meant Victor Cherneko was near the exhibit some time between when Laverne locked up the church for the night and the next day when I found Forbis's body.

Chapter Ten

"You're a peach, Stan."

"Nah." He shrugged off the compliment, but I wasn't fooled. The tips of Stan's ears turned pink. "You know I don't have much else to do. I don't mind coming in here to the shop. In fact, I'm getting to like these buttons of yours." He had just set down a box filled with buttons on the worktable in the back room and ran his fingers through them. "They kind of grow on you, you know?"

I did know. I just didn't think Stan ever would. "Coming in here two days in a row to watch the shop for me is—"

"An excuse to get this old guy out of his apartment."

"I was going to say too much. You know, Stan, I've been thinking." I had, ever since the day before when I returned to the shop after my visit to Victor Cherneko and Remondo's. "When I first opened the shop, I hired an assistant.

That didn't work out too well." Understatement. Brina was, in a word, a total disaster. Even if that isn't one word. "How'd you like to make it official?"

It wasn't often I got the drop on Stan. He may be a senior citizen, but he's one sharp guy. For once, he was so surprised, he actually flinched. "Me? Work here? You mean like on the payroll? Come on, Josie, you don't have to do that. I don't mind coming in here when you need me so I can help out."

"But I mind asking you to come in here and help out."

"You make me dinner. And you get me Cubs tickets. And you take me over to the diner for Swiss steak and rice pudding."

"Yeah, once in a while. But that's not the same. If we had a more formal agreement, I wouldn't feel so guilty."

He gave me the eagle-eye look I knew he'd once reserved for perps. "Really? You feel guilty?"

"As sin."

He hadn't come right out and said *no*, and that's what I'd expected. Encouraged, I pressed my advantage. "You don't want me to walk around feeling guilty, do you?"

"Of course not, Josie, but—"

"My conscience just can't take it, Stan. My scruples are all in a twist."

He laughed. "I don't think scruples can twist."

"Mine can. They do. And you wouldn't have to work here full time. You'd be bored silly, and there's usually not enough to do to require another full-time worker here. Of course, we also have to consider that you'll still want time for your senior softball team, and for meeting your friends for lunch and for visiting that great-grandchild of yours. I'm thinking . . ." I crossed my fingers behind my back. "Fifteen hours a week?"

He tapped a finger to his chin. "Does yesterday count? Because I was here three hours yesterday and—"

"Yes, yesterday counts. And so does today." I had to force myself not to jump up and down for joy. "I'll pay more than minimum," I added, then because I knew he was going to protest, "You know I can afford it so don't argue. Your schedule will be completely flexible. Each Sunday, we can look at the upcoming week, see what you've got coming up—"

"And what murder you need to investigate."

I ignored this last bit, and no wonder. Just like I had the last time and the time before and the time before that, I hoped this murder investigation would be my last and I wouldn't have to worry about taking time off for sleuthing. "I won't ask you to do any more than you've ever done," I said. "All I would need you to do is watch the shop when I can't be here, and help keep things in order."

"And save damsels in distress."

It was my turn to be surprised and seeing it, Stan laughed again. "Yesterday when you were gone. A lady came in. She was outside sipping an iced tea and she spilled it all over herself. Poor thing! She said she was headed to a job interview and she was really upset."

"So you saved her."

"Well, not exactly saved. I gave her paper towels and let her get cleaned up back here. By the time she left, she was calmed down and she looked just fine. I told her to stop back after her interview and let me know how it went, but she never did. I hope she got the job."

"Well, we can add saving damsels in distress to your job description. So what do you say?"

KYLIE LOGAN

Grinning, Stan stuck out his hand and I shook it. "So," he said, "where do we begin?"

"We're not going to do anything different than we've ever done. I'm just going to run out for a little while and—"

"Investigate, eh?" I knew Stan was a little jealous. He'd been a cop for forty years and it was hard to put that kind of experience aside. "I could help you do that, too."

"You do. I don't know what I'd do if I didn't have you to talk over everything that happens. You give me advice. You help me decide where to go and who to talk to. You help me interview witnesses and suspects. Without you, there's no way I could help out the cops the way I do."

"There you go again, trying to give me a swelled head." Another wave of the hand. "You don't need me for any of those things. That's what you have Nev for."

Nev.

Just the mention of his name made my stomach bunch. But then, I knew where I was headed when I left Stan in charge of the shop for the rest of the afternoon.

"You look like you swallowed a pickle."

Leave it to Stan to bring me back to reality! I shook away the uneasiness that had settled on my shoulders. "It's that obvious, huh?"

He waited for me to say more and while I worked out how to put it into words, I scooped a handful of buttons out of the box in front of him and started sorting. As always with a new batch of buttons, the first thing I did was sort the buttons by color. Later, I'd worry about dividing the buttons according to what they were made of and where and when they were manufactured.

142

"I was doing some research last night," I told Stan. "Trying to find out more about that ceramic button I told you was missing from Forbis's exhibit. I didn't find anything useful, so I came in here extra early this morning and looked through all the books I have here."

"And . . . ?"

My drooping shoulders said it all. "If there was ever another button like it, nobody's written about it, nobody's photographed it. Nobody mentions it in any of the monographs I read about handmade buttons. Nobody references anything like it, or like those letters that were etched onto the button."

"And this has you looking all puckered when I mention Nev because . . . ?"

I sighed. "Because I was thinking. About Forbis. And about the exhibit. And about the whole tie-in with vudon. Forbis was from an island off the coast of Georgia where vudon was practiced back in the day. What if that button has something to do with the religion?"

Stan pursed his lips. "It's possible I suppose."

I finished with the buttons I was sorting but rather than reach for another batch, I brushed my hands together and stepped back from the table. Sorting buttons by color was something Stan could do sitting down and with a cup of coffee at hand, so it wouldn't be too strenuous for him, not like dusting or vacuuming. Besides, until he knew a little more about buttons, I couldn't ask him to do much more than sort. Sorting was a great place to start. All the rest about button history and what each button was made of would come later.

"If I want to know about vudon," I said, "it only makes sense to go to one of the world's recognized experts."

The light dawned and Stan nodded. "Into the lion's den, eh?"

"I'm not exactly sure that's how I'd put it." That hadn't stopped me from dressing with extra care that morning. It was warm out, and I'd chosen a black pencil skirt and a cami the color of pink cotton candy. No, I am not usually a pink person, but I remembered that Kaz had always told me I looked good in pink because of my dark hair and eyes.

It's not like I was trying to show anybody up. Not anybody. But I was concerned with looking presentable and professional and with making a good impression. On top of all that, I didn't want to look like a reject, like some cast-off Nev had let go when someone prettier and smarter came along, someone with a bigger brain than mine.

Pathetic. Yes, I know. Rather than think about it, I gave Stan a few last-minute instructions and grabbed my suit jacket.

"Taxi's already waiting for you," Stan said, walking me to the front of the shop. "You'd better get a move on because the meter's running and you'll spend all your money and you won't be able to afford my huge salary."

When I walked out of the Button Box, there was a smile on my face.

That lasted exactly two seconds.

When I climbed into the backseat of the cab, there was already someone there waiting for me.

"What are you—?" I tried to play it cool, honest. That wasn't exactly easy with Gabriel Marsh smiling at me like a *GQ* cover model.

"It makes perfect sense to share a ride," he said. "I suspect we're going to the same place."

"How would you—?" I gulped down the rest of my words. I knew he'd never give me a straight answer anyway, so why ask the question?

That was about when I realized the cab driver was looking over his shoulder at us, waiting for instructions.

"Field Museum," Gabriel and I said at the same time.

Gabriel sat back, perfectly comfortable and looking as at home in the cab as he had at my dining room table surrounded by Chinese takeout containers.

"You owe me an explanation."

"Do I?" This close, I saw that the skin at the corners of Gabriel's eyes was creased, like he spent too much time in the sun. Those little wrinkles were even more noticeable when he smiled. "I thought you would have figured it out by now."

"Figured what out?"

"That I'm interested in Mr. Parmenter and what happened to him."

"I didn't need to figure that out. You told me that when you stopped over on Saturday. What you need to figure out is that you're not going to find out anything about Forbis Parmenter at the Field Museum."

"Neither are you."

"Which would tell any logical person that I'm going to the museum for a whole different reason."

"Are you insinuating I'm not logical?" When he laughed, he threw back his head. "I'll take that as a compliment. In fact, when you get to know me better, you'll find that I am among the least reasonable people you are likely to meet. I am not so much a man of intellect as I am a creature of passion."

I suppose I actually could have given the whole intellect versus passion thing some thought if I wasn't so focused on what he said about *when* I got to know him better.

Sizzling was poor form. So was melting into a puddle of mush. Rather than do either, I shook my head to help clear it, and when I realized Gabriel was studying my pink cami with far more appreciation than even Kaz ever had, I slipped on my suit jacket.

"Cold?" he asked.

"Icy."

"I'd offer to provide some warmth but something tells me that wouldn't go over well."

"I'd rather have answers than warmth."

"Ask the questions."

"OK." I thought about where to start and figured the beginning was as good a place as any. "How did you know I was going to the museum?"

"Damn!" He made a face. "And just when I declared myself illogical! Now you expect me to lay out my plan and actually have it make sense. Very well, here goes. I knew you would eventually go the museum because, eventually, you were bound to want to find out more about vudon."

"But how did you know it would be today?"

"I didn't."

I may not have been genuinely cold before but suddenly, I was chilled to the bone. "You've been following me."

"You make it sound like some kind of crime."

Since my steady, and slightly sarcastic, gaze didn't seem to make an impression, I said, "It is!"

One corner of his mouth pulled tight. "It's not like I'm a stalker or anything. I'm a—"

"Journalist. Yes, I know." I plunked back against the sticky vinyl seat, my arms crossed over my chest. "And that gives you the right to follow me?"

"It gives me the right to look for answers."

"I told you before, I don't have any. So you're wasting your time."

"Oh, I don't know about that."

I didn't respond to this less-than-subtle attempt at whatever it was he was attempting. How could I? If he was saying what I thought he was saying . . .

Well, just thinking about it made my blood buzz, and this was not the time or the place. Or the man, for that matter.

"I don't know anything about Forbis's murder," I said. "I told you that Saturday night. End of story."

His smile would have been devastating if I thought it was the least bit genuine. "It's not that I don't believe you, it's just that I'm as stubborn as hell. It is my job, after all. I'm just a guy looking for information."

"Information about vudon."

His shrug wasn't as noncommittal as it was simply elegant. "If I intend to write about Parmenter, I need to know all I can about him, and about the exhibit."

This much I figured was true, and it made me wonder how much Gabriel already knew. I weighed the wisdom of saying too much and tipping my hand about the missing mystery button against the chance that I might be reinventing the wheel. I might not have answers for him, but maybe he had some for me.

"Did you take any photos when you were at the exhibit?" I asked him.

"You mean before Parmenter caused a scene?"

"Yes. Before Forbis spilled his champagne. Before he was found dead."

"Before you found him dead." He didn't expect me to say anything so I don't think he was disappointed when I pressed my lips together. "Sorry," he said, and just to clarify that it wasn't my fragile emotions he was worried about, he added, "I didn't take any photos."

"But you did do research, I bet. Before you showed up at the church. You must have if you hoped to look at the exhibit and understand what you saw. When you got to the show, did you notice anything . . . unusual?"

"You mean the argument our Mr. Parmenter was having with someone before he walked into the church."

"Yes, that." Believe me, I hadn't forgotten about that. "Do you know who he was fighting with?"

"Do you think it was strange that his body was found in the box with the loa?"

Don't think I didn't notice that he responded to my question with one of his own. "That was the next morning. I'm talking about at the show. Did you see anything that struck you as unusual?"

"Oh come on! I don't care how much you love buttons. You have to admit, it was all unusual. Weird artifacts covered with weird buttons."

Before I had the chance to defend buttons and the honor of button collectors everywhere, the cab stopped in front of the Field Museum.

Gabriel didn't offer to pay for the cab, so I did, then turned to walk up the wide steps that led to the magnificent building with its massive columns. Gabriel was right by my side.

"Going to see the dinosaurs," he said. When we stepped into the front door, he pulled a pair of sunglasses out of his pocket and put them on.

"Sun's out there," I said, looking over my shoulder and back outside. "Why would you—" When I turned back around, Gabriel was gone.

Good. Fine. Terrific, in fact. I was here on business and I didn't need the distraction that was Gabriel Marsh tagging along.

I paid my admission, grabbed a brochure to get the lay of the land, and headed out to find the museum's anthropology collections. From there it wasn't hard to find what I was looking for. Or, to be more exact, *who* I was looking for. There was a new exhibit being set up under a sign that said "Yoruba" and there smack in the middle of it, wearing khakis along with a museum polo and white cotton archival gloves, and standing in a soft spotlight that added coal black highlights to her hair, was Evangeline.

If she was surprised to see me, she didn't show it. In fact, she lifted her chin and met my steady gaze head on. "You've come to talk about Nev."

"There's nothing the two of us need to say to each other about Nev."

"Really? Is that what you think?" She set down the elaborate beaded belt she was holding. "What can I do for you?"

"I was hoping you could tell me something about vudon. This isn't . . ." I glanced around the soon-to-be exhibit. Behind Evangeline, there were three empty glass-fronted cases with glass shelves, and in front of them, tables, packing crates, and display platforms. "I thought vudon was your thing," I said.

Dressed so casually, Evangeline looked more like a college intern than a recognized expert in a long-dead religion. She stripped off her gloves. "My specialty is vudon, but voodoo and vudon and other related religions can all be traced back to the ancient religions of Africa. The religion of the Yoruba people is one of them. I've had a number of articles published about the similarities and differences. If you're interested in learning more, we can stop in my office and I'll get you a list."

I'd had a number of articles published, too, all of them about buttons and none of them in the swanky sorts of journals where I'm sure Evangeline's research appeared. Rather than admit it, I cast a leisurely glance around the exhibit. There was a mannequin nearby dressed in astonishing robes of brightly colored fabric adorned with seashells and beading, and I itched to get a closer look and promised myself a trip back to the museum when the exhibit opened.

"Did Yoruba beliefs have anything to do with Forbis Parmenter's exhibit?"

A couple of workers came by carrying a large wooden crate, and Evangeline and I backed up and out of the way. "I doubt very much if Mr. Parmenter was intellectually capable of making the connection between vudon and Yoruba," she said. "From what I saw, his knowledge of vudon was rudimentary at best. Is that really why you're here? To ask for my opinion about the exhibit and vudon?"

"You are one of the country's leading experts."

"One of the world's, actually."

"Of course. Just like I am about buttons."

Her smile was stiff. "What is it you wanted to know about Mr. Parmenter's exhibit?"

"I was just wondering, that's all. About what Forbis said. You remember, before he dropped his glass and ran out of the church. He said—"

" 'Le bouton.' Yes, I was standing close enough. I heard exactly what he said."

"Does it mean anything? In relation to the vudon religion?"

There was a pile of brochures on a nearby table and Evangeline picked them up and tapped them into order, then slid them into a holder mounted on the wall. The front page showed a picture of that mannequin at the back of the exhibit, resplendent in its robes.

She was so intent on doing her job, I was pretty sure she forgot all about me being there.

"There's a button missing from Forbis's exhibit," I finally said, and just like I hoped, that got her attention; Evangeline's hands stilled over her work. "I wondered if that button might have anything to do with the button he was talking about, and if that button might somehow be significant to the vudon culture."

"A button missing? Really?" She finished with the brochures before she turned to face me. "How on earth would you know one button is missing among all those thousands of buttons?"

I didn't often twinkle. It was silly and usually a waste of time. Except at moments like this. "I'm an expert, remember."

Her smile froze around the edges. "Is the missing button valuable?" she asked.

My ego kept me from telling her that I didn't have the slightest idea so instead I told her, "It might be. And if there's some connection with vudon—"

"There's not." She slipped her gloves back on. "I can tell you that with certainty because I'm an expert, too. Except that they might have been used to adorn clothing, there's nothing in the vudon religion that attaches any significance to buttons. But then, that's hardly a surprise, is it? Buttons are such insignificant things to begin with."

"Forbis didn't think so." I thought about those buttons on his eyes and the one that had been glued on his lips sometime after his death. "And, you know what, I don't think his killer did, either."

After as pleasant a good-bye as I could manage, I got back downstairs and found Gabriel leaning against a pillar, his legs crossed at the ankles. He pushed off the moment he saw me.

"Where've you been?" I asked.

"A more interesting topic would be where you've been. Yoruba, huh? Want to tell me why you were having that little heart-to-heart with Evangeline Simon?"

I stopped mid stride, the better to shoot him a look. "If you know I was talking to Evangeline, you don't have to ask where I've been."

"You think there's a connection, don't you? You wouldn't have come all the way over here to talk to her if you didn't think there was some connection between Parmenter's mad exhibit and his death."

"Is there anything you don't know?"

"Nope. Except I don't know if she told you anything helpful."

"Do you think I'd tell you if she did?"

At least I got a thumbs-up to acknowledge the fact that I'd finally gotten one up on him.

I got a move on again and we were outside on the steps before I spoke to Gabriel again. "So? You know what I was doing here. You didn't tell me where you were."

"You mean you don't believe I'm wild about dinosaurs?"

At least he gave me enough credit not to expect me to answer. He started down the steps in front of me. "While you were busy with the lovely Ms. Simon, I was searching her office, of course."

"What!" I froze long enough for him to get far ahead of me, and scrambled to catch up with him. At the bottom of the steps, I grabbed his arm. "You broke into Evangeline's office?"

"I didn't break in. Institutional keys are shamefully standard."

My mouth flapped open.

"Oh, come on!" Gabriel slipped an arm around my waist and walked me out to the sidewalk. "Don't look so righteous. And don't pretend you're surprised. She's one of the world's leading experts in vudon. Parmenter's exhibit was all about vudon. There might be a connection."

"What did you find?"

"Not a damned, bloody thing."

"Pardon me for being just the slightest bit skeptical." I tugged out from the circle of his arm so that I could face him. "Come on. Really. What did you find?"

Gabriel sighed and pulled his phone out of his pocket. "Only this," he said. He held the phone out to me and I looked at the photo on it. It showed a square building with a sloping roof. It looked like a—

"Garage?" I asked him.

"Mmmm." He tucked the phone back in his pocket.

"Why did you take a picture of a garage?"

"I didn't take a picture of a garage. I took a picture of a picture of a garage."

I am not dense, but it took me a moment to work through this. "Evangeline has a photograph of a garage in her office."

"Matted, framed, and hanging behind her desk."

"And that's interesting because . . . ?"

Gabriel had taken off his sunglasses the moment we were out of the museum, and in the bright sunlight I saw that his gray eyes had flecks of amber in them. They sparkled at me when he said. "Don't you get it? That's the whole point. It's interesting because it's not the least bit interesting at all."

Chapter Eleven

I FELL ASLEEP THAT NIGHT WITH THE SOUNDS OF DISTANT drumbeats pounding in my head, but at least that wasn't what woke me up before the sun the next morning.

It was my phone, and startled, I glanced at the clock on my bedside table and groaned.

Right before I sat up like a shot.

A phone ringing in the dark will do that to a person. Especially when that person has even half an ounce of imagination and envisions all the worst things possible.

My blood pressure spiked through the roof and my hands trembled when I groped for the phone.

"Josie, I'm so sorry to bother you this early."

It took me a moment to realize that it was Laverne on the other end of the phone. It took less than that for me to collect myself and ask, "What's wrong?"

"I think you better get down here," she said.

"Down—"

"I'm sorry to be so unclear. I'm a little . . ." She drew in a long breath and let it out in a whoosh. "I'm a little upset. Down here to the church, of course. You'd better get down here to the church."

I wasn't sure I wanted to hear the answer, but I asked anyway. "Is there another body?"

"Body? Oh, no. Nothing like that. At least not that I can see."

"Are you in any danger?"

When it took her a heartbeat or two to answer, my throat squeezed. "Laverne?"

"I . . . I don't think so. I'm here in the gallery. I think . . ." I pictured her looking around the interior of the church. "I'm pretty sure I'm alone."

"I'll tell you what . . ." I was already out of bed, and I reached for my jeans and slipped into them along with a yellow T-shirt and my sneakers. "There can't be much traffic this early in the morning. I'll drive over. But it's going to take me at least twenty minutes." I pictured the huge church with its infinite hiding places and shadowy corners. "Wait for me in your office. Can you do that?"

"Yes." I think there was something about having a plan that gave her courage. She sounded more sure of herself, more in control. "I'm on my way there now."

"Good. Stay there. And Laverne, lock the door once you're inside and if you need to, call the cops."

Inside her office was exactly where I found Laverne and it was less than twenty minutes later. But then, like I said, there wasn't much traffic at that time of the day and luckily,

I didn't pass any cops. I don't think they would have appreciated me making an attempt to break land-speed records on Chicago city streets.

"What's going on?"

There was a coffeemaker on top of a filing cabinet in the corner and Laverne had a mug of coffee poured for me practically before I was inside the door and had it closed—and locked—behind me. She handed me the coffee and gestured over to where there was sugar and powdered creamer. "I can't thank you enough," she said.

I wrapped my hands around the mug. It was going to be a hot, sticky day; I knew that the moment I walked out of my apartment. But the warmth of the coffee still felt good, comforting. I savored the aroma that drifted off the mug and closed my eyes, hoping for a calm I hadn't felt on the drive over.

"What's happening?" I asked Laverne. "And what on earth are you doing here so early?"

She pressed a hand to her forehead. "I'm sorry. I shouldn't have bothered you. I saw all the buttons and I just naturally thought of you and I didn't know what else to do and . . ." Laverne was in a tizzy and she's clearly not the tizzy type. She squeezed her hands into fists and held her arms tight against her sides while she drew in another long breath.

"I couldn't sleep," she said. One of her fists beat a staccato rhythm against her hip. "I tossed and turned most of the night, thinking about everything that happened around here and wishing it could all be different, and feeling so sorry for poor Mr. Parmenter and for poor Reverend Truman, too. The reverend, he's being badgered by the media and it's taken so much of his focus away from our congregation. We're a people of prayer and community action, and yet last Sunday, all anyone could talk about before and after the service was the murder, and Reverend Truman, he's going to have a time of it getting everyone to give their heads and their hearts and their hands back to the Lord."

Her fist beat faster, and I knew if I didn't try to rein her in, I was in for trouble. "So you couldn't sleep," I said.

Laverne nodded. "That's right. I kept thinking of everything I had to do today and then I realized that it's Thursday, and just one week ago, I remember hopping out of bed and thinking how exciting it was to have a real art show at the church, and how it would help us draw in people and build our congregation. And then I thought about how all that came crashing down around us. And then . . . well, naturally, since it's Thursday, I remembered that the reverend, he always works on his Sunday sermon on Thursday, and I knew he'd need my help with doing that more than ever this week. He's a good man, and this murder has thrown him for a loop. I was thinking maybe I'd suggest that he base this week's sermon on a quote from Psalm 34. You know, the one that goes, 'Turn from evil and do good; seek peace and pursue it.' And I was so pleased with myself for thinking of that. It's perfect, don't you think?"

She didn't give me a chance to answer. Laverne barreled right on. "And that's when I had another thought. About pursuing peace. Our church, with what happened here last week, our peace was shattered. But that doesn't mean it has to be gone forever, and that's the message we need to get across to the world. And so I thought that once Mr. Parmenter's exhibit is packed up and shipped out of here, we could do a prayer meeting up in the church. You know, as a way of starting over."

"That's a wonderful idea." It was, and besides, I had to interrupt Laverne so she'd take a breath.

Once she did, she plunged back in. "And I thought about how we'd invite everyone from the neighborhood in, and the media, too, and how we'd have a candlelight vigil with prayer and music. Then for sure I was so excited, I couldn't sleep." She had a cup of coffee on her desk and she picked it up but she didn't drink it. "And that's why I came in a little early."

Understatement. The clock on the credenza behind her desk said it wasn't even five yet.

"And I stepped into the church," she continued. "You know, just to sort of imagine all the people who would gather and how we could light candles all around and where we could put flowers and how the reverend, he could use that Psalm as a way of reminding not only our congregation, but everyone in the neighborhood that there are better ways to live our lives than with violence. Peace, that's what we need to pursue. Just like the Psalm says."

"And you walked into the church and . . ."

"That's right." Laverne set down her coffee cup. "I walked into the church. And that's when I saw it. Oh, there's no use trying to explain. Come on." She grabbed my arm and led the way.

A minute later we were standing in front of Forbis's exhibit. When Laverne came in earlier, she hadn't turned on the spotlights over each of the art pieces. The only light in the place came from a hanging fixture above the door that led to the hallway and the dim light of the streetlights that seeped in through the stained-glass windows. Still, it didn't take me more than a half a second to see what Laverne had seen when she walked in.

I flinched.

She patted my arm. "I'll get the lights," she said and she did, the better to illuminate the Congo Savanne statue.

This time, even the ugly, looming loa couldn't keep me at a distance. I hurried over and looked at where the front of the box that held the statue was completely torn away. "It's gone!"

Laverne glanced around the exhibit. "I sure don't see it anywhere. Somebody must have broken in during the night and taken it. But why . . ." Her shoulders rose and fell. "Why take part of the box?"

Good question, and I didn't have an answer. "We've got to call the police," I said.

"I know that. I should have done it first thing except when I saw it had to do with the buttons, all I could think of was you."

This was a compliment, and I appreciated it, but I didn't have a chance to tell Laverne. I was already on the phone with the police dispatcher.

THREE CHEERS FOR the two cops who arrived within fifteen minutes. They called in backup so they could thoroughly comb the church and make sure whoever had vandalized the box—and taken all the buttons on it—wasn't hiding somewhere, and they stopped in Laverne's office briefly to let her know that they found how the burglar got in. A basement window was broken.

"We've been saving to have glass block installed," Laverne told me when the cop left. "Looks like we should have made it a priority."

"At least nothing else was touched." This was a consolation of sorts even if it did bring up another whole question.

Laverne knew it. That's why she asked, "Why would anyone make off with part of a box covered with buttons and leave everything else, like computers and such? There's a flat-screen TV downstairs. You think he would have taken that."

Don't think I hadn't thought the same thing.

Don't think I wasn't already thinking I had the answer.

"I saw a button on that box the night of the murder," I said. "A button that wasn't like any other button I've ever seen before."

Laverne latched onto my arm with both hands. "And you think that's why somebody broke in and stole the box. To get at that button! Josie, you're a genius."

"Not so much." Before she could get too carried away, I unhitched her fingers from my arm. "The button was already missing a couple days after the murder when I came back to the church."

"But not right after the murder?"

I sighed. "I don't know. That morning we found Forbis's body, I didn't even think to look for it. I noticed it was gone when I came back the next time."

"So the killer could have taken that button."

"Yes."

"But we don't know for sure."

"That's right."

"So what are you going to do?"

What I should have told her was that *I* wasn't going to do anything. That murder investigations were up to the police and that Nev was in charge of this one and he knew what he was doing.

What I said instead wasn't something I intended. It just sort of popped out. "You didn't go out for coffee with Richard last Thursday after the art exhibit."

Laverne pulled in a sharp breath. "Don't be silly, Josie. I told you—"

"I know what you told me, but I know it's not true. Richard was with Victor Cherneko that night."

Her eyes widened just enough for me to realize this was news to her.

"You don't know what they were doing together?" I asked her.

Laverne didn't answer my question. Instead, she twined her fingers together. "I can imagine what you think. About me."

Since I hadn't had a chance to finish that first cup of coffee, I'd poured another when we got back to Laverne's office and I drank down the last of it. "I think that an old friend asked you for a favor and you obliged him. I think you did it because you didn't imagine that it could make any difference."

"That's right." She hung her head. "I should know better, shouldn't I? You think a woman my age would. But you see, when Richard came back into my life . . ." She rounded her desk and sat down behind it. "Back when Richard and I were in college, a lot of people didn't approve of us dating. White man, black girl. You can imagine."

I could, and I didn't like it.

"When I got that call from him saying he was going to

be in Chicago, asking if I'd like to get together . . . well, things are different these days, and I thought . . I thought maybe our relationship could be different, too."

"Is it?"

"It's . . ." She took a moment to find just the right word. "It's nice," she said. "Oh, I know he's not a cutie pie, not like that policeman boyfriend of yours. But then, that's never why I liked Richard in the first place. He was considerate, kind, fun to be with. He still is."

"And when he asked you to lie, did you think he was being considerate, kind, and fun to be with?"

Her shrug said it all. "I didn't know what to think. But like you said, I didn't think it would make any difference."

"Did he tell you why it was important?"

"He told me that after everything that happened at the show, what with Forbis running away and everything being ruined, he told me all he wanted to do was go back to his hotel room, grab a shower, and hit the hay. I had no doubt that's exactly what he did."

"If you thought that's where he was, why do you suppose he'd ask you to lie about it?"

"Because once we knew Forbis was dead . . ." Laverne gathered her thoughts. "Once we knew Forbis had been murdered, Richard said the police were bound to ask us about our alibis. He said that because I went home myself and he went to his hotel room himself, neither of us had an alibi and that would make us both look fishy. He said if we covered for each other, no one would be the wiser. I figured, no harm, no foul. I knew I went right home after I locked up the church that night, so obviously, I wasn't the murderer.

And I had no reason not to believe Richard. He surely didn't kill Mr. Parmenter." As if she'd been punched in the stomach, Laverne winced. "Wait a minute! You think he did!"

"I never said that." I didn't, so I made sure I kept my tone even and my words non-accusatory. "I'm only trying to get the facts straight. Where Richard was and who he was with, those are facts. And I need to verify them."

Laverne sat back and crossed her arms over her chest. "Well, he didn't do it."

"You know that for a fact."

"I know he's not the kind of man who would kill another human being, then glue buttons on his eyes and mouth." She shivered. "That would take some freaky thinking, and Richard, he's not like that. He's ordinary, just a regular guy."

I slipped into her guest chair. "Any idea what this regular guy was doing with Victor Cherneko?"

She shook her head. "I doubt they even know each other. Are you sure your information is right?"

I thought about my three sources: Gabriel, Victor himself, and the bartender at Remondo's. "What kind of package could Richard have been delivering to Victor Cherneko after the art show?"

Laverne ran her hands through her hair. "Now you're making me crazy with all these questions! Richard gave Cherneko a package? You saw this? Here at the church?"

"I didn't see it. But other people did. And no, it didn't happen here. It happened after. When Richard told you he was at his hotel."

"Richard never mentioned any sort of package to me."

"Maybe he didn't want you to know too much. In case someone came around and started asking questions."

"Someone like you." I don't think Laverne held this against me. She was far too practical for that. "Truth be told, I didn't believe Richard, not completely. Oh, I know he ended up back at his hotel. I have no doubt of that. But I thought on the way, he might have gone out looking for Mr. Parmenter. He cared about the man very much, you know."

I had only seen Richard and Forbis together once, in that one brief encounter before the show. The way I remembered it, Richard was overly friendly and Forbis was downright snippy. That may have been artistic temperament talking, but I didn't think so. "I don't think they liked each other," I told Laverne.

"Don't be silly. They've worked together for a couple of years and they always got along. Ask Richard."

"I intend to." I glanced at the clock and yawned. It was nearly time to open the Button Box, and I was in serious need of a couple more hours of sleep that I knew I wasn't going to get. I rose from my chair. "Would you do me a favor, please, Laverne. Don't tell Richard we had this talk."

"I don't know if I can—"

"Please." I wasn't especially good at pleading but I gave it my level best. "You're not doing him any favors by trying to cover for him. Not until you find out why he thinks he needs an alibi in the first place."

She bit her lower lip, thought about it, nodded.

"Thanks." I moved toward the door. "I've got a lot to think about and I should call Nev and tell him what happened here." Not that it had changed a whole lot, but I looked at the clock again, anyway. "I'll wait a bit. No use disturbing his sleep, too."

"What do you make of it, Josie?" Laverne followed me

to the door. "Why would someone break in and destroy the artwork? And if that was his goal, why not destroy more of the pieces?"

"I'm pretty sure he didn't care about the art. I think this has more to do with the buttons."

"Like that unusual one you said was on the box." Laverne pressed her lips together. "Why didn't this fellow just take the buttons the night he killed poor Mr. Parmenter?"

I had asked myself that question, too, and the answer wasn't all that hard to come up with. "Remember," I said, "the person who killed Forbis took the keys from Reverend Truman's office. Have you had the locks changed here at the church since the murder?"

Laverne grimaced. "We talked about it. And I know we should have done it. But we looked at the budget and that sort of extra expense is something we can't afford. It's our fault, isn't it? If we had done that, the exhibit wouldn't have been vandalized."

I could understand how her thinking got all mixed-up. There was a lot to think about, it was early, and neither of us had had enough sleep. I put a hand on her shoulder. "Don't you see, it's just the opposite. The murderer stole Reverend Truman's extra keys the night he killed Forbis. And you haven't changed the locks since. That means that if the murderer came back here and took the front off that loa box, he wouldn't have had to break in through the basement."

"You mean . . . ?" Working through it, Laverne scrunched up her nose. "Are you saying . . . ? What do you mean, Josie?"

"I mean that the person who broke in here last night wasn't the murderer. If it was, he would have come right in the door, he wouldn't have had to break a window and crawl in through the basement."

"So you're saying we have two different criminals on our hands. One is a murderer and the other one is a burglar."

"Exactly."

"And the burglar, all he took was the front of a box that was covered in buttons."

"Yes."

"And the front of the box that was covered with buttons—"

"Is the front of the box where I saw a button that was very unusual, a button that wasn't there when I came back to get a better look at it."

Laverne put her hands to the side of her head and tugged at her hair. "My brain is spinning! What does it all mean?"

I couldn't say. Not for sure. But I had a theory. In fact, I had two.

The first was that the person who broke into the Chicago Community Church was looking for the weird button. And whoever it was, he was a little out of the loop. He didn't know that button was already missing.

And the second?

That was a no-brainer.

Richard lied about his alibi, and he asked Laverne to lie to cover for him.

To me, that made him look pretty darned guilty.

Chapter Twelve

BART McCROMB LOOKED MORE LIKE A FIGHT PROMOTER than an art gallery owner. He wasn't much taller than me (which, for the record, is not very tall) and he weighed at least two-fifty. He had broad shoulders, a short neck, and a nose that sat crooked on his face, as if it had been broken a couple times and reset in a hurry. His mouth was broad, but then it had to be to accommodate lips that reminded me of bologna slices. The moment I walked into the door of the Mango Tango Gallery, he stuck out one massive hand in greeting.

"Welcome." The diamond stud in Bart's ear winked in the light of the spots trained on the huge oil painting that dominated one wall of the gallery. Tropical flowers. Maybe. Or it might have been a painting of fish. Whatever, bright splashes of color flashed across the canvas, orange and purple and blue and chartreuse. I appreciate color. I did not, however, own a wall anywhere near big enough for a painting that size. I wondered who did.

"You've visited us before?" Bart asked.

"No. First-timer." The gallery walls were brick and painted a particularly vivid shade of yellow that provided a showy background for the other, smaller paintings displayed all around us. The one just over my right shoulder showed a village scene with a pink adobe church in the background and a fountain, brick walkway, and flower carts out front. It would look great over my fireplace, and I noted the price and promised myself a little shopping therapy was in order. After all, I had been up since before the crack of dawn and I'd worked hard all day.

"It's a beautiful gallery," I said, more to myself than to Bart, but he heard and grinned like a Miss America contestant. "I'd heard—" I didn't want to put him off, not when I hoped he could help me make sense of everything that happened at the Chicago Community Church, but I couldn't help myself. Naturally, I thought of Richard and how he'd claimed he'd moved Forbis's exhibit from Mango Tango to the church because this gallery was—

"Somebody told me Mango Tango was a dump," I said. "Obviously, they were not talking about the same place."

"I'm glad you like it." There was an open bottle of Cabernet on a glass-and-stainless-steel table in the corner and Bart poured a glass and offered it to me. Luckily, Mango Tango had evening hours on Thursday and I was able to come back to Wicker Park after the Button Box was closed. It had been a long day, and I planned to head right home when I left the gallery. I gladly accepted the glass of wine.

I sipped and strolled, admiring the paintings, the art glass, and a couple of small wood carvings. I was the only customer at the moment, so with his own glass of wine, Bart walked along at my side. He was as subtle as the silver tie he wore with his charcoal suit—there to answer questions if I had any, but not pushy at all.

If only he knew my questions weren't going to have anything to do with art.

And everything to do with Forbis.

I was studying a photograph of a beat-up bicycle leaning against a graffiti-covered wall when I decided it was time to make my move. "I know you were out of town. I stopped in last week."

"Ah, St. Croix." Bart tipped back his head and smiled. "Sunshine, blue skies, and gorgeous beaches. Off season, of course, but that's not such a bad thing. Fewer tourist means more peace and quiet."

"I thought . . ." Another sip of wine, just so I didn't seem too eager. "I stopped by last week because I thought there was supposed to be an exhibit here, *Vudon Me Wrong*."

It wasn't my imagination. Bart's shoulders went rigid and his chin shot up. "*Supposed to* being the operative words in that sentence. Do you know about that exhibit?"

"Do you know about the murder?"

We had strolled our way around the gallery and were back where we started from, at that glass-topped table. He set down his wineglass and crossed his arms over a chest as wide as the Dan Ryan Expressway. "Why do I get the feeling you're not really here to talk about art?" he asked.

I set down my wineglass, too. "I'm glad we don't have to

dance around the subject," I said, and I truly was relieved. "I don't like to play games."

"So you are here to talk about Forbis Parmenter."

"Well, yes. And to buy that painting." I pointed toward the village scene. Hey, when in search of information, it doesn't hurt to spread around some goodwill, and some cash. "We'll worry about the painting later. For now, I was wondering if you could tell me why Richard Norquist told me Mango Tango was a dump."

Bart laughed, but not like it was funny. "Richard's the one who said that? I guess I'm not surprised. The guy is a first-class jerk."

This did not tally with the considerate, kind, and fun-to-be-with man Laverne had told me about.

"I'm glad I came over to see the gallery for myself," I said in an attempt to smooth Bart's ruffled feathers. "Richard was wrong."

"About a lot of things." He refilled both our glasses and though I hadn't finished mine in the first place, I knew a peace offering when I saw it. I sipped and thought about the right way to approach the subject. It was obvious Bart was an upfront kind of guy. And it was just as obvious there was no use beating around the bush.

"Forbis Parmenter's exhibit was supposed to here," I said. "It got moved to the Chicago Community Church. Can you tell me why?"

"Can you tell me why you care?"

"I can tell you I'm working with the police to try and figure out what happened to Forbis."

He lowered his chin. I couldn't say for sure, but I had the

feeling this was his way of acknowledging the fact that if I had the authority and I was asking the questions, he'd be willing to answer. There was only one way to find out.

"Who decided to move the exhibit from here to the church, Forbis or Richard?"

"It sure wasn't Forbis's decision. Forbis was . . ." He glanced my way. "You met him?" he asked, and when I said I had, he smiled. "Then you know what I'm talking about when I say he was the stereotypical artiste. Forbis didn't much care where his work was shown, as long as the spotlight was on him. And he didn't handle the arrangements for the exhibit to be here in the first place. Richard did that."

"Richard came to you and asked you to host the exhibit?"

"No, no. Nothing like that. As a matter of fact, I'm the one who originally approached Forbis about an exhibit. I'd heard the buzz, you see. Anyone with their ear to the art rail had. About a year ago, I heard about this wild artist who covered things in buttons. I saw pictures of his pieces and I'll tell you what, I was intrigued. Buttons are a little out there, of course, but—"

In the interest of full disclosure I told him buttons were what had drawn me into the investigation. "I'm something of an expert," I said.

"Then it makes sense you'd want to know more about the chain of events." He rolled the wineglass in his hands. "I first met Forbis down in Nashville. Like I said, about a year ago. He had an exhibit down there at a small gallery and I'd heard so much about him, I wanted to see for myself if it was all true."

"Was it?"

"His playful use of color? His eye for detail? His wild

abandon when it came to buttons? Yes, every word of it was true. That particular exhibit was the one where Forbis covered household goods with buttons, and I took one look at the kitchen table and KitchenAid mixer covered with buttons and I was hooked. I knew my customers would be, too."

"So you asked Forbis to come here to Chicago and show his work."

"He was thrilled. He was more than thrilled. Nashville is all fine and good, you understand, but it's not exactly a city known for its art or its galleries. Chicago, on the other hand . . . Forbis knew if he had a major show in Chicago, his future as an artist was pretty much assured. Forbis told me he didn't actually bother with the day-to-day details of the business, so he handed me off to Richard. I met with him and we agreed on dates for the show and that was that."

"Except it wasn't."

"Exactly. A few weeks ago, I made a trip down to Jekyll Island to see the vudon exhibit before it left Forbis's studio. You know, so I could think about how best to display things and lighting and such. I wasn't disappointed by what I saw. Those ceremonial drums . . ." Bart's eyes twinkled with the fire of artistic appreciation. "And that loa in the box!" He looked my way to make sure I knew what he was talking about.

I put out a hand, my palm flat. "I don't need to be reminded of that particular piece," I told him. "That's where Forbis's body was found. I was the one who found it."

"I'm sorry." He laid a hand briefly on my arm. "I read about the whole thing, of course, and even if I hadn't, every gallery owner here in Chicago is buzzing about it. I got plenty of calls while I was down in St. Croix, and I heard the details, but I never stopped to think that a body just isn't found. Somebody finds it. That must be a terrible experience."

"And not something I like to think about." I shook my shoulders to get rid of the cold chill that had settled there. "So you went to Jekyll Island . . ."

"That's right. And I saw Forbis's pieces and I was thrilled. Richard and I made an appointment to meet the next day and get everything finalized."

"So it sounds as if things were working out well."

"They certainly were." Bart looked at me over the rim of his wineglass. "That's a very long-winded way of answering your question. You asked who moved the exhibit from here to the church. Was it Richard? Or was it Forbis? Well, I don't know who actually trolled for another exhibit space and ended up with the church, but I can tell you I know who told Forbis and Richard to get lost. That was me."

"You cancelled? Richard told me—"

"Let me guess. That's where the dumpy gallery comment came in."

I nodded.

Bart shook his head in disgust. "Leave it to Richard. I guess he had to save face."

"Because you told him they couldn't have the exhibit here. But why, if you loved Forbis's work so much?"

Bart finished his wine and set down his glass. "How much do you know about galleries?" he asked.

"You mean other than that I always see something in them that I want to buy? Very little."

"We may spend our days surrounded by wonderful art, but gallery owners have to have a practical side, like all small business owners. When an artist displays at a gallery and makes a sale, the standard cut is anywhere from a third to a half. My cut is fifty/fifty. Overhead, you know. Of course I discussed that with Richard. In fact, he signed an agreement that stated it quite clearly. But that last day I was in Nashville . . ." Bart heaved a sigh.

"The last evening I was there, I met Richard for a drink. He got to the bar before I did, and he was on the phone when I arrived. Just so you know, it wasn't like I was eavesdropping or anything. His back was to me, he didn't know I was there. When I walked up to the table, I couldn't help but hear Richard. He was obviously talking to Forbis. He reminded Forbis what a big deal it was to have a show in Chicago. And then he told Forbis that big-city galleries do things a little differently from the other galleries they'd worked with. He told Forbis I was getting a sixty percent cut."

"But you said—"

"Fifty-fifty standard. That's right."

I let this sink in for a moment. "So you cancelled the showing."

"Right then and there," Bart said. "Well, as soon as Richard got off his call with Forbis, anyway. That's why the comment about Mango Tango being a dump doesn't really surprise me. Richard had to tell Forbis something to explain why the show wasn't going to be here. He certainly couldn't tell Forbis it was because I wasn't willing to go along with his scheme, because then Richard would have to admit he was skimming ten percent off the top of every sale and putting it in his own pocket."

I DIDN'T LIE to Laverne. Not exactly anyway.

Not that I wouldn't have been justified, I mean with the

way she'd bought into Richard's cooked up alibi and the way Richard, apparently, had been living a lie since even before he stepped foot in Chicago.

Instead of making up a story, I told Laverne that I was concerned about the panel on the front of the loa box and the missing buttons (true) and asked her if I could look around the church again (hey, it wouldn't hurt) and oh, by the way, I wondered if Richard was going to be around since Forbis's artwork was damaged and I was sure there must be police reports to file and insurance claims to fill out.

I was in luck. At least that's what Laverne said. Richard would be at the church the next morning, taking care of all the details.

Perfect timing, especially since Nev was able to join me.

It was early when we met in the parking lot of the Chicago Community Church. The sun was barely above the tall steeple and already the air rippled with heat. My headache was back, and I blamed it on the high humidity and told myself that, headache or no headache, I had to finish up and get over to the Button Box as soon as possible. Stan would open the shop, but this was the day of his monthly lunch at Clark Street Dog with other retired cops and that, I knew, was written in stone. So was what Stan would order: a Polish sausage sandwich with mustard and grilled onions along with cheese fries. I also knew he'd spend the evening complaining about heartburn.

What with the heat and the headache, I wanted to be cool and comfortable all day. But I was finally going to see Nev, too, and I wanted to look my best. I chose a khaki skirt and a pink short-sleeve blouse. Yeah, pink again. I wondered if Nev would notice.

He didn't.

"I appreciate you calling me about this," he said, swinging out of his unmarked car, his eyes on the church. "Like you told me on the phone yesterday, you've been busy. You found out why the art exhibit ended up here and not at that swanky gallery. And you found out Richard was with Cherneko after the show."

"There's a lot we still don't know." I didn't need to remind him. The fact that things still didn't make sense explained the little vee of worry between Nev's eyebrows. "Obviously, something's going on between Victor Cherneko and Richard Norquist. They wouldn't have met at Remondo's after the art show otherwise. And as far as Richard trying to cheat Forbis out of ten percent of the profits from any sales of his artwork—"

"Yeah, that's all important. But what I meant is that you've been busy at the Field Museum."

"Oh." Not the most elegant comeback. But then, my brain froze at the same time as my feet did. Witty was too much to ask at a time like that. When I stopped cold, so did Nev.

"You talked to Evangeline," I stammered.

"She told me you stopped by."

"You're the one who's always told me that when you want information, you shouldn't waste time with somebody who might know only some of it. You go right to the top. I hoped she could help me out. You know, when it came to vudon."

"Really? Is that really why you went over there to talk to her?"

Why did I suddenly feel like I was in an interrogation room down at the police station and Nev was interviewing me from the other side of a gray metal table?

I shifted my purse from one shoulder to the other. "Why else would I go to the museum to talk to Evangeline?"

"She was uncomfortable."

"Because I stopped to talk to her?" Call me insensitive, but I laughed. "You're kidding, right? What, I'm intimidating? Because I asked about a subject she's supposed to be an expert about?"

"She is an expert. And I'm just telling you what she told me. She thought you were being . . ."

"What?" I'd stepped closer to Nev and raised my chin even before I realized it, but by that time, it was too late to back down. "I was being what?"

How on earth he could wear a raincoat when the temperature was already licking eighty, I didn't know, but I did see Nev's shoulders rise and fall inside his coat. "All she said was that she was uncomfortable. She thought you were there to talk about . . . you know, about you and me. About our relationship"

"Well, she was wrong and besides, why would I talk to a complete stranger about my relationship with you? If I was going to talk about my relationship with you, I'd talk to you."

He pushed a hand through his hair. Even if I didn't know Nev was knee-deep in a case, I would be able to guess from his hair. It was a little past needing a cut and if he paid more attention, he could have made it look halfway presentable. But when Nev is busy, his hair is the last thing he thinks about. Even before he got out of the car, I saw that there was a curl flopped over his forehead and now it stuck up at a funny angle right above his left eyebrow. One of these days, he'd worry about personal grooming again. That is, when he wasn't distracted by his case.

Unless he'd been distracted by something—or someone—else that morning?

The thought was unworthy of me, and I slapped it away. "How's LaSalle?" I asked him.

"LaSalle's fine. LaSalle's always fine. You know him, he's a tough street dog. Nothing ever bothers him."

"Really." I slipped past him and to the door of the church. "Then why did he have to go to the vet?"

"Oh, that." Nev reached around me so he could open the door and he stepped back so I could walk inside first. "He's fine now."

I didn't budge. "But Evangeline's not. She's uncomfortable because I went to the museum to talk to her."

"I told you, Josie, I'm just reporting the facts."

"And the fact that you've talked to her—"

His exasperated sigh interrupted me. "She called. What did you expect me to do, hang up on the woman?"

Honestly, men can be so clueless sometimes. Well, if he didn't know the answer, I was duty bound to give it to him. I breezed through the door at the same time I said, "Hang up on her? Yeah, that's exactly what you should have done!"

Chapter Thirteen

It was a good thing we found Richard standing near Forbis's artwork. With questions to ask him, Nev and I didn't need to worry about talking to each other.

Nev wasn't in the mood for preliminary chitchat. Which was fine by me. Practically before Richard had a chance to look our way, Nev said, "We've talked to Laverne Seiffert, Mr. Norquist. We know your alibi for the night of the murder doesn't hold up."

Richard's mouth dropped open, and though she was nowhere around, he glanced toward the hallway door anyway, the hallway that led to Laverne's office. "Laverne wouldn't—"

"She did." I climbed the single step and walked closer to where Richard stood with a clipboard in his hands in front of the ceremonial drums. "Asking you to lie for her was a lousy thing to do. Laverne's a good woman. It wasn't fair for you to take advantage of her feelings for you and put her in that position."

Richard's mouth flapped open. "I didn't. That is, I never—"

"Laverne believed you when you said all you did after the show was go back to your hotel," I informed him. "She trusts you. So you can imagine that she was plenty surprised when I told her the truth. You know, about how you weren't at the hotel at all. You were with Victor Cherneko."

The clipboard slipped out of Richard's hands and clattered to the floor. He didn't stoop to retrieve it. "You know—"

"That you lied to us." Nev walked up to my side. "I shouldn't have to remind you, Mr. Norquist, but in case I do, lying to the police about a murder investigation is serious business. You could be charged with—"

"Charged?" Richard's face went ashen. His hands flew around him like frenzied butterflies. "No, no, you've got it all wrong. I didn't do anything."

Instead of mentioning the lie again, Nev simply stared at him.

Richard ran his tongue over his lips. "OK. All right. So my story wasn't exactly on the up-and-up. I didn't mean to deceive anyone."

This time, both Nev and I gave him a look. Deceive? That's exactly what Richard intended and he knew it.

"What I meant to say . . ." His shoulders sagged. "I knew that if you thought I was with Laverne, you'd realize I couldn't have killed Forbis. I mean, Laverne is salt of the earth. You know that, right? With her to vouch for me, you'd have to know I couldn't have had anything to do with Forbis's murder. Me? Kill Forbis? That's just . . ." There was a little too much forced humor in his laugh. "That's just crazy!"

"But why not just tell us where you really were?" I asked Richard. "Wouldn't that be far simpler? You and Victor Cherneko, you could have provided each other with alibis."

"Unless they were doing something they didn't want us to know about." Leave it to Nev to think like a cop. His suspicion paid off. At least, I thought it did when Richard gulped so loud, the sound echoed in the church, as loud as—

I thought of the night of the opening and about that argument we heard before Forbis walked into the gallery. I'm not a gambler (I leave that up to my ex, Kaz, who is an expert at it even if he is usually not very successful), but I decided to take a chance.

"You were the one we heard arguing with Forbis before the show opening."

As if asking for divine intervention, Richard squeezed his eyes shut. "Yes," he said. "You're right. That was me. I didn't say anything to you about it because I knew if you found out I had a falling out with Forbis . . ." His eyes flew open and his gaze shot to Nev. "If you knew Forbis and I were fighting, I was afraid that would make me look guilty."

I guess it was a police technique, one I told myself I'd have to remember and use to my advantage some time. Nev let him stew for a couple minutes before he said, "What's making you look guilty is all this lying. Maybe we should take a ride down to the station and—"

"No! No!" Richard backed up a step. Yeah, like that would save him from Nev if Nev decided to haul him to the hoosegow. "If you'll just let me stay here and wait for the insurance adjuster, I'll tell you everything."

It was Nev's turn to back up. He did, and gestured toward the pews, and Richard plodded down the step ahead of us and sat down in the first row. Nev and I joined him, me to Richard's left and Nev on his right.

"Let's start with before the show," Nev said. "What were you and Mr. Parmenter arguing about?"

As if it was immaterial, Richard waved a hand. "It was a business disagreement. That's all. Nothing important."

I scooted forward in my seat. "A business disagreement that had something to do with you telling Forbis that the Mango Tango Gallery was taking sixty percent of every sale when they were really only taking fifty?"

Richard's eyes went wide. That is, before he pressed a hand to his forehead. "No! Forbis didn't know anything about that. He couldn't have. He'd never—" Realizing he'd almost said too much, Richard's head shot up.

"He'd never found out before. Is that what you were going to say?" Nev asked him. "Because my guess is this wasn't the first time you cheated Forbis out of his share of the profits. You'd done it before. In other cities. With other galleries. Bart McComb, he's the first one who figured out what was going on, and he's an honest businessman. He wasn't about to get mixed up in a scheme like that."

Richard considered his options and realized they were pretty much slim and none. He squeezed his fingers to the bridge of his nose. "Y . . . yes. You're right. I've done it before. In other cities. With other galleries." He snapped his gaze to Nev. "It's not exactly like I've taken millions. The sales were all small, and Forbis didn't need the money, anyway. He's got tons of family money that goes way back, all the way back to when his family ran the hops plantation on the island where he lived. Believe me, Detective, we're talking nickle and dime. That's all it amounted to. Nickels and dimes."

Nev sat back. "I don't need to believe you. We'll subpoena your financial records, Mr. Norquist. We'll find out exactly how much you stole from Forbis Parmenter."

"Stealing isn't murder," Richard grumbled.

"But if you're lying, and Forbis really did find out what you were doing . . ." I threw out the theory just to watch Richard squirm, and I wasn't disappointed. "If he found out and he threatened to turn you in, that could be what you were fighting about before the show. It's also a really good motive for murder."

Richard jumped to his feet and yelled, "No!" and the word bounced back at us from the church's high ceiling. His breaths came hard and fast, and for a moment all Richard could do was try and control himself. When he finally did, he dropped back down into the pew. "It was the church. We were fighting about the church. I'd promised Forbis this glamorous art venue and when he got here and saw this place . . ." Richard looked all around. "Well, it didn't exactly fit with Forbis's delusions of artistic grandeur."

"And he let you know it."

In response to Nev's comment, Richard nodded. "He fired me. Right then and there."

"But you—" It went without saying, but I couldn't help myself. "You were here in the church for the opening ceremony. You had the cement so Forbis could place the button and—"

"Yes," Richard said. "I couldn't exactly walk out, not when I had a role in the evening's festivities. Whatever you think of me . . ." He slid a glance from Nev to me and gave us an opportunity to say that he wasn't as bad a person as all this made him sound. We didn't. "Well, whatever you think,"

Richard grumbled, "you should know that I took my job seriously. And I had to save face with Laverne. I said I'd help out that night and I intended to help out, no matter what Forbis said."

I thought back to that scene I'd witnessed between Forbis and Richard at the opening. "Forbis wasn't happy about it."

"No, he wasn't. But I knew he couldn't say much in front of other people. Besides, I was sure the opening would go well, and I hoped once we made a few sales, Forbis would be in a better mood and he'd see that this wasn't such a bad venue after all, and then maybe he'd change his mind and give me my job back."

"And if you got the sales you were hoping for, you'd get to skim another ten percent," Nev put in.

Richard had the decency to at least look embarrassed. "I told Laverne the church would get twenty percent of the profits. I told Forbis they were taking a fifty-fifty cut."

I was speechless. Stealing from a church was one thing, stealing from a woman who was supposed to be a friend . . .

I swallowed down my revulsion and stuck with the facts. "Well, if Forbis fired you . . ." I slid out of the pew and strolled over to where Richard had dropped that clipboard. The papers on it were invoices from a shipping company. "You're probably not the one who should be in charge of sending Forbis's work back to . . ." I flipped through the papers. "This is all going back to your home in New York!" I yelled, wheeling around, my fists on my hips. "You were going to steal it all!"

"You've got it wrong." Richard didn't bother wasting this argument on me. He stood and looked at Nev. "There's no one at Forbis's home on Jekyll Island to receive the shipment.

So there's no use sending the artwork back there. I thought if I sent it to my place—"

His explanation was cut short when Nev stood up, too. "Now that we know that your employer fired you, where the artwork goes and how it gets there isn't up to you anymore." He gestured to me and I gave him the clipboard. "I think this is all going to have to be worked out by attorneys now."

"Sure. Of course." Richard hung his head. "I'll just go back to my hotel and—"

"You're kidding, right?" Nev clamped a hand on his arm. "You've just admitted to stealing from Forbis Parmenter. And don't tell me I can't take you in because you didn't commit any of the acts here in Chicago. We'll let the prosecutors figure things out and worry about the details later."

Nev didn't say good-bye. But then, he was pretty busy hauling Richard to the door. If he wasn't so preoccupied, I would have pointed out that he might already have enough to officially charge Richard in Cook County. That is, if that package Richard delivered to Victor Cherneko was what I thought it was.

And listening to how Richard had been ripping off Forbis for years . . . well, I was pretty sure I was right.

I GOT TO the Button Box in plenty of time for Stan to make his lunch date. That was a good thing because by noon, when I knew he was already over at Clark Street Dog, dark clouds had gathered in the skies above Chicago and the air crackled with the kind of electricity that proceeds a whopping thunderstorm. At least I didn't have to worry about him traveling in the rain.

I wouldn't have much foot traffic that afternoon, that was for sure. Anyone who was smart would be inside, and to tell the truth, that was fine by me. Without customers to distract me, I had the opportunity to take care of a few Internet orders, a slew of e-mail, and some research I'd promised to do a couple weeks earlier for a group of Revolutionary War reenactors who were looking for authentic British regimental buttons for their uniforms. Once they found out what the buttons cost, I had a feeling they'd opt for reproductions.

By the time I was done, it was nearly four o'clock and I heard rumbles of thunder in the distance. It was the first time I remembered that it was my week to mind the small courtyard behind my brownstone and the one next door, the tiny green space my fellow merchants and I used when we needed a little fresh air and sunshine. There was nothing I could do about the coming storm, but I wanted to make sure the pots of flowers we kept out there around a little park bench were pushed into a corner so they couldn't blow around.

Did I think about Angela Morningside when I went out to the courtyard? Absolutely. Poor Angela was a customer who was killed behind the Button Box and I was the one who found her body. As always when I was back there, I bowed my head and said a little prayer. Done with that, I grabbed the pots of begonias and petunias to tuck them away.

It was the first time I noticed that there was something leaning against the back of the brownstone.

Buttons, hundreds of them, though since the sky was getting blacker by the moment, they didn't glow nearly as much as they had under the spotlights in the Chicago Community Church gallery.

Just as the first giant raindrops plopped to the ground, I grabbed the panel that had been ripped off the loa box and raced inside.

IT WAS NEARLY six and time for the Button Box to close, but I wasn't in a hurry. Most Friday nights, Nev and I tried to get together for a drink and dinner or, if he was working on a case, at least for a cup of coffee. But when I saw him earlier that morning, he hadn't said a word about dinner. It's not like I was bitter or anything, but I will admit to wallowing in just a bit of self-pity. It was raining cats and dogs and thunder crashed and rattled the shop's front display window. It was Friday night and I had no one to spend it with and no place to go.

Maybe that wasn't such a bad thing . . . A smile relieved my grim expression. Truth be told, I was having a blast examining the buttons that had been left behind the shop.

The buttons.

Minus the ochre button that I suspected was "le bouton," the one that had caused such a stir when Forbis saw it.

I had hauled the panel into my back workroom and, careful to keep from touching the panel too much and getting my fingerprints all over it, I took pictures of the buttons and, yes, I called Nev to let him know someone had dumped the buttons where I was sure to find them. He didn't answer his phone and I left a message.

I took another picture, and I don't know which was brighter, my camera's flash or the particularly vivid streak of lightning I saw from the open door of the workroom. My camera poised over the buttons, I waited for the crash of thunder that was sure to follow.

It was a doozy, and when the last echo finally died down, I went back to work taking photos.

Or at least I would have if I didn't hear my front door crash open.

I hurried out to the front of the shop and got just about to my desk when another bolt of lightning flashed and the lights inside the Button Box flickered. Fortunately, they didn't stay off. When they blinked on again, Evangeline was standing inside my front door.

She put her shoulder to the door and pushed it shut and when she was done I watched her brush raindrops from the sleeves of her black raincoat.

"I thought you might be closed," she said.

"I was just going to put up the sign." The "Closed" sign (the word spelled out in buttons) was propped near the door and I pointed that way. Yeah, it was a lie, I mean, about me closing, but there was no use admitting to Evangeline that my Friday night was going to be spent lonely and alone and that the company of buttons would help alleviate my melancholy.

Another streak of lightning split the sky.

"I can't believe you came out on a night like this." I walked toward the door, reminding myself that I always had been a gracious business owner. It wasn't easy to smile, but I managed. "What can I do for you?"

Evangeline slipped out of her coat. She obviously hadn't come from work. Or maybe she had and she was headed somewhere where a short sparkly dress in shades of teal was

.

de rigueur. Even against the backdrop of the front display window and the stormy weather beyond, she looked as fresh and as beautiful as a flower.

"I've been thinking," she said, "about the other day when you came to the museum and asked about vudon."

"You mean the day you told Nev you felt threatened by me?"

"I believe the word I used was *uncomfortable*. But then, you can hardly blame me for feeling that way. The news is filled with stories about jealous exes who try to take their revenge out on their rivals."

My stomach clutched and my smile faded. "Except I'm not a jealous ex. And you're not a rival."

The sequins on her dress flashed in the next flare of snake lightning. "Of course I told Nev how your visit made me feel. I'm surprised he mentioned it to you."

"I think it was because it struck him as being pretty unlikely."

"Why? You don't think you can be intimidating?" Evangeline took a few more steps into the shop, glancing around as she did. "What an interesting place," she said. I guess it was supposed to be a compliment. "Nev told me you sold buttons, I just never expected anything so . . . quaint."

"I'd think an anthropologist would have more of an appreciation for the historical significance of buttons. Clothing has always been a reflection of the society in which it was worn."

"You don't need to defend your little shop. I understand completely." She offered me a smile, but it was hardly enough to make up for the *little shop* comment.

My shoulders shot back. "What can I do for you?" I asked her again.

Evangeline set her purse down on the guest chair in front of my desk. "Actually, I thought maybe I could do something for you."

I pressed my lips together. Better that then letting *you've got to be kidding* escape them.

"I know, I know." Evangeline waved one hand in a way that told me she knew exactly what I was thinking. "If I were you, I wouldn't believe I was going to help you, either. I mean, there's the whole ex thing and the rival thing and—"

"I'm not an ex and you're not a rival." Even though I raised my voice just a tad and stared at her when I said it, I figured it wouldn't hurt to add, "Am I clear?"

"As crystal." Her smile was crystalline, too, and nearly as brittle. "I was actually thinking about what you asked when you came to the museum the other day."

"The day I was being threatening."

"The day I felt uncomfortable, yes. You asked about vudon, and you mentioned a button that you thought was missing from Mr. Parmenter's exhibit. You wondered if there was any connection."

Lesson learned here: Though it is tough, I am actually able to put aside personal animosity when it comes to a case. In fact, I hoped I wasn't suddenly salivating. "You thought of something?"

"Not really." She sashayed past my desk to look at the filigree buttons in the glass-topped display case nearby.

Yes, it was one-upsmanship, but I couldn't help myself. I strolled over there, too. "Someone once described filigree as lace made with gold and silver threads," I said. "They're intricately made with whorls of metal."

"Yes. Filigree." Studying the buttons, Evangeline nodded.

"From the Latin *filum*, which means thread, and *granum*, which means seed."

I pretended this wasn't news. "As you can see, filigree buttons come in all sorts of sizes and shapes. There are domed." I pointed. "And some shaped like rectangles. Some that are shaped like flowers, even some realistics. They're quite beautiful."

"Expensive?"

"That all depends on what you think is expensive." I crossed my arms over my pink blouse and leaned back against the display case. "And why you're really here. I asked if you'd thought of something and you said you hadn't. So why—"

Evangeline tossed her head. "I didn't think of it. But your visit got me thinking. I did some research. Well, actually, I did a lot of research."

"Why?"

Her sparkling laugh was nearly lost beneath the next boom of thunder. "Well for one thing, I'm insatiably curious, especially when it comes to vudon. The button you mentioned wasn't anything I'd ever heard of and I wondered if the story could possibly be true and, if it was, how I'd missed hearing about it or reading about it. For another—"

"You certainly didn't do all that research to help me."

"No. I did it to help Nev."

"Then why don't you tell Nev what you found out?"

"Oh, I will." She touched a hand to her sparkly dress and I don't think I was being overimaginative; she was sending the message that she was meeting Nev, that she had dressed carefully and spectacularly just for him.

I ignored it. "The button?" I asked.

"Yes, well . . . like I said, I'll tell Nev, but I thought you should know, too, since you're the button expert. I thought once you knew what I found out, you might want to stop back at the museum and look through my research."

"Why?"

"I told you, I thought—"

"No, I mean why are you doing this for me? Why share the glory with me?"

"Oh, that." She slipped into her raincoat. "I just thought you should know, that's all."

"Know?"

Evangeline sauntered to the door. "What you're getting into, of course."

I refused to play the game; I stood my ground. "What exactly am I getting into?"

"The button." She already had her hand on the door and she turned back to me. "I found some mention of it in an old journal that belonged to a houngan."

This was one instance where I didn't mind showing my ignorance. "Houngan?"

"A vudon priest, and just so you know before you get creeped out, the houngan works for good. It's a bokor, a sorcerer, who does evil work like casting curses."

"But in this case . . . is the button the one I saw the night of the show?"

"I can't say for sure." Thunder underscored Evangeline's words. "But in his journal, the houngan talks about a button. A very special button. And remember, many of the enslaved people who eventually worked the plantations on Jekyll and other Barrier Islands were originally from Haiti. Many of them were French-speaking. The houngan certainly was. In his journal, he talks about what he calls le Bouton De Malheur, the Button of Doom."

The tingle that ran through my body had nothing to do with the electricity flashing through the air. I hugged my arms around myself. "What does it mean?" I asked Evangeline.

"I don't know for sure. I'll have to do more research, but if le bouton Mr. Parmenter was talking about is the same as le Bouton de Malheur . . . Well, the houngan is quite clear about that. He says that any person who is given the button will meet a quick and ugly death."

Chapter Fourteen

"You don't really believe in this crazy Button of Doom thing, do you?"

Yes, me asking for Evangeline's opinion was a little surreal (not to mention disturbing), but hey, she'd invited me to stop in at the museum and talk to her—about the button, about Forbis, and about vudon. Whether it was weird, or uncomfortable, or humiliating (and it was all those things), I wasn't about to pass up the opportunity to ferret out more information regarding the case. Evangeline may not have all the answers, but even if she had just some of them, I would be (gulp) grateful.

"I don't know if it matters what you and I believe." When I arrived at her office on that Saturday morning, Evangeline had offered me tea, and now she poured from a pretty blue ceramic pot. "You must add some of this." She pushed a small jar of amber honey across her desk to me. "It really brings out the flavors of this herbal tea."

She was right.

Oh, how I hated to admit it.

I sat back to savor my tea and took a moment to glance around her office. It was pretty basic: two walls of shelves filled with books, a desk stacked with more books, a couple exotic (were they vudon?) carvings set here and there. Did Gabriel hand me a line when he said he'd broken into the office to look around during my last visit to the museum? I'd like to think so. In fact, I would have convinced myself the story was nothing more than macho preening if it wasn't for the picture hanging on the wall behind Evangeline's desk. A photo of a garage. Matted and framed and hung in a place of honor. The same photo Gabriel had shown me and thought was so intriguing simply because it was so mundane.

"That's an interesting picture!" Three cheers for me, I managed to keep the saccharine out of my voice way better than Evangeline had the night before when she strolled around the Button Box and complimented me on my cute *little* shop. "Does that building have some significance to you?"

As if she had to be reminded what I was talking about, Evangeline glanced over her shoulder. "Oh, that. The photograph was left here by Dr. Roddy, the man who had this office before me. I have no idea what the building is. One of these days I need to find a picture I really like. Then I'll hang the new one and take down this old one. Until then, I suppose I should be smart and create some sort of storyline to go along with the picture because people always ask. Maybe I should say the building is part of the old family homestead."

"Or there's treasure buried beneath it."

Too late, we both realized we'd actually relaxed enough to laugh together, and we clamped our mouths shut.

"So . . ." In an effort to look casual, I sipped my tea. "You were saying . . . about the Button of Doom."

"Le Bouton de Malheur, yes." Evangeline had long, slim fingers and she wrapped them around her teacup and sat back. "I was saying that what the two of us believe probably doesn't matter in the least. In fact, what the whole world believes may not matter. Maybe all that counts is what Forbis Parmenter believed."

"You mean about the button and the vudon connection and the legend that says if you're given the button you're going to die. If Forbis was a believer in vudon—"

"No. Not possible." Evangeline's mouth thinned. "If he was, he never would have ridiculed the religion like he did."

"So you don't think the exhibit was some sort of tribute to vudon. It was—"

"A joke!" Evangeline's top lip curled. "No man who claims to respect a religion would take its sacred implements and cover them with buttons. No offense intended," she added after it was already too late. "But you know what I mean."

"That buttons are commonplace, and covering things like sacred altars and drums—"

"And the loa. Don't forget the loa. No man who had reverence for those things would put them on display like that. Parmenter was pretty much asking for people to poke their fingers at his work and laugh."

"Or he was showing that something as unglamorous as a button could become part of something sacred and mysterious."

Another lip curl, and I knew what it meant. I could throw out all the theories I wanted, but it was obvious, at least to Evangeline, that I had no basis for even trying to offer an opinion on a subject I knew so little about.

"So you think he was dissing vudon." I finished the last of my tea and Evangeline refilled my cup. When I reached for the honey, she smiled. "Do you think someone might have taken offense to that? That some practitioner—"

"Vudon is an ancient religion that originated in Africa. And the particular brand of it practiced on the Barrier Islands never had many believers to begin with. If you're asking me if someone who believed in vudon might have killed Parmenter, I'd say it was unlikely. Then again . . ." Thinking, she cocked her head. "As an anthropologist, I've seen it over and over . . . old beliefs don't always die out, even when the modern world thinks they have." She shook her shoulders. She was wearing a lightweight sweater and pants the same color as her ebony hair. "I know Nev has already talked to members of the Haitian community on the north side. There, they call the religion *vodou*. That's spelled v-o-d-o-u. It's similar, to vudon, yes, but there are differences between its beliefs and those we think of when we think of New Orleans voodoo. There are differences between vodou and vudon, too. That might explain why none of the Haitians claim to know anything about a Button of Doom."

"That's too bad." My comment did double duty. It was too bad we couldn't learn any more from the Haitians, and worse if what Evangeline said was true. If Nev investigated the vudon/vodou connection on his own . . . if he never even bothered to tell me about it . . . if he never shared what he'd learned with me . . . if he had consulted Evangeline instead . . .

"I said, don't you think that was very smart of Nev?"

I shook away the bitter thoughts that filled my head and popped back to the matter at hand. "Very smart," I said. "But then, he's that kind of guy."

"Always has been," Evangeline commented.

I shifted in my seat and decided to get back to what we were supposed to be talking about. "What you said, about Forbis not being a believer in vudon . . . Even if he didn't practice the religion, he might have heard the story of the Button of Doom, right?"

"Parmenter was how old?" Evangeline asked.

I shrugged. "I don't know for sure, but I'd say he was close to eighty."

"And eighty years ago . . ." She rummaged through the books on top of her desk and when she didn't find what she was looking for, she got up and scanned the bookshelves. She came back carrying a slim volume with a beat-up red leather cover and she flipped through its pages. "Yes. Here." She pointed to a page, but even though I sat up and leaned forward, she didn't turn the book around so I could see what she was talking about.

"This monograph talks about the lives of the last remnants of the vudon community. They were the descendants of the enslaved people who once worked on the plantations on the islands. Once the slaves were emancipated, many of them left the islands, but some stayed and set up small farmholds of their own. The last of the community dispersed back in the 1940s."

"When Forbis would have been a young man."

Evangeline snapped the book shut. "I've studied the oral story traditions of the Barrier Islands and I've heard people talk about how the descendants of the enslaved people and the descendants of the plantation owners would mingle from time to time. And no doubt a family with money like Parmenter's had cooks and cleaning people, and they were probably descendants of believers in vudon. Perhaps they were practitioners themselves. I'd say it's very possible that a young man of Parmenter's artistic sensibilities would be interested in the culture and in the stories those people told."

"Like the story about the Button of Doom."

Evangeline nodded. "If he knew the story, if he believed it—"

"And if he saw the button on one of his pieces, and he knew he didn't put it there—"

"It would explain why he got so upset at the art show opening."

Oh, how I hated to agree with her! But hey, I'm a big girl. And I can actually act like one when the situation calls for it. "He was startled."

"He was frightened."

"And as it turns out, it was for good reason. And once Forbis was dead . . ." I thought through this piece of the puzzle. "Whoever put the button on the loa box in the first place took the button with him. That would explain why the button underneath it was tacky." Evangeline didn't know this part of the story so I filled her in. "Whoever wanted to scare Forbis didn't want us to find the button because it would have been a clue."

"If the button you remember really is le Bouton de Malheur."

If.

Such a small word and so many possibilities.

I reached in my purse and retrieved my drawing of the button, smoothing it out on Evangeline's desk. "This is what I remember the button looked like. I don't suppose any of your books has a picture of the button."

"Not a photograph." The book she wanted was at the top of the pile on her desk and Evangeline flipped it open next to my drawing. "This is what I discovered, how I learned about the Button of Doom in the first place." She poked one finger against the black and white drawing in the book. It showed a button much like the one I'd seen on the art piece.

"These figures . . ." I ran a finger over the symbols incised on the button. "I thought they were letters of some sort."

Evangeline glanced at my drawing. "Yes, you used wavy lines to indicate them."

I leaned forward for a better look at the drawing in the book. "But they're not letters. Not from our alphabet, anyway. Do you know what they mean?"

Evangeline turned the book around for another look. "There's little written history of the vudon culture. Myths and legends, stories and prayers were passed down from generation to generation orally. Part of the reason, of course, was because many slaves were illiterate. But there's more to it than that. Vudon was sacred. And secret. If its beliefs were written, they could be discovered by the slave owners, and practitioners couldn't risk that. They valued their beliefs too much."

"What you're telling me is that you don't know what those symbols mean."

Evangeline closed the book. "Sorry. I wish I could be of more help."

"You've helped." I finished my tea and stood. "There's a lot I need to talk about with Nev."

A slow smile brightened Evangeline's expression when she stood, too, and walked me to the door. "Don't bother," she crooned. "I've already filled him in. About everything."

THE HEADACHE CAME back full force that Saturday night, and by the next day, there was no doubt what was going on—I had the flu. Yes, I know . . . the flu in summer? Hey, it might be rare, but tell that to my pounding head, my achy muscles, and a fever that spent the day hovering around one hundred and one.

I followed the rules and drank plenty of fluids. I turned off my phone, stayed in bed, and slept for hours, sure that if I laid low, I'd be fine by Monday morning.

I wasn't. In fact, I felt even worse. I dragged myself into the Button Box anyway. There was no way I could ask Stan to cover for me again, not on a day when he had a senior softball game scheduled, and besides, I didn't want to scare him off. We had an agreement, yes, but if I started taking advantage of him and cramping his retiree lifestyle, he'd change his mind about helping out at the shop. And I wouldn't blame him.

Lucky for me, it was Monday, and not a busy day. I made tea and sipped it to soothe my burning throat, and except for the time I had to come out of hiding and wait on a customer who wanted buttons for a scrapbooking project, I pretty much stayed in the back room.

It was quiet in there, and since the room had no windows,

the sunlight that streamed through my front display window had no way to sneak in and hurt my eyes. Not that I could keep my eyes open. It wasn't even noon and I was so tired, I couldn't think straight. Sure I'd hear the little brass bell above the front door if a customer came calling, I laid my head down on the worktable.

Just for a minute, I told myself.

I would close my eyes for only a minute.

I fell asleep instantly, but in this case, sleep did not equal rest. My fevered brain spun out of control, and I dreamed about a leering loa and beating drums. Symbols like the ones on the Button of Doom flashed in front of my eyes in neon colors and even though my skin burned, my insides felt as if they'd been filled with ice.

In the dream, I was standing in a place where the air was hot and damp. It was dark and I was alone and I wanted to run, though what I was trying to escape, I couldn't say. All I knew was that I was so scared, my knees refused to hold me up.

I had to get out of that place, but I couldn't move my feet. I could barely take a breath.

I gasped and fought for air, and when I recoiled from the fear and flinched, I stumbled out of the dream and into a not-quite-awake state where inky shadows lurked in every corner of my workroom and the high-intensity lamp attached to the side of the table loomed over me like a sneering face.

Startled, I sucked in a breath and thrashed my arms in an effort to make the face go away. Bad enough I missed by a mile. Worse, because waving my arms around like that threw me off balance. The tall stool I sat on tipped and, half-asleep and feeling like I was moving in slow motion,

I compensated with too much oomph and too little in the way of coordination. With a screech against the tile floor, the stool went out from under me and the floor rose up to meet my nose.

I guess I yelped when I landed hard. That would explain how Gabriel knew where to find me.

"What the bloody hell . . ." I didn't see him race into the workroom (nose to floor, after all) but I heard him. He paused in the doorway for maybe a half a second to assess the situation and then he was down on the floor on his knees beside me.

"What happened? Are you all right? Did someone—"

I waved a hand, but I didn't dare sit up. How could I when I'd have to explain that all that happened was that I got carried away by a dream?

"You're sure you aren't hurt?" He looped an arm around my shoulders and like it or not, he forced me to sit up and eased me far enough back so that I could lean against the worktable. "Your nose is bleeding," he said.

Now that he mentioned it, I could feel the moist heat and the stickiness under my nose, and when Gabriel went to the sink and came back with wet paper towels, I didn't argue. I did as he told me and tipped back my head and he gently cleaned up the blood, then laid the towels across the bridge of my nose.

"You're burning up."

"Flu." It must have been the way my head was tilted, because my voice sounded funny, even to me. Like there was a pillow over my face. "Don't get close . . . I've . . . got . . . flu."

"Then what are you doing here?" He dabbed at my nose

and I guess it wasn't gushing or anything because he finished up, grabbed another batch of paper towels he'd brought over from the sink with him, and whisked those over my cheeks. They were wonderfully cool and I sighed. "You should be home in bed."

"Can't. On account of . . . softball game." The touch of the moist towels was heavenly, and I closed my eyes, sinking into the sensation. "If I was retired, I could work here."

"Have you been drinking?"

I opened my eyes to find Gabriel's nose about two inches from mine. His dark brows were low over his eyes and he was looking at me like I was some kind of lunatic.

"Not going to make a scrapbook," I said. Those weren't the words I meant to say, somehow I knew that instinctively, but that's what came out. "I have too much tea."

He put a hand to my forehead. "It must be the fever talking. I'll call a cab and take you home."

"No." He already had his phone in his hands, and I plucked it away from him. My fingers were slick with sweat, and it slipped right out of my hand. "Have to . . ." What did I have to do? I thought about it for a moment. "Have to keep the shop open."

Gabriel sat back on his heels. "I doubt if anyone's going to come looking for buttons at this time of the night."

Now I knew for sure that something was wrong, because he was talking nonsense. I sat up and when he put a hand on my arm to try to keep me from moving, I swatted it aside. If I scooted forward—I did, and on my butt, too—I could just see the clock that hung on the wall near the back door.

"Nine o'clock?" I was still dreaming. I must be. There was no way it could be—

"Nine o'clock." I grabbed Gabriel's hand. "No. Can't be. I put my head down . . . for a minute."

"How long ago?"

Why did he have to talk so loud? And be so demanding? I let go of Gabriel so I could put my hands over my ears.

He snatched them away and held on, his gaze riveted to mine. "Do you remember what happened, Josie? Do you know how long you've been asleep?"

"Before . . . noon. But how . . . ?"

"That's what I want to know. Tell me everything that happened."

"My head . . ." I squeezed my eyes shut. Nine o'clock explained the long, dark shadows here in the back room and the fact that from out in the shop, there was no sun streaming through the front window. "My head hurt. And I was so . . . so tired. I put my head . . . down. Just for a minute. That's when I heard the drums."

"Drums?" Gabriel didn't have to stare at me like that. Like I was some sort of lunatic. "You heard drums? You mean outside? Or were the drums on the radio?"

I shook my head and decided instantly that it was not the best course of action. Even when I stopped, the room kept up a shimmy in front of my eyes. "Drums. In my dream."

"What was the dream about?"

Did I shrug? I meant to, except it seemed like such an effort and I wasn't sure I could muster up the energy. "Chasing. Running. And the loa."

All the emotion washed out of Gabriel's expression and in the weird half-light, his face looked as if it had been chipped from granite. Like a sculpture on a tombstone. His lips twitched. "You dreamed about a loa. Which one?"

I tried for another shrug and gave up halfway. My eyes drifted closed. "Dunno. He was chasing me, I think. He was behind me and I was . . ." My breath shuddered through my body. "I was scared."

"Josie."

I didn't think I had time to drift off, but when I opened my eyes again, Gabriel's hands were on my shoulders. He gave me a shake. "You need to wake up," he said. "There's something going on, and I don't like it."

"I don't like . . . either. Flu . . . stinks."

That morning when I got out of bed, I was so chilled to the bone that I'd put on a Chicago Bears sweatshirt along with my jeans. Gabriel pushed the sleeves of my sweatshirt up and turned my hands over, the better to see the insides of my arms. He grumbled a curse and got up long enough to snap on the high-intensity lamp and swivel its gooseneck over the side of the table to put me in the spotlight.

"This isn't the flu." He studied my arms again, and even though my eyes felt as if they were filled with sand, I looked, too. There were tiny pinpricks of red rash all over my arms.

"Measles?" I asked.

"I wish." He pulled my sleeves back in place and brushed my hair back to take a look at my neck. Apparently, whatever he saw there wasn't very encouraging because he jumped to his feet. "You need water. Plenty of water." I knew there was some in the mini-fridge over near the coffeemaker and before I even had a chance to tell Gabriel about it, he was back with three bottles. "Drink them all," he instructed. "Now." When I didn't move fast enough, he cracked one open and put it in my hands.

"Do you have a blanket?"

I shook my head.

"Then how about a coat? Or a raincoat? Or—"

"There's a tablecloth." I waved vaguely in the direction of the metal storage cabinet on the far wall. "I use it . . . it's for . . . display."

Though I didn't remember seeing him leave to get it, Gabriel came back with the tablecloth, unfolded it, and draped it around me. He tucked it behind my shoulders to keep it in place and got down on his knees so he could look into my face. "Tell me, Josie, has anyone given you anything odd lately?"

"I got the flu."

His smile was so quick, I wondered if I imagined it. "I was thinking of something more concrete. A gift of some sort."

Even with the blanket around me, I shivered. "No. Nothing."

"How about at home? Did anyone send anything to your apartment?"

"You brought lo mein."

"Not me." Gabriel got up and turned on the overhead lights, and I thought my head would burst. I pulled the tablecloth over my face and closed my eyes and I heard him rummage through the storage cabinet and comb through the refrigerator.

"Damn and double damn." By the time I heard him grumble the curse, he was standing in front of me, his fists on his hips. He glanced around the workroom. "Are you feeling sicker here than you were at home?" he asked, then because I didn't answer quickly enough, he raised his voice and asked again, "Are you sicker here than you were at home?"

Blame it on the flu. Or whatever it was I had. I am not the type who is easily intimidated, but when Gabriel's baritone voice echoed through the workroom, I couldn't help myself. I burst into tears.

He scraped his hands over his face and dropped down on his knees beside me. "I'm sorry. I didn't mean to—"

"It's OK. Really." I sniffled. "I . . . just . . . can't . . . help it."

He put a hand on my shoulder. "I know." He was back on his feet and did another turn around the workroom. There were cabinets below the sink, and one by one he opened them, got down on his hands and knees, and looked inside.

It should come as no surprise that I am an orderly person, but apparently, even my system of a-place-for-everything-and-everything-in-its-place wasn't enough for Gabriel. He scooped everything out of the first cupboard and piled it on the floor and when he didn't find whatever it was he was looking for, he started in on the second cupboard.

"I can . . . help." I pushed off from the floor with the intention of going around to the other side of the worktable, but my legs wouldn't hold me.

"You stay put," Gabriel said over his shoulder. "And I'll—"

As if they'd been snipped with scissors, his words stopped cold and I heard him release a long, slow breath.

"I'm pretty sure I know what's wrong with you," Gabriel said. He came around to my side of the table, looped his arm around my shoulders, and helped me to my feet. My knees were rubber, but Gabriel was a strong guy. He kept his arm around me and propped me against the table. Sweat beaded on my forehead and he used a corner of the tablecloth to blot it away.

"I'm calling a cab," he said, and he did, and when he was

done, he explained, "We're going to go see a friend of mine. We've got to take care of this and we've got to take care of it now."

"But what . . . Why . . . ?"

Gabriel pulled something out of the back pocket of his jeans. "I found this," he said, "tucked away in the cupboard." It was a fabric doll, about eight inches tall, and dressed in black, like I had been at the opening of Forbis's art show. It was even wearing a string of pearls like I had. There were buttons where its eyes should have been, and another button directly in the center of a mouth that had been embroidered with red floss.

My mouth went dry. "Is that—"

"Yeah." When I tried to take a step and nearly collapsed, Gabriel lifted me into his arms and carried me to the front door. "It's a voodoo doll."

Chapter Fifteen

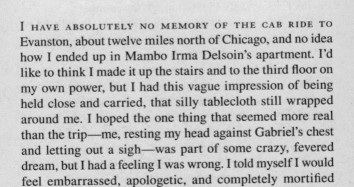

I HAVE ABSOLUTELY NO MEMORY OF THE CAB RIDE TO Evanston, about twelve miles north of Chicago, and no idea how I ended up in Mambo Irma Delsoin's apartment. I'd like to think I made it up the stairs and to the third floor on my own power, but I had this vague impression of being held close and carried, that silly tablecloth still wrapped around me. I hoped the one thing that seemed more real than the trip—me, resting my head against Gabriel's chest and letting out a sigh—was part of some crazy, fevered dream, but I had a feeling I was wrong. I told myself I would feel embarrassed, apologetic, and completely mortified later—if my head ever stopped pounding and I lived that long.

I did know that it was dark by the time we walked into the apartment, and somewhere inside my fuzzy head, I realized that didn't matter. There were dozens of candles lit on the end tables in the living room, and more flickering in the dining room where Gabriel deposited me on a chair and backed away. The soft, swaying light threw dancing shadows against walls that were awash with a vibrant palette of colors— soothing aqua, sizzling red, yellow as warm and as welcoming as the sun.

And I remember Mambo Irma's face. She was a stick-thin Haitian woman and at least seventy, but her skin was as smooth a girl's, and her brown eyes sparked when she looked into mine.

"How long?"

Her voice was soft, but strong, and somehow, I knew she wasn't talking to me. Good thing since I didn't have the energy to answer. My hunch was right; over Mambo Irma's shoulder, I saw Gabriel zip through the room.

"Too long," I heard him reply. His voice faded like he was on his way somewhere else. Or maybe that was just me drifting in and out of consciousness.

Mambo Irma sat down across from me and took my hands in hers. I think she was about to speak, but whatever Gabriel was up to, he was making a racket like he had when he rummaged through the cupboards back at the Button Box, and one corner of Mambo Irma's mouth pulled tight. My fever was sky-high, my head felt like it was about to burst, my eyes ached, and my breaths came hard and fast. Still, I knew exactly what that expression meant: men!

"What you are doing, Gabriel?" When she turned in her seat, Mambo Irma didn't let go of my hands. "Come over here and sit down and tell me what is happening."

When Gabriel crossed into my line of vision, his arms were full. He set down a tall candle in a glass holder.

"For Eleggua," he said, and I figured my hearing had been affected by my fever, that's why what he said didn't make any sense. "Light it, Mambo. You've told me so yourself, he has to be honored first at the ceremony and we have to get started. Now."

"Yes. Yes." There was no urgency in Mambo Irma's voice, not like there was in Gabriel's. I didn't know if this was a good thing or a bad thing, but I did know that her steadiness and the gentle touch of her hands comforted me. I was in a good place, a safe place, and I closed my eyes. "We will get started when it is time to start," I heard her say, and I might have been half out of it, but I still smiled. Gabriel Marsh was so cocksure. Leave it to a tiny woman wearing a blue turban and a long white dress to put him in his place!

"Here's a candle for Chango."

When Gabriel set something else on the table with a clatter, I flinched and my eyes flew open. He'd already put another candle down next to that first one, and now he added a third. "And another for Oggun."

"Oggun, yes." Mambo Irma smiled. She had a couple missing teeth. She patted my hands. "Oggun gives protection from harm. And we will call on him for his help."

"I've got your firewand, too." Gabriel set down what looked like a magic wand from a fairy tale, only this one was made of wood and painted red with yellow lettering along its handle. "And your dark stones." He unloaded those on the table. "And your wish papers and—"

"Gabriel!" Mambo Irma didn't raise her voice. She didn't

have to. One look from her pinned Gabriel in place. "It may be that the rest of the world dances to your tune, *mon chou*, but Mambo Irma does not work on Gabriel Marsh time. I work only on God's time. Now . . ." She let go of me long enough to hold out her hand to Gabriel. "Give it to me."

He handed over the voodoo doll he'd found back at the shop.

Her eyes closed, Mambo Irma cradled the doll in both her hands and after a minute, she lifted one hand and, keeping it an inch or so above the doll, ran it the length of the figure. She shook her head. She clicked her tongue.

"It is a strong trick performed by a powerful bokor." Mambo Irma looked my way. "You know what this is, *cherie*?" It's a good thing she didn't wait for me to answer, because I couldn't find the words. "A bokor is what you would call a sorcerer. A person who performs black magic. He has used the doll to put a spell on you."

Yeah, right!

That was what I meant to say. What I wanted to say. But the words wouldn't come. They were blocked by the sudden knot in my throat that was just as painful as the claw that clutched my stomach.

I didn't have time to consider it. Just then, the door opened and a tall, heavyset man walked in carrying a drum like the ones I'd seen in Forbis's exhibit. He chose a seat in a corner of the dining room and Mambo Irma signaled him to begin. Slowly and ever so quietly, he started in on a rhythm.

Mambo Irma turned back to me. "The spirits will be liberated by his drumming hands," she assured me. "First . . ." There was a brown glass bottle on the table and she opened it and wet her fingers, then dabbed them to my forehead. "First I anoint your third eye for peace of mind, for clarity and protection. Next, I will do a reading to understand what is happening with you. Then, only then, can I cleanse you of this curse. Gabriel!"

When she called him, Gabriel walked into my line of vision.

"You know what must be done," she said. "Only those of clean spirit can be present for the ceremony. *Mon chou*, you must leave."

SUNSHINE BRUSHED MY eyelids. It was wonderful and welcoming, and enjoying the sensation, I stretched and realized I was tucked in bed.

My eyes drifted open.

"My bed." My voice was rough, my mouth was dry. "My bedroom." I smiled and sunk back against the pillows. I don't think I'd ever felt so content, not since I leaned my head against Gabriel's chest and—

I sat up like a shot and my gaze ping-ponged through the familiar room all the way over to where Gabriel watched me from the wingchair in the corner.

That was the exact moment I realized I was wearing a yellow nightgown spotted with brightly colored polka dots.

"You didn't . . ." I stammered. "You wouldn't dare."

A slow smile crossed his face and he stood up and sauntered over. "You don't really think I'm that much of a freak, do you? Wait!" He put out a hand. "Don't answer that. But just so you know . . ." He perched himself on the edge of the bed. "I talked to Stan and Stan talked to Adele Cruikshank."

Adele was my next-door neighbor, and as nosy a woman as ever lived. I dropped my head in my hands. "And you and Stan had Adele come over here and get me dressed for bed. She'll be talking about this from now until forever."

"She'd be talking about it longer than that if we didn't get her involved. She saw me carry you up the stairs and into the apartment on Monday night. If I hadn't asked for her help, no doubt she would have filled in the blanks for herself. You can imagine the story."

I could.

I did.

I turned away so Gabriel wouldn't see my cheeks get pink, then cleared my throat and prayed I didn't sound as breathless to him as I did to myself "What did you tell her?"

"That you had the flu, of course. Which is exactly what I told Stan, by the way. It seemed a better plan than explaining about the voodoo curse."

The curse.

The memory of Monday evening's events washed over me like a cold wave, and I shivered and wrapped my arms around myself. It was all such a jumble! I remembered disjointed scenes: candles, colors, burning up. I remembered being afraid until I looked into Mambo Irma's eyes and heard the drumming. The music was nothing like the unrelenting drumbeats that had haunted my dreams these past few weeks. This was more rhythmic, organic, like my heartbeat. Instead of causing my blood to boil, the sound gave me something to hang onto, something to concentrate on while Mambo Irma performed her ritual.

I shook out of the memory and this time when I spoke,

I made sure to keep my eyes on Gabriel. I wanted to gauge his reaction. And his capacity for bullshit. "Do you think it really was a curse?" I asked him.

"I've seen stranger things."

"Stranger things than vudon curses?"

"Yes."

"And Mambo Irma?"

"I hope you're not saying she's a strange thing." He leaned forward. "She'll know if you talk about her," he whispered. "And she won't be happy."

Startled, I sat back, and Gabriel laughed. "Only kidding," he said. "Maybe. I wouldn't put anything past her. Mambo Irma is a remarkable woman."

"Then I didn't dream the visit to her apartment? I didn't dream her?"

"She's as real as I am."

"And how real are you, Gabriel?"

He considered this for a moment, and I actually thought he might answer. That is, until he smiled. "Are you hungry?"

"Starved." I was, and hallelujah, my headache was gone. I swung my feet over the side of the bed. "I'll make eggs."

"Absolutely not." He put a hand on my shoulder. "If Mambo Irma finds out you've been out of bed, she'll have my head. And believe me, she will find out. Here." There was a bottle of water on the table next to the bed, and he opened it and handed it to me. "She told me to make sure you drink plenty of water today."

"And you always listen to Mambo Irma."

"If I know what's good for me."

I took a few long sips, then breathed in deep and let the

breath out slowly. I'd been feeling bad for so long, I'd forgotten what it was like to feel well. "Want to explain how you know her?"

"Mambo Irma?" Gabriel's shrug was hardly noticeable. He was wearing jeans and a T-shirt and there was a shadow of dark beard on his chipped-from-granite jaw. "She's a friend."

"Who happens to know how to lift a vudon curse."

"Technically, she knows how to lift a vudou curse, since she's Haitian and that's what they call the religion there. Good thing she's ecumenical, eh? A full-service curse lifter." He patted my knee. "I've got the coffeepot going and all the ingredients for a full English fry-up." Before I could ask, he explained. "Bacon, eggs, tomatoes, mushrooms. And toast. All the things we civilized Brits eat early in the morning."

"Is it early?" Because of the way the sun streamed in through the bedroom window, I couldn't see the numbers on the clock radio. "I've got to get dressed and get into the shop. Who knows how much business I missed yesterday when I fell asleep in the back room."

"Just for the record, you weren't exactly asleep. You were in more of a stupor. You know, because of the spell that had been put on you. It was magnified by the doll. Do you know how it got hidden at the shop?"

I combed my fingers through my hair. "I can't imagine."

"And also for the record . . ." Gabriel got up and I hoped he was headed into the kitchen to get me a cup of coffee because the aroma floated into the bedroom and it smelled divine. "You didn't miss any business yesterday at the shop."

"And you know this how?"

"Because yesterday was Tuesday," he said.

"And today is—"

"Wednesday. You've been asleep for more than twenty-four hours."

I threw my hands in the air. "I don't need the Button Box to close down because some crazy person put a crazy voodoo doll in my shop. What about—"

"Not to worry. Stan was there all day yesterday. He took care of everything." Gabriel disappeared down the hallway and called back to me, "One egg? Or two?"

I DON'T OWN a wicker tray with legs suitable for serving breakfast in bed, so don't ask me where Gabriel got the one he brought into the room a few minutes later. He helped me sit up and fluffed the pillows behind me, unfolded a linen napkin and handed it to me, and pulled over the wingchair so he could put his own plate of English fry-up on the bed.

Either he was an excellent cook or I was just incredibly hungry. I finished my bacon, toast, eggs, and mushrooms in record time and started in on the tomato. It had been cut in half and broiled with a pat of butter on the top and it, too, was delicious.

I washed it all down with a second cup of coffee and leaned back against the pillows. "Thank you," I said.

"You're very welcome." Gabriel whisked the tray away and set it on the floor, then stacked his empty plate on top of mine. "I'm all about helping out damsels in distress."

"And you stayed here with me. All of yesterday?"

"I ran out for a bit. To get clean clothes and buy tomatoes and such." (He pronounced it to-mah-toes and I decided right then and there that's what made them taste so much better than regular old tomatoes.) "Adele was here when I wasn't. And Stan came in for a bit last night. I had a hard time keeping him away until I reminded him that he needed his rest if he was going to run the shop today."

"He's a sweetheart."

"He adores you."

Adore.

Something about the word made me wonder if Nev had called, but I didn't ask. Later, I'd check the missed calls on my phone. If he'd been looking for me, he'd be frantic by now. Of course, if he hadn't . . .

A cloud blocked the sun for a moment and the bedroom was thrown into shadow.

"Cold?" I didn't realize I'd shivered until Gabriel tugged the blanket over my shoulders. "You mustn't try to do too much. Mambo Irma's orders. She said it's to be expected if, once in a while, you still feel . . . you know . . . weird."

I had felt weird a moment earlier when I thought of Nev, but thank goodness, the sensation passed. The sun came out again and when it did, Gabriel got up and crossed the room. There was a black backpack on the floor in the corner and he unzipped it and took out a book with a blue cover. It was about the size of those Bibles that get tucked away in hotel rooms, and when he sat down, he set the book on his knees.

"Mambo Irma said I had to keep you quiet and not get you excited. About anything."

"She's smart."

"She's as suspicious as hell and she doesn't trust me as far as she could throw me. Though, come to think of it, she's a skinny little thing but she's plenty strong. She could probably give me a good toss."

I glanced at the book. "OK, so I promise not to get too excited. About anything. But the fact that you warned me when you got out that book you're holding tells me it's something you think I'm going to get excited about."

He lifted the book and for a moment, seemed to reconsider the wisdom of showing it to me. He gave up with a sigh and handed the book to me. "It's Forbis Parmenter's diary," he said.

The book was already in my hands and it slipped onto the blankets. "Forbis's diary?" I stared at the book, then lifted my head so I could give the same sort of bewildered look to Gabriel. "How did you get it?"

"Don't ask."

"I'm asking. How did you get it?"

"You don't want to know."

"Actually, I do."

"Actually . . ." He sat back. "You've been through a lot thanks to old Forbis. You were hexed, and it could have gotten very serious, indeed, if I hadn't shown up when I did. You should know . . ." He crossed his arms over his chest. "The truth is a slippery thing, and not always something I deal in. But I'm going to tell you the truth because you deserve it with all you've been through. So here goes. The truth." He pulled in a breath. "I left Chicago for a bit last week. I went down to Jekyll Island, to Forbis's family home. That's where I got the diary."

"Richard Norquist says he had to have Forbis's artwork delivered to his home in New York because there's no one at Forbis's home."

Gabriel's eyes sparkled. "Right. No one home. Thank goodness."

It took a moment for what he was implying to sink in. "You mean you wanted to be down there when no one else was around? Did you . . . Gabriel, did you break into the house? Like you broke into Evangeline's office? Are you telling me you stole the diary?"

He made a face. "*Steal* is such a nasty word. Let's just say I appropriated the diary. In the name of the investigation."

"Let's just say that might make sense if you had anything to do with the investigation."

"Let's just say I do. Then again, if you're not interested . . ." He whisked the book off my lap.

"You know I am." I snatched it back from him and held on tight. "And something tells me you've already read through it."

"Cover to cover."

"And . . . ?"

"And most of it is utterly dull in the way only the diary of a man who believes his own PR can be dull. Forbis Parmenter thought he was going to be the next Andy Warhol."

"And I can see how an arts journalist would find that fascinating. Except . . ." I flipped through the pages. They were covered with loopy handwriting that curlicued over the pages with no regard for lines or margins. "Except something tells me your interest goes deeper than simply writing an article about Forbis. And don't tell me you're hoping for a book contract," I added. "Even if that's part of the truth, that's not all of it. If it was, you wouldn't keep popping up in my investigation." No matter what he was going to say, I knew I had to ask, "Did you kill Forbis?"

Gabriel threw back his head and laughed. "I'm a lover, not a fighter. How about you?"

"I didn't kill him."

"That's not what I meant." He leaned near enough for me to catch a whiff of the almond and ginger bath gel I kept in the shower. I'd bet anything he'd used my bottle of expensive shampoo, too, the one that contained Champagne grapeseed oil. "What I meant," he crooned, "is are you a lover?"

What with the way my heart suddenly thumped out of control, it was almost like being vudon cursed again.

I smoothed a hand across the sheets. "I'm a lover of the truth. What is it in Forbis's diary that you thought was so interesting?"

Maybe he *was* a better lover than a fighter, because he gave up without an argument. He reached over and flipped the book to the back pages. Someone (Forbis?) had cut up a folder and added a pocket there, and Gabriel pulled out two yellowed newspaper clippings from it.

Carefully, he unfolded them. "This one is about Forbis's father, Beau Parmenter. He died back in 1947 when Forbis was still a young man. Cause of death?" Gabriel slid a finger over the article until he found the paragraph he was looking for. "According to the sheriff who investigated the elder Mr. Parmenter's death, there were no signs of foul play."

This didn't seem so odd to me. "A heart attack? Some other disease?"

"That's the easiest answer and exactly what I was thinking until I read further. 'Sheriff Mason Grant speculated that Mr. Parmenter had been frightened to death.'"

"That's not possible." I took the article out of Gabriel's hands and read it for myself. "Forbis's father died of fright? And Forbis died of fright, too? That seems a little too coincidental, don't you think?"

"You have no idea." Gabriel unfolded another article, this

one even more yellow and brittle than the first. "This one is about George Parmenter. Beau's father."

"Forbis's grandfather."

Gabriel nodded. "He was a prominent man in the area, and only forty-two when he died. Naturally, the news made the papers. Want to guess at the cause of death?"

"No!" Not *no, I didn't want to guess. No, I didn't believe it.* I leaned closer to Gabriel so I could read the article and saw that, as strange as it was, it was true. " 'Frightened so powerfully his heart gave out and he expired.' " I read the pertinent words with a mixture of awe and disbelief. "Three generations of Parmenters all frightened to death?"

"And who knows how many before."

"But that's just crazy!" I watched Gabriel carefully replace the articles. "Don't you think it's crazy?"

"I think . . ." He returned the diary to his backpack. "I think if you promise not to tell Mambo Irma, you could probably get up and take a shower and get dressed. There's some really great shampoo in there," he said, pointing to my bathroom. "Smells like it has Champagne grape-seed oil in it."

Chapter Sixteen

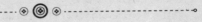

It's amazing what a long, hot shower and a two-hour nap can do for a recently vudon-hexed girl.

Refreshed, revived, and wearing khaki capris and a red T-shirt instead of my yellow nightgown, I was ready to take on the world.

All right, so not the world, exactly. But I sure felt ready to talk about the investigation again, and about the Parmenter family's strange tradition of being frightened to death.

My resolve might have stayed firm if I hadn't walk into the kitchen and been greeted by the incredible aroma of pizza.

Double pepperoni!

It was steaming and gooey with cheese and I didn't wait for Gabriel to hand me a dish. I scooped a slice out of the box and dug in.

"You're hungry. That's good. But . . ." He had been leaning against the granite countertop and now he swung around to grab a bottle of water. "Don't forget. Mambo Irma says—"

"Plenty of water. Yes, I promise." I took the water out of his hands, but I didn't bother opening the bottle until I wolfed down that piece of pizza and another one after. "I feel as if I haven't eaten in weeks."

"You'll be back to your old self in no time at all." He polished off a piece of mushroom, sausage, and green pepper, brushed his hands together, and tackled a piece of pepperoni.

Satisfied, at least for the moment, I took my bottle of water and sat down at the kitchen table. I waited until Gabriel came over and took the chair opposite from mine before I asked something I'd been thinking about in the shower as I let the Champagne grape-seed nourish my hair. "Why are you being so nice to me?"

He was mid chew, so he held up a finger to tell me I'd have to wait for an answer. "You mean about saving your life?" he asked after he'd swallowed. "All in a day's work."

"But it's not. Not really. Certainly not for a journalist who writes about art show openings. And did you save my life? I mean, I know I felt awful, but . . ." Blame it on the fog that had been clogging my brain for days. Though I knew I'd felt lousy and though I hadn't forgotten the nightmares that plagued me, I'd never thought of the curse as really serious, really . . . deadly.

My stomach soured and I sat back in my chair.

Gabriel brushed a strand of mozzarella off his chin. "It's over now," he said. "So it's best if you don't think about it any longer."

"Yeah, but—"

"It's not going to happen again," he assured me, though how he knew that I was wondering if another curse might be headed my way, I don't know. "Mambo Irma, she made sure of that."

"She's that powerful."

"She is." He grabbed a bottle of water for himself. "And you're lucky we went to her for help. Another mambo might know the right prayers and the words to the ceremony, but Mambo Irma said that trick against you—"

"Trick." I'd heard the word before and remembered Mambo Irma using it back in her apartment. "What does that mean?"

"To trick someone is to use the left hand of vudon. You know, black magic."

"And you know this, how?"

He pursed his lips. "I know a damned lot of useless information. What I'd like to know . . ." He leaned forward. "What I'd really like to figure out is who cursed you like that. You have a powerful enemy, Josie. Who do you suppose it is?"

"An enemy?" I lifted my hands, then let them drop. I'd wondered about this, too. "I've met other button dealers who weren't happy because I outbid them at auction for buttons they wanted, but cursing me because of something like that seems a little extreme. I've helped put a couple of murderers behind bars, but none of them seem to be the type who would be into vudon. Then there's—" I clamped my lips over the name that I'd almost let escape.

There was Evangeline, of course.

That's what I was going to say.

Evangeline who seemed to use every opportunity she got

to remind me that she and Nev had once had something special.

"Who?" Gabriel demanded.

"Nobody. It's nothing." I got up to get another piece of pizza and while I was at it, I brought over both boxes, so Gabriel could grab another slice, too. "Besides, the last time I saw her, she was perfectly nice to me. And she was helpful, too, as far as information regarding vudon. She's not even close to what I'd call an enemy."

"If you say so. Then what about—"

Gabriel didn't have a chance to finish asking the question. My phone rang and since it was in my purse in the dining room, I headed that way.

It was Nev.

"Hey!"

"Hey," he said back. "Are you busy?"

I glanced at the clock. It was a little before five and Nev probably thought I was at the Button Box. "Not so busy," I said, avoiding the subject of being home and why I was there. Then again, I obviously wasn't the only one avoiding. If Nev thought I was at the shop today, he mustn't have known I wasn't there the day before.

I slugged down a drink of water to squelch the bitter taste that filled my mouth. "What's up?" I asked him.

"Well, I thought you'd like to hear the latest. I just got the lab report." In the background, I heard him shuffle papers. "You know, the results of the tests on that smudge of white stuff we found in Reverend Truman's office and up in the choir loft at the church."

So much had happened in the days since Forbis's murder, I'd nearly forgotten that little detail.

Nev put a hand over the phone and said something to someone. "Hey," he said again, talking to me this time, "I've got to go. My lieutenant wants to have a meeting. But just so you know, that smudge of white, it was theatrical makeup."

"Makeup?" When I told him good-bye and got off the call, I tapped my phone against my chin and made my way back into the kitchen. "Why would anybody wear theatrical makeup to the church?" I asked myself, and Gabriel. "There was nobody there in costume that night."

His eyes lit. "There was no one we know of who was there in costume. Not anyone we saw."

I knew exactly what he was getting at, and I sat down to think it over. "If Forbis really was frightened to death, you think it might have been by someone wearing a costume."

He pulled out his phone. "What color theatrical makeup?"

"White."

"Exactly."

He flipped the phone around and I looked at the image on the screen and sucked in a breath.

The Congo Savanne I'd seen made of buttons was scary enough, but this drawing—one that showed the loa as huge and glowering and with the red fire of hate glittering in his eyes—was positively terrifying.

"It makes perfect sense." I didn't like the way my voice shook, but then, I didn't like the chill that ran up my spine when I looked at the picture of the loa, either. I glanced away, and I guess Gabriel got the message, because he put his phone screen-side down on the table. "If someone wanted to scare Forbis, it makes perfect sense that they'd dress like the scary loa. Imagine seeing that coming at you. Seeing it come to life. The poor man!" I could picture the scene, Forbis crouched in the choir loft, frightened by the sight of the Button of Doom. And the loa, alive, horrifying—and hunting him.

I shook the thought away and came back to reality to find that I'd wrapped my arms around myself. Gabriel watched me closely.

"It makes even more sense when you think of the old legend," he said. "You did say the police believe Forbis was killed in the choir loft, right?"

I nodded.

"And there's an old legend that you'll find no matter what branch of the religion you look into—voodoo, vodou, or vudon. It says that the only way to find protection from a loa who seeks to crush your bones and devour your soul is in the voice of God. What does that mean? I can't say. But I do know that if I was desperate and very much afraid, I might think the voice of God—and protection of some sort—could be found in the choir loft."

It was a theory that explained everything, but I didn't bother telling Gabriel that. I was too busy listening to all the questions that spun around inside my head.

"You seem to know an awful lot about stuff an arts journalist shouldn't know about," I blurted out. "Even back at Mambo Irma's. What was that bit about Eleggua—"

"The spirit of the crossroads, yes. He opens and closes doors and is called on to remove evil and misfortune."

"And Chango?"

"He'll protect you against enemies."

"And Oggun."

"Another protector. Like I said . . ." Gabriel's smile might have been devastating to a woman who hadn't already been involved in her share of murder investigations. To this one. . . . well, let's just say I'd always been a pragmatist and being involved in murders had only served to ramp up my logical side. Not to mention my suspicious one.

That didn't stop him from turning up the fire of his smile a notch. "I know all sorts of useless information."

"Like about firewands and wish papers and where to find the most powerful mambo in Chicagoland. Call me crazy . . ." With a look, I dared him to even think about it. "But that seems like a mighty big stretch for an arts journalist." I pressed my palms to the table and leaned forward. "Unless you're not really an arts journalist."

Gabriel scraped his hands over his face. "I like you," he said from between his fingers. "You're smart and you're pretty and you're gutsy and that's a rare combination in a woman."

I forced myself not to notice the tingle that started up in my bloodstream and waited for more.

"But—"

I cut him off before he could even get started. "I'm smart. You said so yourself. I know there's something else going on, so don't hand me some line about how you just happen to know a lot of weird things for no reason at all. I'm going to keep asking questions, Gabriel, until I find out the answers."

He steepled his fingers. "But—"

"And I'm the one who got tricked by black magic, remember. As far as I'm concerned, that means I've already gone above and beyond in the name of this investigation. You owe me an explanation."

"It's like this . . ." Gabriel was quiet for so long, I thought he might leave it at that, but when his gaze met mine and he drew in the tiniest breath, I hoped it meant we'd turned a corner.

"What if I was something else?" he asked. "Something other than an arts journalist? I'm not saying that's true," he pointed out. "This is just speculation. But let's pretend it is true, just for a moment. Let's pretend I'm someone who takes special commissions from various discerning collectors. Let's say I'm a person who finds things that other people really want."

Don't ask me how I knew, I just did. Deep in my bones. Down in my gut. As sure as I knew it was Wednesday, and we were in Chicago. "Things like the Button of Doom."

His smile was so quick, I might have imagined it. I for sure didn't imagine that he didn't ask what the Button of Doom was or what I was talking about. "Do you believe there really is such a thing?"

"Do you believe I could have been on the bad end of a vudon curse?"

"So if there is such a button . . ." He paused to choose his words carefully. "If there really was such a thing and if a collector of oddities in Shanghai wanted that button badly enough—"

"No!" Honest to goodness, I wasn't sure I believed in such nonsense. At least I never had until I saw that voodoo doll. But just thinking about someone getting their hands on the Button of Doom made my breath catch. "Nobody can actually want the Button of Doom. Evangeline told me that the legend says that anyone who's given the button will die a quick and terrible death."

"Given it, yes. But not if he seeks it. Not if he pays for it.

Not if he wants to get his hands on it because he's convinced its power is real and he can use it against his rivals."

I wrinkled my nose and considered the possibilities. From every angle, it looked like nonsense. "You don't really think that's possible, do you? That somebody would use a button to gain the upper hand on some rival? It's like some crazy plot for an Indiana Jones movie."

Gabriel pushed his chair back from the table. "I think it's worth considering. After all, we're just dealing in a hypothesis anyway, right?"

I got the message and reined in my skepticism. "OK." A deep breath helped calm me. "So *hypothetically* . . ." I emphasized the word just as he had. "Hypothetically, if there was someone who wanted the button and if there was someone else who was trying to get that button for him, how did you . . , I mean, how would that person even have known the button was going to be at the exhibit? Obviously, Forbis didn't even know, and it was his exhibit. He was scared out of his wits when he saw the button. That tells me he wasn't the one who put it there."

"Hypothetically . . ." Gabriel grabbed another piece of pizza. Something told me he wasn't as hungry as he was simply looking for something to do and something to distract him from my questions. He folded the slice in half and looked at it as carefully as if he'd never seen a piece of pizza before. "If that person knew there was an exhibit about vudon in town and the exhibit had something to do with buttons, and if that person had heard the legend of le Bouton de Malheur, he might have thought it was worth checking out. He might have thought he would never be lucky enough to actually get his hands on the button, because after all, in certain circles and with certain collectors it's quite a famous and desirable thing. But when he saw the way Forbis reacted when he got close to the exhibit . . . well, that person might be very smart, you know." His shoulders shot back just a tad. "He might have figured out that the only thing that would make Forbis Parmenter get all wonky was that very famous button, a button that I suspect was given to his father and his grandfather before him. And maybe once that person realized that, he made a call to that man in Shanghai, the one he knows who collects oddities of all sorts."

Semantics aside, I saw exactly what was going on.

"You don't really care who killed Forbis. You don't really care that there was a hex put on me. All you want is to find the button."

"Not me." He chomped into the slice of pizza. "Truth be told, I'm as curious as the next guy as to who killed Forbis. And as for you and that curse . . . I happen to care very much. Which explains why I ordered pizza for dinner, and oh, by the way, finish that bottle of water and have another one."

"I don't want another bottle of water."

"Mambo Irma insists." Gabriel leaned back in his chair and reached over to the counter for another bottle. He tossed it to me. "Are you always so obstinate?"

"Are you always so evasive?"

"Do you really think it matters? If you're helping the cops find out who killed Forbis—"

"Then what happened to the button is a critical piece of the puzzle. Because it was there at the exhibit the night the show opened. I saw it. But I know it wasn't there a couple of days later. And if I needed it, I now have positive proof

234

because the entire front of the loa box was ripped off and left behind my shop and there's no sign of the Button of Doom."

"So someone else is looking for the button." Gabriel thought this over. "Interesting, and it all goes back to the same place we started. Who wanted to hex you?"

I drummed my fingers against the table. "I'm beginning to think it might have been you."

"Really?" I didn't think it was funny, but Gabriel did. When he saw that I was as serious as a heart attack, he wiped the smile off his face. "Why would I want to hurt you?"

"To get to the button."

"But you don't have the button." He reached across the table and snatched up my hand in his and his eyes snapped to mine. It was evening, and light slanted into the kitchen from the window above the sink. It made his gray eyes look darker and brought out flecks in them, like iron. "Do you?"

"If I did, I'd know who killed Forbis."

"Well then you see, we do both want the same thing." Gabriel laughed, and though he loosened his hold, he didn't let go of my hand. In fact, he slipped his fingers through mine. "Tell me, who are your suspects?"

"You?" I didn't actually believe it, but I figured it was worth a try.

Gabriel shook his head . "Not me. Anyone else?"

"Richard Norquist for one. Forbis fired him and they fought before Forbis came into the church. And Nev says Laverne Seiffert, but I don't believe that for a minute."

"Because . . . ?"

"Because she's too nice."

"Not logical, but I'll accept that as an explanation for a moment. Who else?"

"Well, there's Victor Cherneko."

"Aha!" His eyes lit. "He has a factory in Haiti."

"I know."

"And from what I've heard, a rather unhealthy interest in the occult."

This was news, and I turned it over in my head. "None of that explains why he'd want to hurt me with a voodoo doll. He hardly knows me. In fact we only spoke once, when I returned an onyx stud that belonged to him. One I found at the church."

"Someplace where it shouldn't have been?"

I nodded.

"He may feel threatened," Gabriel pointed out. "The trick might have been designed to send a message about how you should mind your own business."

That much made sense, but Victor Cherneko, patron of the arts, as some sort of vudon bokor . . .

"I'm not buying it," I told him. "Why would Victor want to kill Forbis?"

"You mean other than that multimillion dollar stink of a lawsuit they were involved in?"

I guess the look on my face said it all, because Gabriel smiled. "That nice policeman boyfriend of yours seems to have forgotten to mention that to you."

"Then I . . ." I was out of my chair before I even stopped to think where I might be going. "I've got to talk to Cherneko." I glanced at the clock on the microwave. "It's just after five. I bet he won't be at the office"

"No." Gabriel still had his phone in front of him and he navigated his way through a couple of screens. "But he will be here."

He turned the pad around so that I could see the screen and a homepage done in gorgeous shades of green with touches of teal and red.

I glanced from the screen to Gabriel. "Forest?"

"A new gallery. It's supposed to be beyond fabulous. Tonight is the opening reception." He looked me up and down. "Do you own anything stunning?"

"You don't think button sellers can be stunning?"

Gabriel stood. "Not what I said. But if we're going to fit in, stunning is the word of the night." He'd already turned to head out of the kitchen when I caught him by the arm.

"We're going to the opening? How do you know Cherneko is going to be there?"

His smile warmed the air between us. "The opening of a grand new gallery? Of course he'll be there. You can take my word for it." He gave me a wink. "I'm an arts journalist, you know."

Chapter Seventeen

I AM NOT A FLASHY DRESSER, BUT I GUESS I DID A PRETTY good job of getting ready for the art show opening because when I walked out of my bedroom in the nipped-waist, black lace, sleeveless dress with the short, slightly flared skirt, Gabriel's eyes lit. Then again, I suppose I had the same reaction when I saw him. While I was getting ready, he'd gone . . . where? . . . and when he came back, he was dressed in a tux.

"Well, you can't expect me to go to an opening like tonight's in jeans," he said in response to my open-mouthed appreciation.

Slack jaw is not a good look for me. I snapped my mouth shut, then reminded him, "You went to Forbis's opening in jeans."

"That was at the Chicago Community Church. Forest is a little more upscale."

He was right.

From its Michigan Avenue address to the valet parking out front, Forest was a whole different ballgame. While the website was drenched in warm colors that gave off earthy vibes and there was a sort of green tree thingy just inside the front door (tapestry? sculpture? I wasn't sure) that played on the theme, the gallery itself was an eye-popping extravaganza of high ceilings, stark white walls, and stainless-steel accents. A jazz trio played in the far corner of the room and servers in black pants and white shirts circulated with tiny appetizers and glasses of champagne.

I am no bumpkin, but in a room where every man wore a tux and every second woman had on more jewelry than I have owned throughout my lifetime, I can't say I felt at home.

Not so Gabriel. By the time we got to the halfway point in the long gallery, he'd already returned the greetings of a dozen or so of our fellow guests. While he was at it, he scooped two glasses of champagne off the tray of a passing server and handed one to me at the same time he asked, "What?"

I guess he knew what I was thinking. Or maybe he saw the question in my eyes.

"You know everyone." As if to emphasize the point, a dowager type loaded down with diamonds put a hand on his arm and greeted Gabriel. "Everyone knows you."

"Of course they do." His smile was as bright as the sparks off the elderly woman's jewels. "I attend all these things. Arts journalist, you know."

I imagined a wink going along with the comment, but truth be told, I wasn't looking Gabriel's way. My attention had been caught by the art installation that dominated the center of the room. Center of the room and up.

My gaze naturally went right there, and I found myself looking at the accouterments of a full, formal English tea—china cups and saucers, silver teapots, lace-covered table and all. All upside down and facing us from where they were stuck to the gallery ceiling.

No doubt, some artist's idea of turning tradition on its head.

"So . . ." I looked from the ceiling to the other artwork around us. "What does your arts journalist self have to say about Forest?" I asked Gabriel.

"Eclectic." At the same time he said this, Gabriel checked out a way-bigger-than-life bronze sculpture of a lobster riding a pony. "If I were writing about the event, I might even throw in words like *idiosyncratic*, *whimsical*, and *haunting*."

"You might." I took a tiny sip of champagne and strolled nearer to an installation of garden tools covered with mud. "If you were an arts journalist."

Gabriel stepped back to give the tools a better look. "Commonplace and weathered. Still, they brim with yearning and are aquiver with history." He slid me a sidelong look and warmed it up with a smile. "Arts journalist enough for you?"

I suppose it was, and told myself to stop obsessing. Who—or what—Gabriel really was and why he was really mixed up with Forbis and the Button of Doom didn't matter at the moment. Not as much as locating the button—and the murderer who'd probably taken it off the loa box.

As if in response to the thoughts swirling through my

head, I caught a glimpse of Victor Cherneko across the gallery. Gabriel saw him, too, and side by side, we headed over to greet him.

"Oh . . . er . . . Ms. . . ."

"Giancola." I filled in the blanks for Victor and believe me, I didn't hold it against him that he didn't remember my name. A man who lived in the stratosphere barely had time, much less memory, for those of us mired on terra firma. "We met when I returned your onyx stud."

"Of course! Of course!" A lifetime of cocktail parties, board meetings, and dinners at the country club had served Victor well. He must have known we hadn't run into him simply by chance, yet he was as gracious as if we'd met at the polo grounds. "I was grateful that you took the time to bring the stud back to me. They were a gift from my wife for our thirtieth anniversary and you know how women can be about things like that." He looked Gabriel's way for support and, not finding it, Victor glanced around. "So . . . what do you think of Forest?"

"Idiosyncratic, whimsical, and haunting," I said. "But what I'm really wondering is why I found your shirt stud under those ceremonial drums in Forbis's exhibit back at the church. You couldn't possibly have been near those drums—at least not until after everyone left the church that night."

Victor's face turned to stone. "You're not saying—"

"I'm saying it's curious. And I bet the cops would love to hear all about it."

Oh yeah, I was playing hardball and that's not like me at all, but then, with a guy like Victor, I was pretty sure I had to. A man didn't get to be a billionaire because he had warm

241

and fuzzy tendencies. Or because he happened to suddenly feel like sharing his secrets with some woman he hardly knew.

I knew this. But I also knew that billionaires don't like to have their luxury boats rocked. If I was going to get anywhere with Victor, I had to push the envelope and make him more than just a tad uncomfortable even on what was essentially his turf.

I guess my strategy worked because Victor cleared his throat and stepped back from the crowd and toward a doorway that led into a service corridor alongside the gallery. Gabriel and I followed.

When the door closed behind us and shut out the hum of conversation and the soft beat of the music, Victor shifted from foot to foot and tugged at his left earlobe. "You two . . ." His gaze zipped from me to Gabriel and back to me. "You're not saying . . . well, you couldn't possibly be!" His laugh echoed against the high ceiling. "Why would I possibly want to—"

"Mr. Parmenter was supposed to complete a commission for that new headquarters building of yours."

This was news to me, and I hoped the look I shot Gabriel told him so; I didn't like being blindsided.

But I wasn't about to admit it in front of Victor. "The mural in your lobby . . ." I picked up on the hint from Gabriel and ran with it. "It was supposed to be done with buttons. When did Forbis back out?"

Victor scowled. "After it was too late to do anything about it. I had no choice but to open the building with that damned blank wall sticking out like a sore thumb. But you don't think . . ." When a waiter walked by on his way into the gallery, Victor deposited his empty champagne glass on the man's tray. "Give me a break, you two. You can't possibly think that Forbis backing out of a contract gave me reason to kill him. Kill him in court, yes. I planned to sue the pants off that goofy man. Imagine him telling me that he didn't have time for me anymore. That he didn't have time to complete the mural. It's unfathomable! But I certainly didn't kill him to exact some sort of revenge. I'll find another artist. Believe me, with what I'm willing to pay to get that mural completed, they're lined up like pigeons on a telephone wire."

"Still, it must have been plenty aggravating," I suggested. "Not to mention humiliating. Especially with Forbis's art star rising."

Victor's opinion came out as a grumbled *harumph*. "I know art. I have a house full of it. And the money to buy more. Why would you think that I had any appreciation for Forbis and his silly buttons? Yes, yes, it would have been quite a spectacular mural in the new building, one wall entirely covered with buttons. It would have been unique. And people talk about unique. Forbis had sent sketches. A Chicago skyline. A rendering of Lake Michigan. If he'd been able to pull it off, and all in buttons, it would have been something to talk about, all right. But that other stuff of his? The drums and the statues and the household utensils covered with buttons? Silly."

"And valuable," I suggested.

"Possibly." Victor threaded his fingers together. "I honestly don't know. I never cared enough to look into it."

I gave him the moment, and another one after that. Then again, as a once-upon-a-time theater major, I knew the value of timing. As a button dealer who was sometimes a detective, I also knew that waiting for the exact right moment before I said another word could do more than just about anything to advance an investigation.

I let another heartbeat pass then said, "If you didn't think Forbis's works were valuable, why did you have Richard Norquist stealing them for you?"

Victor was a big guy, so I guess it was a good thing that when the starch went out of him, he collapsed against the wall. I didn't much like the thought of picking him up off the floor.

"How do you . . . how did you . . . ?" He gasped like a fish out of water. "You can't possibly know—"

"But I do." When I took a step closer, I had to look up to look Victor in the eye. "I know Richard Norquist was skimming off the top of Forbis's art show sales. And that tells me that Richard is a conniving little thief. That means he's not above swiping whatever he can get his hot little hands on. And what he got his hot little hands on . . . that's what he brought you at Remondo's the night of the murder, wasn't it?"

Victor didn't have to answer. The fact that his face went ashen pretty much told me everything I needed to know.

"Richard brought a package to the bar. He left without it." Victor knew this, of course, but I figured it wouldn't hurt to explain this part of the story to Gabriel. "That package went home with you, Mr. Cherneko, and I know what was in it." (OK, so I didn't, not for certain, but hey, like I said, timing is everything and this wasn't the time to sound unsure of myself.) "Richard stole one of Forbis's smaller works and you bought it from him. When the police find out—"

"Really, Ms. Giancola!" A waiter came in from the gallery

and the noises of the party and the music overlapped with Victor's harsh whisper. "Keep your voice down," he said and he put a hand on my arm.

For exactly one nanosecond.

But then, that was because Gabriel stepped between me and Victor so fast, I don't think poor Victor knew what had happened until he realized that instead of looking into the sweet but determined eyes of a button dealer, he was staring into eyes as gray as they were steely.

"OK. All right." Victor flattened himself against the wall. "I didn't mean anything by touching Ms. Giancola. I only thought I'd remind her—"

"Whatever you're going to remind her . . ." Gabriel's words were half growl, all warning. He backed away from Victor and stood at my side. "You can remind her from right where you are."

"Yes, of course. I didn't mean . . ." Victor coughed. "What I meant, of course—"

"What you meant is that you know you could help clear things up," I suggested, hoping to take advantage of a contrition I knew wouldn't last long. "All we're looking for is the truth, Mr. Cherneko. If you had nothing to do with Forbis's murder, you won't mind sharing it."

"That . . ." Gabriel crossed his arms over his chest. "And your interest in le Bouton de Malheur."

What was that I said about the right words at exactly the right time?

Victor's spine accordioned. His mouth fell open. He rubbed his hands over his face. "How do . . ." He looked at us through his fingers. "How do you two know about the button?"

"Oh, come on, Victor!" Gabriel gave him a friendly slap on the shoulder. "You think you're the only one with an interest in island legends? Josie here . . ." He glanced my way. "She knows about the button. I know about the button. Forbis Parmenter, he certainly knew about the button. But then, so did his father and his grandfather."

Victor nodded, but no words came out of his mouth. Not for a few moments, anyway. Finally he sputtered, "Like you said, it's just a legend. That's all. There isn't anyone who takes that sort of thing seriously!"

"Except I bet you do." This was me, and yes, I was going on nothing but instinct alone. Three cheers for me, because it worked.

Victor passed a hand over his eyes. "All right. Since you know so much, I might as well tell you. Then you'll see . . ." He twitched his shoulders. "Yes, I know the legend. I first heard talk of it in Haiti. There was a story about a special button that had been made there two hundred years ago, a button with special powers. Le bouton was taken to Jekyll Island when the houngan who owned it was transported there as a slave. And yes, I know what happened to Parmenter's father and grandfather. They were given the button."

"And died terrible deaths soon after," I reminded him.

Victor nodded. "The button was the reason I was at that tacky little excuse for an art show in the first place," he said. "I mean, really, the Chicago Community Church?"

I really had never wanted to wring the man's neck. At least not until I saw the way his top lip curled when he talked about the church.

"I've been interested in Mr. Parmenter's work for a while and thanks to Mr. Norquist's . . . er . . . assistance, I've been able to obtain a couple pieces of it for my own private collection," Victor went right on. "When I heard Parmenter was coming to town, I was mildly interested. When I heard he'd made vudon the theme of this show . . . well, I doubted it was possible that the Button of Doom would be there, but you can't blame me for being curious. An artifact of such age and such power . . ." His shoulders shot back and his chin came up and Victor had to rein himself in. "Well," he said, "I knew it wasn't likely that the button would be there, but I thought it was worth taking a chance and showing up to see."

"And did you see it?" I asked him.

Victor pressed two fingers to the bridge of his nose. "I didn't need to see it. I saw Parmenter's reaction when he walked up to that loa exhibit. I knew the button was there."

"And you stole it," I said.

Victor's smile was slow and sinister. "There are some people who believe le Bouton de Malheur has great power. Power to vanquish enemies and eliminate all opposition. Any man who had that sort of power could easily use it against his rivals."

"If you believe such things," Gabriel said.

"Yes, of course." Victor's smile was quick. "But the only way to find out . . ." He splayed his fingers and held out his hands. "I made my fortune taking chances and I wasn't about to pass up one like that. After Parmenter ran out of the church and the party broke up, I went into the men's room and stayed there for a long, long while. I thought that by the time I came out, the coast would be clear and I could take a look around the exhibit and figure out which of those buttons Parmenter was looking at when he lost his nerve."

"And did you see the button?" I asked him.

Victor ran his tongue over his lips. "I saw . . ." He squeezed his hands into fists. "When I got over to the exhibit, I saw Parmenter's body on the floor. I understand that's not where you eventually found it, Ms. Giancola. That tells me the murderer heard me coming. He was still there. Right nearby, and when he saw me, he hid. I didn't know that at the time, of course, I only know that Parmenter laid there, all pale and waxy and with buttons glued to his eyes and his lips and . . . I panicked. Of course, I panicked. At least for the moment. I don't know what I did, I suppose I might have . . ." He clutched both of his hands to his heart. "I suppose I made some sort of gesture and that's when I lost my shirt stud, that's how you found it under the ceremonial drums. All I know for sure is that I ran out of that church as fast as I could."

" 'At least for the moment.' " I glommed onto the words that seemed so out of place in his story. "Does that mean you went back?"

Victor nodded. "The next morning. By then, I thought I could deal with seeing the body again. My plan was to get into the church, get the button, and be gone by the time anyone else was around, but you . . . You and the police were already there."

"You were wearing Bob the maintenance man's uniform!" I pointed in an aha! sort of way. "No wonder Bob thought there was a zombie around."

"Did he?" There was no laughter in Victor's voice. "I

obviously didn't get close to the exhibit that day, either, so I didn't have a chance to look for le Bouton de Malheur, but as you can see, I'm not the one who killed Parmenter."

"You didn't give up, though, did you?" Another thought hit and just for good measure, I added another aha! gesture. "You didn't know that the button was already gone. But you did know that you didn't have the luxury of picking through that exhibit, button by button. You broke into the church and ripped the front off the loa box. Then when you realized the Button of Doom wasn't there, you dropped the box at my shop because you knew I'd get it back where it belonged."

"Yes." Victor lifted his chin and moved toward the door. "I'm more than willing to pay a fine for trespassing and destroying Parmenter's work. So go ahead and report me if you like. But while you're at it, make sure you tell the cops that I didn't kill the man. I couldn't have. By the time I saw him after the show broke up, he was already dead."

When the door swung closed behind him, Gabriel and I exchanged looks. "When he mentioned he was willing to cop to what he'd done, he forgot to mention stealing Forbis's artwork," I said.

Gabriel grinned. "It's kind of nice to think of the cocky bastard getting his due. You'll tell your policeman friend?"

"Yes." I pulled out my phone to check the time. "Only it's kind of late. Nev's pretty much an early bird." I pushed open the door to walk back into the gallery. "I'll wait until tomorrow and—"

And what?

Honestly, at that moment, I couldn't remember. But then, that was because I found myself face to face with Nev.

Nev and Evangeline.

I'm not sure who was more surprised to see who. Or is it whom? And did it matter anyway when Evangeline and I exchanged startled and oh-so-embarrassed looks?

Lucky for me, Gabriel was either unaware of the mortified vibes or he really didn't give a flip. "Hey," he pumped Nev's hand, "we were just talking about you."

"We were just . . ." Nev had a canapé in one hand and he popped it in his mouth. "That is, we heard about the opening and we thought we'd stop in and . . ."

"Talk to Victor Cherneko. Yes, I figured." Did I? Or was I just trying to save a situation that was obviously headed down the tubes? Maybe I was simply trying to save my own suddenly flaming face. "He went thataway." I pointed toward Victor's retreating back. Last I saw them, Nev and Evangeline were headed after Victor.

I headed for the door.

"You're going to tell him aren't you?" Gabriel asked, scrambling to catch up with me. Can a short woman with short legs really move that fast?

"Tell him . . ."

"Everything Victor told us. When it comes to the police, Cherneko might not be in much of a talking mood."

I glanced over my shoulder to where I saw Nev chatting it up with Victor. But only for a moment. I pushed through the door and took a long, deep breath of outside air.

"So you are going to tell him everything, aren't you?" Gabriel asked again.

"There's nothing more important than solving the case," I said.

"Which means you're more than willing to share."

"I always have been before."

I didn't bother to add the words that finished the thought and swirled in my head to the funny beat of the hurt and disappointment that mixed it up on my insides.

Except this time.

Chapter Eighteen

AFTER ALL HE'D DONE FOR ME, THERE WAS NO WAY I COULD ask Stan to mind the Button Box for another day. The day after the opening at Forest, I got to the shop early and told myself in no uncertain terms that there was no suspect, no investigation, and no distraction that was going to make me leave.

I stuck to my guns and luxuriated in all the wonderful, mundane tasks that made the shop so special to me. By one, I pulled out the ham salad sandwich I'd brought with me for lunch and sat down in the back room with it and a nice tall glass of iced tea. I actually might have been able to enjoy both if there wasn't something niggling at the back of my mind.

Gabriel's phone.

I'd found it on my dining room table when he dropped

me off at my apartment and left for parts unknown the night before.

"Who forgets their phone when phones are so important these days?" I asked myself, and not for the first time.

Just like I asked myself if I was brazen enough to poke through the phone and, hopefully, find some clue on it as to how I could contact Gabriel and get it back to him.

I gave the phone a one-fingered nudge that sent it spinning on my worktable, not sure if I admired myself for, at least so far, not snooping, or if the fact that what felt like a violation of privacy to me simply meant I was too much of a wimp.

Before I had a chance to figure it out, the bell above the front door jingled.

"I'll be right with you," I called out, and I hopped up to run a brush through my hair and smooth on a fresh coat of lip gloss.

I always greet customers with, "Welcome to the Button Box," but this time when I walked out of the back room, the words never made it past my lips.

Nev stood near my desk.

"Hey."

"Hey," he said back. He didn't smile. "I was in the neighborhood and I wondered if you could get time away for lunch."

"I just ate."

"Oh, OK." Nev shifted from foot to foot. "You know, I've been thinking . . ."

"About the case. Of course." I reminded myself that this was my shop—my turf—and I didn't need to feel uneasy or embarrassed or unsure about anything. Which actually might have been encouraging if I didn't feel uneasy, embarrassed, and unsure. Especially when I made the mistake of glancing up into Nev's blue eyes.

"I can explain about last night," he said.

"I'm sure you can. But I don't need to hear it."

"You do." He stuffed his hands into the pockets of a beige sport coat that he wore with a shirt and tie that were nearly the same color, along with brown pants. Maybe it was the steamy temperatures outside, but he reminded me of a vanilla ice-cream cone. "I was at the gallery last night to talk to Victor Cherneko. He's got Haitian connections, you know, and I just figured—"

"You figured it was only natural to have someone along who's got the inside track on the culture and the customs. Like I said, Nev, you don't owe me an explanation."

"But I do owe you an update." It wasn't my imagination. As soon as Nev pulled out the little leather notebook he carried around, he was back in his cop-element and feeling far more comfortable than he did when he was trying to tiptoe through the Evangeline minefield.

Fine by me. I knew once we were talking about the case, I'd feel more comfortable, too.

He planted his feet and read from the notebook. "Listen to this. Cherneko admitted that he was inside the Chicago Community Church the night of the murder after everyone else cleared out. But he swears he's not the one who killed Parmenter."

I think Nev expected a bigger reaction than the simple nod I gave him. "He told me that, too, but I bet he forgot to mention to you how he and Richard Norquist have been skimming artwork from Forbis's collection. Richard steals them, Victor buys them."

"That did slip his mind!" Nev made a note of it. "I can see you were at the opening last night for the same reason I was. As usual, you're better at making people talk."

It would have been nice to get lost in the gleam of admiration in his eyes. Just like the old days. Except this wasn't the old days. "I'm not better at it," I told him, "just less threatening. People are more willing to open up to me because they don't think it's going to hurt them in any way. They're not intimidated by me like they are by you. It's the whole cop thing, you know."

"Exactly what I was thinking." Nev tapped his pen against his notebook. "That's why I was wondering if we could get together and . . . you know . . . do what we've done with the other cases we've worked on together. We've gathered our suspects and then you've taken over, explaining how you worked through the investigation and what you discovered about the case. I think having a button dealer call them out about their behavior and their motives catches them off guard, no offense intended. We've always caught our murderers that way before."

Really, there was no offense taken, because I knew exactly what Nev meant. Besides, I liked the thought of working hand in hand with him again. Or at least I would have if I could get that image out of my mind—the one of a wide-eyed Evangeline, so surprised at seeing me at Forest.

I played it cool. And not because I was trying to be coy. I needed to keep calm for my own sake, not for Nev's. I was still stinging from seeing him with Evangeline, and I didn't want to fool myself into thinking I could forget that, simply because I fell in with his plan. At this point, I couldn't afford to forget that we were talking about two separate things: our investigation, that was one thing. But my relationship with Nev . . . well, that was something else altogether.

I told myself to keep focused on the investigation and strolled over to the old library card catalogue files that held my glass buttons. "Who did you have in mind?" I asked him.

"Cherneko, of course. And now that I know about what he and Norquist were up to, I need him in on this for more reasons than I thought. Parmenter left him high and dry about some big project in that new building of his, you know. I figured a man like Cherneko holds a grudge as big as his ego. I thought that gave Cherneko motive. But if Parmenter found out that he was buying stolen artwork from Norquist and threatened to have him arrested. . . well, that gives Cherneko motive number two. Oh yeah, Cherneko's on my suspect list. Then there's Norquist, of course."

"Forbis fired him."

"And he was stealing."

"And he'd been skimming the profits of the shows for a long time. If Forbis found out about that—"

"Another motive for him." Nev made a note of it. "And then, of course, there's Laverne Seiffert."

"What?" I am not the type who usually confronts authority, but really, this was ridiculous and I told Nev so. "Laverne's a sweet woman."

"She had the opportunity. She was the last one to leave the building and we know she doesn't have an alibi. And she knows where all the extra keys were kept. It would have been easy for her to pop into the minister's office and take those extra keys, stash them somewhere to make it look like someone had stolen them, and then use her own keys to get back into the church. I've had my eyes on Laverne since day one."

"But we've got to consider motive." I crossed the shop to stand nearer to Nev. "You've always told me that, Nev. You've always said that why a killer does what he does is as important as what he does in the first place." Even I cringed at this convoluted logic, but sharp guy that he is, Nev followed right along. "Laverne doesn't have a motive. She barely knew Forbis."

"But she did know Richard."

"Which doesn't mean—"

"You heard her yourself, Josie, she's nuts about Richard. If she knew Forbis fired him—"

"She's not going to be so nuts about him once she finds out what a lowlife Richard really is." I made a face. Poor Laverne. A woman concerned with social justice wasn't going to tolerate a man with sticky fingers, no matter how many bittersweet memories she had of their days together in college. "She didn't do it," I told Nev.

"Maybe." I saw him write down Laverne's name anyway, and every scratch of his pen only served to remind me how unreasonable he was being. "Either way, we can invite Laverne to our little suspect powwow. She knows more about Richard than any of us do. Even if she's not our murderer, she might be able to help us on that front."

"I agree there. But I don't agree that she looks guilty," I added just so he knew he hadn't changed my mind.

"So . . . great." Nev flipped the notebook closed. "What about tomorrow evening? That will give me a chance to get in touch with everybody. I'll invite them here, tell them you're having a sort of private memorial for Parmenter. Wine and cheese, that sort of thing. I can say you want to do it here at the shop because of what buttons meant to Parmenter. Does that make sense?"

"Only if you invite Evangeline, too."

I waited for the firestorm I expected would result from this suggestion and when it didn't come, I bent at the waist and looked up into Nev's face "Evangeline? You do remember her, right?"

He's a tall, rangy guy. He shook himself like a Labrador coming out of a lake. "I thought you said you understood. I thought you said I didn't owe you an explanation. Evangeline was with me last night because I thought she could provide some insights into Cherneko's interests into Haitian religions, but other than that, come on, Josie. You know she's really not involved in the investigation. I can ask her to come if you think there would be some benefit, but I hate to put her out like that. I'm guessing she'd be pretty bored."

"Are you trying to make this as hard as it can possibly be?" I groaned and tipped my head back, thinking about the best way to ease into an explanation. "Oh heck!" I slapped a hand against my thigh. "I'm done playing games, Nev, so here's what I think. If you're going to drag Laverne here because she looks like a suspect to you, then I think Evangeline has to be here, too. As a suspect."

He looked as stunned as if I'd started talking Martian. That is, until his mouth thinned. "You're talking crazy."

"I'm talking sense. Forbis's show was about vudon, and nobody knows more about vudon than Evangeline."

"Which doesn't mean she had anything to do with his murder."

"Which doesn't mean we can't poke around in that big brain of hers just a little."

"No." It was as simple as that. At least to Nev. He spun around and headed for the door. "I'm not going to insult Evangeline by making her come over here and—"

"And what? Show respect for Forbis at a private memorial service?" I followed on his heels. "That is what you're going to tell everyone else, right? Why shouldn't she hear the same story?"

"Because I don't tell Evangeline stories. And I don't let her get mixed up in murder investigations."

"No, you leave that for me."

Admit it, it was a great parting shot.

Too bad Nev had already banged out the front door and never heard it.

AFTER NEV LEFT and I spent an appropriate amount of time fuming, I decided to rearrange the biggest of the glass display cases at the front of the store. I emptied it and carefully stowed away the mother of pearl buttons that had been in there, then cleaned the glass until it sparkled. I filled the case with wooden buttons, decided they looked too dull and heavy to match the summer sunshine, and emptied the display case again.

Buttons, buttons, buttons.

Buttons, I knew, would keep my mind off the little tiff Nev and I had, and I went through drawer after drawer of buttons, looking for exactly the right ones to feature in the display.

I decided on lacy glass, those wonderful old buttons with

painted backs and fancy molded surfaces that sometimes mimic the texture of fabric.

I arranged the lacy glass buttons one way, then another. I scooped them out of the display case and tried again, grumbling to myself all the while. It was Nev's fault. Nev and Evangeline. Though what exactly was their fault—the fact that I couldn't think straight, or the fact that I couldn't make the display look the way I wanted it to—I didn't know.

I did know I wasn't happy with the lacy glass button display.

Grumbling some more, I stepped back and wondered what I could do that would look different, interesting, and I thought about that installation I'd seen at Forest the night before, the tea service stuck on the ceiling.

"Buttons stuck to the sides and top of the display case!" I swooned and really, that should have told me something right there. As much as I love my buttons, I am usually not obsessive (well, at least not too obsessive) about displaying them. I'm pretty sure I was knee-deep in what psychologists call transference, and perfectly willing to transfer my frustrations about my relationship with Nev to my button-display capabilities. I got on the computer and did a little research to see how an artist could possibly stick a tea service to the ceiling.

By the time I was done, I still didn't have the display case done.

But suddenly, I had an idea about Forbis Parmenter's murder.

NOTICE I SAID *idea*.

At this point, all the pieces hadn't fallen into place yet.

That didn't happen until I forced myself to calm down, put away the lacy glass buttons in a pleasing manner that had nothing to do with sticking them to anything anywhere, and got a bottle of water in the hopes that deep breaths and hydration would help me make sense of everything I'd just discovered.

That's when I saw Gabriel's phone still sitting there on my worktable, and that's when I knew I had to throw caution to the wind and take the chance of being a busybody and looking through his phone.

Good thing I did.

Because with what I found in his picture file . . .

Well, that's when I knew for sure what was going on, and who killed Forbis Parmenter.

Chapter Nineteen

By the time I got where I was going, I was hoping Nev would be with me or at least that he'd be on his way, but no matter how many times I called him (and believe me, I called him a lot of times), he refused to pick up.

"Be that way," I mumbled, shoving my phone back in my pocket and telling myself it was for the last time. "You'll be plenty sorry."

Oh, how I hate it when I'm right!

See, Nev was already there. On the floor, his back propped against a wall. The second I saw him, my heart bumped and my adrenaline kicked in. I'd been thinking I'd assess and evaluate and get the lay of the land before I took the chance of letting anyone know I was there, but those plans pretty much went right out the window when I saw that Nev's eyes were half-closed, his color was off, and his chin was on his chest.

"Nev? Are you OK? What happened?" I was on my knees next to him in record time and I checked his pulse. It was slow and steady, but his skin was clammy. I chafed his hand between both of mine. "Nev, can you hear me?"

Except for an eye flicker, he didn't respond, and I didn't hesitate. I stood and reached in my pocket for my phone.

"That's a really bad idea."

Like I was about to let a voice from out of the dark stop me? My fingers slipped against the numbers: 9-1 . . .

"I said it's a bad idea." Evangeline stepped into the light of the single spot that shone over the Field Museum Yoruba exhibit, and, dang, I would have gone right on dialing if that light didn't glint against the barrel of the gun in her hand, the one she had trained on Nev.

"You wouldn't." My voice bumped over the words, and the hand poised above my phone trembled.

Not so Evangeline's. As cool as a cucumber and as emotionless as if she'd been carved from rock, she motioned for me to drop my phone on the table of Yoruba divination trays on my right.

I did as I was told.

"I was hoping this would be quick and easy," she said. "I'm sorry you showed up and ruined it."

"Nev got here before me. He knew before I did, didn't he?"

"He suspected. He didn't know. Not until that very last moment when I stepped so close to him and raised my lips to his." Evangeline tipped her head back and closed her eyes. Just as quickly, she snapped them open again and her smile was sleek. "That was when I stuck him with this." She took a syringe out of her pocket and tossed it on the table next to my phone. "Oh, you should have seen his face then. That's when he knew for sure, and by then, it was too late."

My mouth went dry. "Is he . . . will he be . . ."

"He'll be fine. At least that was the plan. All I wanted to do was knock him out for a while. The security guard won't get to this section of the building until at least ten tonight. That would have given me plenty of time to get to O'Hare and get out of here. But now . . ." Evangeline slid the gun in my direction. "Now you're here and you ruined everything."

"Hey, I don't care if you leave. Go!" I made a little shooing motion that Evangeline ignored. "If that's what you want to do, go ahead. Get going."

Her smile never wavered "I've got time. Poor, sweet Nev will be out of it for another couple of hours and like I said, there won't be a security guard by for a while. How did you get in here, anyway?"

I didn't exactly feel like shooting the breeze, but there was something about having a gun trained on me that made me chatty whether I wanted to be or not. "There's a fundraiser going on downstairs," I said. "And volunteers were coming in through a side door, and while no one was looking—"

"While no one was looking, you decided to come up here and play the hero. Perfect." Evangeline didn't look like she meant it. "You just can't keep your nose out of my business, can you?"

"I never put my nose in your business. Or at least I never wanted to. You were the one who came around and—"

"And took your boyfriend away?" Her teeth were blindingly white and so perfect and even. Evangeline shook her head and in the light of the spot, her hair looked like liquid ebony. "That wasn't hard."

"Because it never happened. Nev and I, we're—"

"Bickering? Fussing? Finding faults where there never were any before?" I didn't think it was funny, but I guess Evangeline did because she laughed. "How easy it is to influence the minds of the weak!"

"A spell?" Even I couldn't believe I was saying it, much less thinking it actually might be true. "You're the one who had Nev and me going at each other. You're the one . . ." Trembling or not, I pointed a finger in her direction. "You stashed that voodoo doll in the Button Box!"

"As easy as pie when that sweet old man was there watching the shop for you. All I had to do was pretend to need help—"

"The damsel in distress. The one who spilled iced tea on her clothes on her way to an interview."

"Smart, huh?" Evangeline pouted. "You weren't supposed to recover so quickly. How did you—"

"I'm allowed to have secrets, too." I took a step toward her. Don't ask me why. It's not like I had a plan to overpower her or anything. At this point, all I wanted to do was get some help for Nev. I guess I thought if I could duck around her . . .

Evangeline stepped to her right to block my path.

I pretended like it was no big deal. "So Nev . . ." I slid a look in his direction. His breathing was shallow and I didn't like that at all. "Did he tell you how he finally figured out that you were the one who murdered Forbis?"

"Sorry. He never had a chance. But since you figured it

out . . ." She jabbed the gun in my direction. "You can explain. Then perhaps I can learn from my mistakes."

"Why, you planning on murdering somebody else?"

She didn't think it was funny, but then, I guess I didn't, either. I gathered my courage and my wits. "Forbis's grandfather and his father were killed just like he was," I said. "They were given the Button of Doom—"

"And after that, it's so easy to scare someone to death." Her shoulders rose and fell in a delicate little shiver. "Once the seed of fear was planted in their brains—"

"And you were disguised as a real, living Congo Savanne on the prowl and looking to find Forbis."

"You figured that part out, did you?" Evangeline was impressed. "And the rest?"

"The button part was easy. You used museum wax." I wasn't sure of this, but when Evangeline didn't protest, I knew I was right. "It's the same stuff artists use to display delicate glass works. It holds on tight and comes off easily. That's how you stuck the Button of Doom to the Congo Savanne box, and that's how you removed it after you killed Forbis."

"And I suppose you have some half-baked theory about why I'd want to do that?"

I pretended to consider this. "I can't say if it's half-baked or not. I can say I saw the first glimmers of a reason the moment I saw those buttons on Forbis's eyes and lips. I wondered if his murderer was sending a message about how Forbis needed to be quiet, but that wasn't it at all."

"He didn't see," Evangeline muttered. "He didn't speak the truth."

"About vudon."

266

"He should have known better than to make fun of a religion that's sacred to so many people."

"People like you."

"And my ancestors before me." When she looked my way, she grinned. "Surprised? You shouldn't be. My great-great grandmother was born a slave on a Barrier Island plantation. She was a mambo, a woman who—"

"I know what a mambo is." There was a perverse sort of pleasure in not telling her how I knew. "And your family has always owned the button. That's how Forbis's grandfather and his father—"

"They bought up our land, the land we worked hard for after our people were freed. They told us to leave. They broke up the community."

"That's not all they did." I remembered what I'd seen on Gabriel's phone. "There's a big old building on Forbis property. It looks like some kind of garage."

Evangeline narrowed her eyes. "You can't know—"

"But I do. Because I've just seen a picture of that building and it's the same as that picture you have hanging in your office. The one you told me wasn't important at all. But that's not true, is it, Evangeline? Forbis's grandfather, and his father, and Forbis when he was a young man . . . they all worked to build that garage. And they built it over where the plantation slaves were buried."

"They disrespected my people, and they disrespected my religion. My grandmother knew what she had to do, she took care of the old man. And my mother made sure she took care of his son."

"And your job was to make sure Forbis suffered the same fate."

She smiled. "Once he saw le Bouton de Malheur, it was easy."

"But it's still murder."

With a snort, Evangeline moved past me. "And you're going to stop me?"

I glanced down the darkened hallway. I knew there was a stairway nearby, and there were people downstairs at the fund-raiser. If I could get to them and to the security guards who I knew were there, too, I wouldn't need my phone, I could get help for Nev. I took a step in that direction.

"Don't do it."

I whirled just in time to see Evangeline bend over Nev. She had a syringe in her hands. Not the same syringe . . . I looked to where that one was still on the table.

"I didn't want to have to use this," Evangeline said. "After all, everything I did to you, I did so that Nev and I could be together again. But really, you're not leaving me any choice." She jabbed the syringe into Nev's thigh and he flinched.

"There." Evangeline brushed her hands together. "Now here's the way this is going to work. I'm leaving. You can follow me, screaming your head off the whole time and that's fine if that's what you want to do. But if you do . . ." She sashayed past me. "By the time you get back here, I guarantee that drug will be in Nev's bloodstream. It's a vudon drug. Very strong. And if you waste a minute, Josie, he's going to be dead."

"You couldn't . . . you didn't . . ." I pushed right past her to get to Nev's side. I got down on the floor and held his hand. His pulse was shaky now and I looked up at her through the tears that filled my eyes. "There's no way you'd kill him. You said what you did, you did so the two of you could be together."

"That was before I knew I needed time to get out of here." As calm as can be, she walked to the front of the exhibit. "Here's the trick, Josie, you can come after me like I said, or you can use that time to head into my office. There's a syringe there. Top desk drawer, right-hand side. It's the anti-dote to what I just gave Nev. The only antidote. Only . . ." She stepped down from the raised platform that held the exhibit. "If I were you, I wouldn't waste any time sitting there blubbering."

I didn't.

Even before the sounds of her heels stopped echoing down the hallway, I was on my way to Evangeline's office. The door was open and my fingers slick with sweat, I flicked on the lights and grabbed her phone.

I called 911. I called Nev's lieutenant. I called down to the main desk of the museum. Then I looked for the syringe, but when I got back to Nev, I didn't administer it. I didn't need to and that was OK. By then, I heard the sirens.

WHEN THE BELL over the front door of the Button Box jingled, I headed out of the back room.

"Nev!" I raced to the front door and threw my arms around him. "Why didn't you call to tell me you were out of the hospital?" I asked him. That is, right after I kissed him a couple times just to show him how relieved I was to see him on his feet again. "I would have come to get you."

"That's OK, after three days of being in bed, I couldn't

wait to get out of there. Besides . . ." He squeezed my hand. "You spent plenty of hours there these last few days. I didn't deserve that."

"Baloney!" I twined my fingers through his to draw him further into the shop. "You look good," I said, and it was true. His color was back, his eyes were clear. "Did the docs ever determine what was in that syringe?"

He shook his head. "Nothing they've ever seen before. Some mix of herbs and oils and . . ." A shiver twisted over his shoulders. "It's crazy. The whole thing is just crazy."

"Crazy but true." This wasn't the time to dance around the most uncomfortable parts of the story. "Evangeline, they couldn't get her to talk and tell them what she gave you?"

Some of that nice, healthy color drained out of Nev's cheeks. He walked over to my desk and sat down in my guest chair, his elbows on his knees. "At least they found her at O'Hare before she got away," he said. "As for her talking . . ." His shoulders rose and fell. "She claims she doesn't know what any of us are talking about, that she didn't give me anything. In fact, she more than hinted that you were the one who gave me the drug."

I flinched as if I'd been slapped and Nev leaned forward to catch my hand. "Her fingerprints are on the syringe," he said. "So she doesn't have a leg to stand on. I just wish . . ."

"I know," I said. "Me, too."

When he let go of my hand, I went around to the other side of the desk and sat down.

"Josie . . ." Nev pushed a hand through his hair. "I'm so sorry you got mixed up in this. If I'd known Evangeline was that unstable—"

"You didn't know. You couldn't have."

"I thought . . ." He made a face. "If I thought she still felt . . . you know . . . that way about me, I never would have gotten near her again. Then to find out she cast some sort of vudon spell so that you and I would fight . . ." He shook his head. "It's crazy. But at least . . ." Nev popped to his feet. "At least we know now why we were fighting all the time. It wasn't us. It was the spell. We're still . . . we're still as good together as ever."

I stood, too. In the days Nev had been hospitalized, I'd been trying to work this thing through in my head. All the times I thought about it, I had this great speech that explained everything I wanted to say. Now, all the pretty words deserted me in an instant. "I . . ." I stammered. I cleared my throat and started again. "I've been thinking about it, Nev. A lot. I don't know if I believe in vudon spells, but I do know this. If we're meant to be together . . . if we're right for each other . . . if you're the one for me and I'm the one for you . . ." There was no easy way to say it. I drew in a long breath that wedged against the painful lump in my throat.

"If we really love each other," I said, "then even a vudon spell shouldn't be enough to keep us apart."

This was something he hadn't thought about. I could tell because his blue eyes darkened and he looked down at the floor.

I stepped around the desk. "You know I'm right."

"I do." He looked up at me. "But that doesn't mean I like it. And it doesn't mean we still can't see each other, right? I mean, just because things are a little rocky now, that doesn't mean we can't still talk and have dinner together and—"

I reached for his hand and squeezed it. "Of course we can."

Nev's smile was quick. "I've got to get going," he said,

heading to the door. "My lieutenant wants to talk to me and the department shrink needs to see me, and I can't wait to get home and see LaSalle. My mom's been taking care of him, but I know the fuzzy guy misses me."

"We all missed you." At the door, I gave him a kiss on the cheek. "We'll talk," I said, and Nev walked out.

I PLAYED IT all wrong.

I said stupid things.

I could have explained myself better. I should have.

The words and the remorse and the guilt spun through my head as I watched Nev walk away, and I went into the back room to dry my eyes. Of course, I wasn't the only one who'd been awkward and unsure. If only Nev had said that of course magic couldn't keep us apart. If only he'd swept me up into his arms and kissed me, we could have started over right then and there.

Only he didn't.

I grabbed a bottle of water, but I hadn't even had a chance to open it when the bell above the front door rang again.

Nev!

My heart knocked against my ribs and I raced to the front of the shop.

"Gabriel!"

He strolled into the shop and tossed his black backpack on the guest chair Nev had so recently vacated. "Sorry to disappoint you."

Did I look disappointed? I wiped the expression from my face. "I was just surprised, that's all. I thought you were someone else."

"That nice policeman boyfriend of yours? I just saw him out on the street. He must be fairly pleased with the way things worked out. Evangeline is behind bars and his case is closed. Thanks to you."

"Thanks to you." I'd put Gabriel's phone in my top desk drawer and I got it out and handed it to him. "If you hadn't forgotten your phone—"

His laugh cut me short. "I didn't forget it."

My mouth fell open. "You took that picture of the Parmenter garage when you were down at Forbis's, and you wanted me to find it so I'd know there was a connection between Forbis and Evangeline."

"It worked."

I thought about the one still missing piece of the puzzle. "It would work better if the cops could find the Button of Doom."

"Ah yes, the button. Too bad about that, but my guess is Evangeline will spill her guts eventually. She'll want the cops to know how smart she was to do everything she did."

"And then they'll know where the button is." I kept my eyes on his. "Unless there's a certain buyer in Shanghai who—"

"Tripe and onions! I was just speculating. You don't think any of that was real, do you? But what is real . . ." He grabbed his backpack and flung it over his shoulder. "I'm leaving town and wanted to stop and say good-bye."

On the heels of Nev walking out, it seemed an especially painful bit of news. Until I realized that Nev walking out had nothing to do with the way I felt about Gabriel. "You'll be back?" I asked him.

"Only if you want to see me again."

"I do."

"Then I'll be back." He walked to the front door and I followed him. "By then, maybe we'll have all the answers we need about the Button of Doom. And until then—"

Honestly, I never saw it coming. Not that I could have done anything about it, anyway.

Gabriel slipped his arm around my waist and pulled me close so hard and so fast, I barely had time to catch my breath.

Good thing he was holding onto me. If he wasn't, I would have melted right onto the floor when he kissed me long and hard.

When he was done, Gabriel grinned down at me. "I'll send you a postcard," he said, and he was gone.

Chapter Twenty

THE BEST THING ABOUT MURDER INVESTIGATIONS IS THEM being over.

I spent the next couple of weeks luxuriating in the wonderful nothingness of looking after the shop and concentrating on buttons.

Yes, I did talk to Nev. Twice in fact. One time I called him just to see how he was feeling and the other time, he called me to ask some questions about what had happened with Evangeline the night he was drugged. We didn't talk about a date or dinner and that was fine. We would. When we were ready.

Until then . . .

The front bell rang and I looked up from my desk to find the mailman and the day's delivery. We passed the time like we always do and when he was gone, I shuffled through the stack: a flyer for a button auction, an invitation to a local merchants meetings—

And a postcard.

There was nothing written on the back of the card but my address, but the front of the card . . .

I flipped it over.

The picture showed a towering skyscraper with a unique opening at the top. It reminded me of a bottle opener.

But it wasn't even the unique building that made me gasp with surprise. It was the words superimposed at the bottom of the picture:

Shanghai World Financial Center

STUDIO BUTTONS

Le Buton De Malheur—the Button of Doom—is, of course, fiction. A button that's supercharged with magical powers? Unlikely in the world outside of books.

However, if there were such a button, it would be what folks in the button collecting world call a studio button. Studio buttons are those special, sometimes one-of-a-kind buttons that aren't necessarily made to fasten clothing but are instead designed for collecting. They're the work of artists such as wood carvers, enamalists, beaders, etc., and they're not mass produced like factory-made buttons.

Many collectors specialize in studio buttons and it's no wonder why. Check online to see some of the fabulous studio buttons available and if you're looking for studio buttons, keep your eyes open at art galleries and craft shows. I once found some wonderful buttons at a pottery studio. The potter kept her bits and pieces of clay and turned them into wonderful, funky buttons in all colors, shapes, and sizes. Come to think of it, some of them were incised with mysterious-looking lettering. Could it be . . . ?

For more information about buttons and button collecting, go to www.nationalbuttonsociety.org.

Turn the page for a preview of Kylie Logan's
new League of Literary Ladies Mysteries . . .

A Tale of
Two Biddies

Coming February 2014 from
Berkley Prime Crime!

"IT WAS THE BEST OF THYMES, IT WAS THE WORST OF thymes!"

I was mid-munch, a shrimp dripping cocktail sauce on its way to my mouth, and I needed one second to grab a napkin to keep the spicy sauce from landing on my new yellow T-shirt and another to focus my eyes—from the one bunch of gloriously green herbs that had just been thrust in front of my nose, to the bunch of dried-out herbs next to it, and beyond, to the ear-to-ear grin of Chandra Morrisey.

"Get it?" Chandra was so darned proud of her little play on words, she hop-stepped from one sandal-clad foot to the other, those small bouquets of thyme jiggling in her hands like maracas. I swear, I thought she'd burst out of her orange capris and the diaphanous lime green top studded with sequins. "Do you get it, Bea? It was the best of thymes . . ."

She held the freshest bunch of herbs at arm's length. "It was the worst of thymes." The other bunch was well on its way to drying out, but she showed off that one, too. "You know, just like the first line of *A Tale of Two Cities*."

"I get it!" I grinned, too, because let's face it, it was a balmy evening in the middle of July and I was sitting on a dock on an island in Lake Erie with the women who were once just neighbors and were now my friends, enjoying the Monday before a huge tourist week celebration for merchants and residents that had been organized by the local chamber of commerce. What was there not to grin about?

I finished off that piece of shrimp and popped out of the folding chair where I'd been lounging. Of all four of us in the League of Literary Ladies—South Bass Island's one and only library-sanctioned discussion group—Chandra was the least likely to actually read one of our assigned books. I didn't hold that against her. What Chandra lacked in literary ambition she made up for in sheer exuberance, a wacky take on everything from her wardrobe to her love life, and a skewed look at the world that included crystals, incense, and tarot cards.

That's why I was careful to keep the skepticism out of my voice when I asked, "So, what do you think of Charles Dickens?"

"Best of thymes, worst of thymes." As if it would hide the fact that her answer was as evasive as the look she refused to give me, Chandra stuck out each hand again, and the pungent, woody scent of thyme fragranced the evening air. *The smell of dawn in paradise.* That's how Rudyard Kipling had once described the aroma of thyme. I couldn't say if he was right or not; I only knew that I'd lived on the island for six months since escaping an ugly stalking incident in New York, and things were going well. Just as I'd once dreamed of doing, I'd turned my life not just around, but completely on its head, and created a new career and a new, peaceful existence for myself. My bed-and-breakfast—Bea & Bees—was booked from now until the end of summer, and I'd settled into a life that was slower paced and far more satisfying than the mile-a-minute stress mess I'd lived in New York. For me, relocation was the right choice. For me, South Bass Island was paradise.

Even if once in a while, there were reminders that even paradise had its perils.

A blast of wind off the lake snaked its way up my back and in spite of the heat, I shivered. One murder does not a paradise destroy, I reminded myself. Just like I reminded myself that thanks to me and the other Ladies, that murder that had happened a couple of months before had been solved, the perp caught, and order restored to paradise.

It wasn't going to happen again, I told myself. This was the heartland, not the big city, and I was grateful for that.

Just like I was grateful that Chandra had remembered to bring the thyme from her garden. I gave myself a swift mental kick to get my thoughts out of the past so I could concentrate on the present and the party atmosphere that enveloped the docks and spilled over into DeRivera Park across the road. Except for the slip next to Luella's that was empty, our fellow islanders were everywhere, chatting, unwinding, and gyrating to the beat of the steel drum band playing near the entrance to the dock. People milled around us, comparing notes about the tourists and how good (or bad) their business had been so far that summer. They shared plates of the food, and recipes when they were asked, along with a camaraderie that could only be forged on a four-mile long spit of land three miles north of the Ohio mainland.

Party, I told myself, and took a deep breath. Paradise, I reminded myself, letting that breath out slowly. This wasn't the time to think about murder, and it sure wasn't the place. Just to prove it to myself, I grabbed the good-looking bunch of thyme from Chandra, stripped the elfin leaves from their stems, and sprinkled them on the salad I'd brought as my contribution to our potluck dinner.

"Did I hear someone say it was time to eat?" Luella Zak jumped off her thirty-foot Sportcraft boat and joined us on the dock. "Kate's coming," she added, glancing over her shoulder toward the fishing charter she captained. "She's just opening the wine."

"One red." Like Chandra had with the herbs, Kate held out the bottle for us to see and joined us around the folding table we'd set with a cheery red, white, and blue cloth and red acrylic dishes and glasses. "One white. Both from Wilder Winery. I hear they make some darned good wine."

Kate ought to know. She was a Wilder and owned the winery.

"Oh no, you know the rules!" If Kate wasn't holding those bottles, I think she would have swatted Chandra's hand when Chandra eyed up the salad and reached for a plate. "Toast first. Eat second."

"Toast first." I handed around glasses and Kate filled them. "What are we toasting?"

"The chance to relax a little before another busy week," Luella said, and raised her glass. Luella was in her seventies, and as tough as any skipper I'd ever met. She was short, wiry, seasoned by the lake on the outside, and as gentle as a lamb on the inside. Of all of us, she was the one who loved books and reading the most, and she'd willingly joined the League, not been coerced into participating like the rest of us had. "I'm always grateful for fishermen, but I'm just as grateful to be on dry land once in a while and let my hair down."

"You got that right, sister!" Chandra squealed with delight. She spun around, taking in all our fellow revelers and raised her voice. "Here's to a great party!"

"And the opportunity to enjoy good wine." Kate lifted her glass. "And good food."

"And good friends," I added. A few months ago, their reactions would have been predictable. Kate would have rolled those gorgeous green eyes of hers. Chandra would have looked as sour as if she'd bit into a lemon. Luella was as steady and predictable as the lake, but where she made her living was not; then, like now, she simply would have nodded. Fortunately, things had changed since the days when Kate, Chandra, and I were hauled into court for our neighborhood bickering and sentenced to a year of discussing books on Monday evenings. I, for one, was grateful.

"Here's to the way things have turned out." I glanced around the circle and smiled back at the friendly expressions that greeted me. "Things are different and I'm so glad."

"To friendship," Luella said, and we clinked our glasses, sipped our wine and filled our plates. Before I had a chance to dig in, though, Gordon Hunter stopped by to chat. Gordon lived on the mainland but had a summer cottage not far from Put-in-Bay, the island's one and only village. He was a mover and a shaker who'd been hired by the chamber of commerce to fill in for an employee out on maternity leave, and if this party he'd organized was any indication, he was going to be good for business.

"*Le fait de s'amuser?*" No, Gordon wasn't French. At least I didn't think he was French. What he was was the driving force behind the Bastille Day celebration planned for the rest of the week. Bastille Day on South Bass Island? Of course, it's not an official holiday, but islanders are always looking for a way to cook up some fun, and tourists are always looking for any excuse to join in. It was a stroke of genius on Gordon's part, and the reason, of course, that the League of Literary Ladies had chosen *A Tale of Two Cities,* the Dickens classic about the French Revolution, as our latest read.

Gordon gave Chandra a friendly poke. "That's 'are you having fun?' for those of you who haven't been to Paris lately."

I had been to Paris. Just about a year earlier in fact, but my French was as rusty as my wanderlust. I took his word for the translation and offered Gordon a glass of wine.

He wasn't a sipper. He took long, quick drinks. Something told me that was the way Gordon attacked all of life. He was a little older than middle-aged, with salt-and-pepper hair, and as suave as a toothpaste salesman. While the rest of us were dressed casually and comfortably, Gordon was decked out in khakis, a white shirt, and a navy blazer with brass buttons. He didn't look as much like a PR guy as he did an admiral.

Maybe he knew what I was thinking because when the guy who owned what was advertised as "the longest bar in the world" came by, Gordon gave him a crisp salute.

"It's going to be a helluva week," Gordon said. He reached

for a shrimp and dragged it through cocktail sauce. "Everybody ready for the crowds?"

"I've got charters every day," Luella said.

"And we're doing winery tours and tastings every afternoon and evening," Kate added. "I put the notice online a couple weeks ago and we're packed for every single one of them."

"My rooms are filled," I put in.

"Thanks again for sending the band my way," I told Gordon.

With the wave of one hand, he acted like it was nothing. "Folks around here tell me you're from the Big Apple, Bea. I figured if anyone could handle a rock band called Guillotine, it was you. They check in yet?"

"Tonight," I told him, and reminded myself I'd have to be back at the B and B by then. "Apparently, rock musicians aren't early risers."

Gordon refilled his glass before he moved on to the next boat and the next group of partiers and watching him, Luella shook her head. "Can't blame the poor guy for drinking. You heard what happened last night?"

I hadn't, but that was no big surprise. My B and B was on the outskirts of what was officially considered downtown, and I was often the last to hear the latest gossip.

This time, though, apparently, Kate and Chandra hadn't heard, either. As one, we pinned Luella with a look.

"Gordon let Richie Monroe help him out on his boat."

Kate's mouth dropped open. Chandra gasped. After six months on the island, I knew Richie well enough. He was fifty years old or so, the guy people called when they wanted small jobs done. Richie shoveled snow in the winter. He ran errands for tourists. He sold ice cream out of a cart on weekends. He carried bags at the grocery store.

I looked from one woman to the other. "I've had Richie do some things for me around the house. He pulled the weeds in the front flower beds. And he cut the grass the weekend my lawn service guys couldn't make it because of a funeral. Richie's reliable."

"Reliable, maybe." Something told me it was no big secret— what is on an island this size?—but Chandra leaned forward and lowered her voice. "But he's not exactly careful."

"Wasn't careful last night." Another head shake from Luella. "He slammed Gordon's boat into the dock. The way I heard it, he did some damage."

Automatically, my gaze traveled down the dock to where Gordon was chatting it up with Alvin Littlejohn, the magistrate who'd sentenced us to be a book discussion group, and his wife, Marianne, the town librarian. "Gordon doesn't look especially upset."

"He's a trouper," Luella said. "And he knows he's got to put on a good show tonight. He put a lot of time and effort into planning this Bastille Day event. He can't let it fizzle. But the way I heard it, he was madder than a wet hen last night. Can't say I blame him. If it was my boat he'd damaged, I would have threatened to wring Richie's neck, too."

"Is that what he did?" It seemed so out of character for debonair Gordon that the comment caught me off guard. "You don't think he'd really—"

"I'm surprised Richie's still alive and breathing, anyway." Chandra's bleached blond hair was chin-length and blunt cut. When she swayed her head from left to right, it stroked her cheeks. "You'd think by now, Mike Lawrence would have gutted Richie like a walleye."

I wasn't so far out of the loop that I hadn't heard this story. Though it had happened the autumn before I moved to the island, Richie's monumental screwup had already reached the status of island legend. "You mean because of how Mike hired Richie to turn off the gas in that fancy new summer cottage over at the other end of the island," I said.

"And how Richie wasn't paying attention to what he was doing, as usual," Kate added.

Just thinking about it made Luella wince. "And how Richie left the gas line open instead of shutting it."

"And that big, fancy summer home . . ." Chandra put down her wineglass long enough to slap her hands together. "Kaboom!"

"Poor guy who owned that house," Kate murmured.

"Poor Mike," Luella commented, and when she looked down the dock, we all did, too, and saw that Mike Lawrence wasn't partying with his neighbors, he was helping one of the dockmasters get a boat berthed. "What with the insurance claim and the owner of the home suing him and the government after him because he was paying Richie under the table and not paying Social Security taxes for him, Mike has lost just about everything he owned, including his contracting business. He's picking up every odd job he can get his hands on, and he's living in a trailer over near the state park. Imagine living in a trailer with a wife and three little kids."

I could imagine it, and what I imagined was cramped and uncomfortable. I made a mental note to see if I could come up with some work for Mike around the B and B. It wouldn't solve all his problems, but it might help.

"Well, look who's here! One of the guests of honor!"

I didn't know there were guests of honor for the week's festivities, so Luella's comment surprised me. That is, until I turned away from watching Mike work and saw who was headed our way on the dock.

Alice Defarge—or was it Margaret?—and talk about a legend! The Defarge twins had lived their whole lives on South Bass and they owned the island's only knit shop. As far as I'd heard, neither of the ladies—seventy-five if they were a day—had officially been named a guest of honor, but the Defarge reference was lost on no one. At least no one who knew anything about the Dickens book. In *A Tale of Two Cities,* Madame Defarge is the iconic figure who sits knitting in the shadow of the guillotine.

Thankfully, our own Defarges were far less ghoulish. In fact, the sisters—who I'd met at various potlucks and island functions—were as sweet and as friendly as can be and this one—whichever one she was—sure enjoyed the reference to being the guest of honor. Her smile was as bright as her snowy white hair.

I adjusted my black-framed glasses on the bridge of my nose. "Alice or Margaret?" I asked Kate out of the corner of my mouth when the old lady neared.

"Alice." As subtly as she could, Kate pointed, indicating Alice's white cotton pants and her sky blue, short-sleeve shirt. "Margaret always wears something pink."

I'm sure I'd heard that before but this time, I told myself not to forget it.

"Isn't this great fun!" In the light of the setting sun, Alice twinkled like a prom queen. Just like her sister, she was a tiny woman with a neat, poofy hairdo and a spring in her step. "I only hope . . ." Her gaze moved past us to the lake. "There are some pretty dark clouds out there. I hope the weather isn't going to spoil our celebrations this week."

"There's a chance of rain tonight," Luella told her. "But nothing for the rest of the week. Will you and Margaret join us for dinner?"

Another blast of wind kicked up over the lake and brought with it the distant rumble of thunder. "Thank you , but . . ." In no time at all, Alice headed back the way she'd come. "I'd better help Margaret get our picnic settled over in the park. Just in case it starts to rain and we need to pack up in a hurry."

"Nice lady," I said when she was gone.

"A real sweetheart," Chandra confirmed. "So's her sister."

"And you'd better be really careful every time either one of them is around," Kate advised, then laughed when she saw the look of disbelief on my face. She grabbed onto my arm. "I'm just saying. Hasn't anybody told you? The Defarge sisters—"

"Are the biggest gossips on this or any other island," Luella said. "There are a lot of people around here who believe that's why they opened their knit shop in the first place. You know, so they'd have a ringside seat right downtown and they could keep an eye on everyone and everything that happens around here."

"They know your business before you know your business," Chandra added. "And there's nothing they like better than telling the world."

By the time they were done with their warnings, my smile was tight. "Then it's a good thing I don't have any business worth discussing."

"Right." Kate split the word into two syllables. Right before she grabbed her dinner dish and took it with her when she went to the boat in the next slip to chat with its owners.

"Anything you say." Chandra had already finished her plate of food, but when she walked down the dock to visit with some of our neighbors, she took the bottle of red wine with her.

"Good luck with that," Luella said, and she, too, walked away, leaving me alone on the dock and wondering what had just happened.

For like a half a second.

That was when I realized I wasn't alone, and the reason they'd all pulled up stakes and fled was suddenly all too evident.

FROM *NEW YORK TIMES* BESTSELLING AUTHOR
JENN MCKINLAY

-The Library Lover's Mysteries-

BOOKS CAN BE DECEIVING

DUE OR DIE

BOOK, LINE, AND SINKER

READ IT AND WEEP

Praise for the Library Lover's Mysteries

"[An] appealing new mystery series."
—Kate Carlisle, *New York Times* bestselling author

"A sparkling setting, lovely characters,
books, knitting, and chowder! What more
could any reader ask?"
—Lorna Barrett, *New York Times* bestselling author

"Sure to charm cozy readers everywhere."
—Ellery Adams, author of the Books by the Bay Mysteries

jennmckinlay.com
facebook.com/TheCrimeSceneBooks
penguin.com